THE MAN WITH THE BLACK BOX

COLIN P. CAHOON

eLectio Publishing

Little Elm, TX

www.eLectioPublishing.com

The Man with the Black Box
By Colin P. Cahoon

ISBN-13: 978-1-63213-264-2
Published by eLectio Publishing, LLC
Little Elm, Texas
http://www.eLectioPublishing.com

Printed in the United States of America

5 4 3 2 1 eLP 20 19 18 17 16

The eLectio Publishing editing team is comprised of: Christine LePorte, Lori Draft, Sheldon James, Court Dudek, and Kaitlyn Campbell.

Publisher's Note
The publisher does not have any control over and does not assume any responsibility for author or third-party websites or their content.

This is a work of fiction. Names, characters, places, and incidents either are the product of the author's imagination or are used fictitiously, and any resemblance to actual persons, living or dead, business establishments, events, or locales is entirely coincidental.

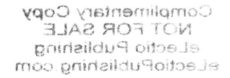

This book is dedicated to my wife, Susan, and my sister, Bonnie, whose support, encouragement and advice made this book possible.

THE MAN WITH THE BLACK BOX

CHAPTER 1
THE RED PACKET

"THIS WON'T DO. This won't do at all."

Jim didn't respond but kept a nervous eye on his fare. The gentleman he'd picked up earlier was standing on the landing of Jim's hansom cab. Having abandoned the cover of his seat, the fool seemed oblivious to the rain sliding off the rim of his top hat onto his black overcoat, and the panic he was inciting in Jim's horse. His arms were wrapped around a leather satchel held tightly against his chest.

"This will not do!" the gentleman bellowed again at the engulfing cacophony of clattering, banging, clinking, and shouting that rose from the crowded London street before him.

"Please, sir, your standing is making her skittish," Jim implored. "She's a little young and not used to such commotion. I beg of you, sir, do please take your seat."

The gentleman looked about at the surrounding congestion, swaying with the erratic motion of the cab induced by the agitated jerking of the horse. "Damn it all, this will not do. What is your name, young man?" he yelled above the din while glaring at the mass of conveyances all in the same gridlocked predicament.

"Jim Talbot, sir. I believe it's to do with some protest march two streets on, sir," he shouted to the back of the gentleman's head. "Please, sir, I need your weight over the wheels and not on her back."

"A protest, yes, quite apparent, I simply asked your name. Master Talbot, I shall remember that," the last part said slightly over his shoulder. "I hired you to take me to my destination in the quickest manner possible. Despite your youth, I trusted your assurances that your horse was of the first rate and up to the task. 'Quickest in all of London,' you said. Now I find myself in the doldrums of a sea of carriages, carts, cabs, and motorcars."

1

The horse interrupted with a loud whinny and snort, shaking her head side to side and bouncing her front quarters a few inches off the ground.

Jim wasn't sure he made out all the gentleman had said, but he got the import. "Please, sir, she's a fine horse, just a bit inexperienced and nervous at the moment. If I could please ask your forgiveness and beg you to take your seat, sir."

"No, this will not do! I'll have to get there on my own." At that, the gentleman, still clutching his satchel with both arms, took a step down toward the wet street.

Before Jim could get out another word, a single pop pierced the din. The horse reacted instantly with a leap forward, followed by a jump back, and then a more determined, frantic leap forward, the last move causing her to ram headlong into the back of a large delivery cart. Next came a guttural scream.

Jim felt the accident, if he didn't quite see it all. The first lurch had knocked the gentleman off his feet and onto the street. He had tried to right himself by grabbing the side of the cab during the backward lurch, but evidently, with the slick street being of little assistance, had only managed to slide his right leg under the cab's carriage while he started to get his weight on his bent left leg. It was during the final forward lurch that the accident occurred. One side of the cab rose up and then back down with a sickening crack. After the crack came the scream, the scream from the gentleman whose right leg was now under the wheel of the cab.

Jim pulled back on the reins and backed the cab, resulting in a final thud as the wheel rolled off the gentleman's leg. Jim jumped from his seat and landed near the injured gentleman, who lay on his left side grasping at his right leg with one arm while clinging to the satchel with the other.

"Sir, I'm so sorry. I think it was a motor car discharging, or perhaps a pistol, I'm not sure, but it scared the horse. I'm so sorry. It's my fault, sir. I should have reined her in a bit tighter."

"What's this, lad? I saw the whole thing."

Jim looked up to see an older man crouching over the gentleman.

"You shouldn't stand in a hansom cab like that, sir, not with such a jumpy horse in the reins and all this hullabaloo. Good Lord, sir, you've broken your leg." The older man pulled the gentleman's pants leg up above his shin. "Lad, look at that. Mother Mary help him, the bone's coming clear through the skin."

As if wired together, Jim felt his eyes and jaw widen in unison. He looked away, holding back the urge to vomit his meager lunch on the pavestone street. "I'm so sorry, sir."

"Why, what 'av we 'ere?" A second man appeared from the traffic, wearing a dingy jacket that was too long for his arms, a battered and greasy cap, and trousers with rips over repaired rips on the knees. "Why, it be a gentleman in distress, he is. Now 'av no fear, Charlie's 'ere now to help you, sir."

The sight of Charlie smiling to reveal a mouth full of brown, broken, and jagged teeth framed by his flabby unshaven face with droopy left eye was alone enough to add to Jim's queasiness. But when the ruffian exhaled a mouthful of putrid rotten-egg smelling breath, it triggered another convulsion in Jim's stomach that he fought back hard with narrow success.

"Let's take a look now, shall we," Charlie added cheerfully as he started feeling around the gentleman's overcoat.

"Leave him be, you rascal," said the older man as he shoved Charlie aside. "You don't mind him, sir. He's just looking for loose change and pocket watches. Lad, we need to get this gentleman assistance. I'm rather lame myself, or I'd be the first to go. So I'm afraid it's up to you."

The rain continued to patter down, rinsing blood from the gentleman's leg and sending it flowing down the street. Jim couldn't tell if he was in too much pain to speak, or maybe just dazed, but the gentleman continued to hold his leg with his body now curled up tighter than before. Jim retrieved the gentleman's top hat and placed it on the man's head as best he could.

"I don't know what to do. It's my father's cab. I can't leave it and the horse. It's all we have."

"Quiet, all of you, don't move," the gentleman barked. He looked up at the group huddled around him, Jim Talbot, Charlie, and the old man. The gentleman's face looked pale but his eyes were alive as he glared at each in turn, scanning them from top to bottom, concluding with a look straight into the eyes of each of them. Then he glanced down at his leg and let out an audible huff. He looked back up at Jim. "I've no choice. Come here, boy. I must tell you something."

Jim leaned in to the gentleman. With fearsome quickness the gentleman grabbed the front of his shirt, pulling them face-to-face.

"Now listen to me, lad. We haven't a moment to lose. You must listen to exactly what I'm telling you."

Jim tried to pull away, but the gentleman held him fast with an iron grip.

"Take my satchel. Now open it. What do you see?"

"A red packet, sir, I mean, a packet wrapped in red cloth."

"Precisely, now close it. A red packet, that's what it's called, and it's important for you to remember. That color has importance, do you understand?"

"Well, no sir, but if perhaps you let loose of my shirt—"

"Master Talbot, this is a couriered packet. They are all given colors. Red means utmost urgency, a matter of great national urgency. Do you understand?"

"I, yes, I think so."

"I don't normally deliver packets, but when I saw the red, I took personal charge of it. Now"—the gentleman paused as he sucked in a lung full of air through clenched teeth—"now, do you remember where we were going?"

"Yes sir, the Foreign Office."

4

"Exactly, this packet is to be delivered directly to Lord Lansdowne at the Foreign Office. If anyone questions you, just show them the red packet. But it is to be delivered to only Lord Lansdowne. You must not relinquish custody of the packet until you've placed it in Lord Lansdowne's hands." The gentleman paused again, bowing his head and taking three long breaths. "Tell me what I just told you."

"I'm to take this packet to Lord Lansdowne in the Foreign Office, and if anyone questions me, I'm to show them the red packet, and deliver it to Lord Lansdowne only. But, sir, I can't. I can't leave my father's cab and horse. It's all we have, sir."

"Listen to me, Master Talbot." The gentleman pulled Jim's face closer into his until their noses were touching and, lowering his voice to a hissing whisper, continued. "You have no choice. For King and country, you must deliver this packet. I'll make sure your cab and horse are tended to." The gentleman turned his attention to the other two men, who were leaning in to the conversation. "Charlie! Or whatever your name is, get away now before I have the constable take you in for theft and vagrancy. Go, now!"

"'Theft and vagrancy,' he says. Humph. Thinks I'm a ruffian, am I? Humph. No good deed goes unpunished." Charlie straightened up his back, placed his hands on his hips, and, with a last smelly "humph" hurled at the gentleman, turned and disappeared into the morass.

"Master Talbot"—the gentleman turned his attention back to the nearby face, lowering his voice again—"reach inside my jacket to my left vest pocket. That's it. Now pull out the contents."

Jim felt a substantial weight of coin in his hand, more weight than he had ever felt in his short life.

"Put it in your pocket. I'm putting my trust in you, Master Talbot. The King is putting his trust in you. The Foreign Office, Lord Lansdowne, for King and country, as quickly as you can. Do you understand?"

"Yes sir, for King and country."

The gentleman released Jim's shirt and dropped his head back onto the street.

Without hesitation, Jim grabbed the satchel, sprung to his feet, and ran at the maze of traffic, leaving the slumped gentleman and his precious horse and cab behind.

"Godspeed, Jim Talbot," the gentleman muttered into a wet paving stone.

* * *

"Lord Lansdowne, there is a young man here to see you, a Jim Talbot."

Lansdowne looked up from his paper, puffing out the mouthful of cigar smoke he had been savoring. "Never heard of him."

"He has a red packet."

Lansdowne set down the paper and placed the cigar in a nearby ashtray. "Well, then, by all means, send him in."

"Yes, my lord."

Lansdowne turned to the other man in the room who had also set down his paper but still held a shot glass at the ready. "Children delivering red packets, perhaps the budget cuts have come closer to the bone than I realized? Well, Charles, we'll just have to see what this is about."

"Indeed."

"My lord, may I present Jim Talbot."

The announcement having been directed to no one in particular, the young man looked back and forth between them, puzzled. "Lord Lansdowne?"

"He's Lord Lansdowne, the British Foreign Secretary," one of them volunteered while pointing with his glass. "I'm Sir Charles Hardinge, the Permanent Assistant Undersecretary of State for Foreign Affairs. Perhaps you can tell us who you are and how it is you came upon a red packet."

The boy gasped for air and then stood frozen, appearing to Lord Lansdowne like a rabbit confronted by two wolves. Lansdowne smiled and looked the lad over. He was dressed in the uniform of a cab driver, but the fit was much too big, and the clothes rather worn. He was a ruddy lad of perhaps fourteen, of average height but rather skinny. He stood panting with his mouth agape, his lower body in the stiff pose of an actor who'd forgotten his lines waiting for stage direction. There was a noticeable fresh bloodstain on his left knee. He clung tightly to a leather satchel, pressed against his chest.

"Sir, my lord, sir, I was instructed to deliver this to you." He pulled from the satchel a packet enclosed in bright red velvet cloth.

"Well then, deliver it to me." Lansdowne smiled and reached for his cigar.

The boy walked purposefully toward Lansdowne. "The courier was injured, my lord. He told me to bring this to you for King and country. I came as fast as I was able."

Lansdowne placed the cigar in his mouth, looked up at the boy, and relieved him of the packet. "Thank you, lad."

The boy paused for a moment, looking befuddled, and then turned to leave. He stopped halfway to the door and turned back around, again facing Lansdowne just as he opened his lips to allow another mouthful of the delicious smoke to slowly waft away.

"I beg your pardon, sir, my lord."

"What is it, lad?"

"The gentleman, what is the courier he was, he says to me that I must deliver the packet for King and country."

"Yes, he was right. You did well."

"Yes, my lord, thank you, sir. But you see, he also gave me these." The boy produced a handful of coins from his pants pocket. "This is far too much for my fare, my lord, sir. I did it for King and country. It had nothing to do with these coins."

"I'm sure you did, lad. What is your name again?"

"Jim, I mean James Talbot, my lord, son of John Talbot."

"James Talbot, you've done well by King and country. Keep the coins. When next I see the King, I shall mention to him your service."

Appearing not to know what else to do, Jim bowed deeply. "Thank you, sir, my lord. I shall take my leave now. I must attend to the injured gentleman and my cab. Thank you, my lord."

Lansdowne allowed a wry smile as he watched the boy march from the room, after which the door was closed behind him, leaving Lansdowne and Sir Charles Hardinge alone with the red packet.

"Well, now, let's see what this is about, shall we?" Lansdowne set his cigar back in the ashtray and examined the packet. "It looks real enough. I haven't received one of these in several months now. I always dread opening them, to be frank." Nonetheless, he unsealed the packet, peered inside it, and pulled out a short stack of papers. As he started to read the first page he felt a knot growing in his stomach. "Good God!"

"What is it, Henry?"

"Good God." Lansdowne paused to compose himself and then read from the papers in his hand. "'Thirty-one March 1905, Kaiser William has landed today in Tangier, Morocco, and is meeting, amidst pomp and ceremony, with Sultan Abdelaziz. The Kaiser has issued a public statement declaring his support for the Sultan's sovereignty over Morocco.'"

"He's insane! The French will never stand for it."

"They can't stand for it." Lansdowne dropped the papers in his lap and stared straight ahead, gathering his thoughts. "He's put them in a box. They either declare war or geld themselves in front of the entire world."

"It's preposterous. Crazy man, he runs around with a Lucifer match and keeps scratching it against powder kegs. He may have scratched too hard this time. How did we not have wind of this in advance?"

"That's precisely what I was going to ask of you. Charles, we can't operate in the blind like this. Why, it's more absurd than children delivering red packets!"

"Quite right. I understand your frustration. There does seem to be a great deal of strangeness of late. I'll look into it straightaway. I'll also instruct Berlin and Paris to watch carefully for any sign of mobilization."

"Preposterous, he thinks he can destroy the *Entente Cordiale*. We must do what we can to stiffen the French spine."

"Shall we send a note of support to Foreign Minister Delcassé?"

"Yes, and please contact the Prime Minister. Inform him that we urgently request a meeting of the cabinet."

* * *

Jim Talbot was relieved as he turned the corner and saw his hansom cab and horse. They were moved off to the side of the road, but not far from where he left them less than two hours before. The street was no longer jammed to a halt, but had returned to something closer to its normal, overcrowded condition. As he got nearer he noted several men loitering about his cab, including a bobby in his blue uniform and tall domed hat.

"Excuse me, Constable. My name is Jim Talbot, and this is my cab and horse."

"See him about it. He wants to talk to you."

"The man with the derby over there?"

"Yes, the inspector. He'd like a word with you."

Jim trotted over to the man with the derby, who was staring intently at a nearby building.

"Excuse me, sir, Inspector. The bobby, he says I'm to see you. I'm Jim Talbot, and that's my horse and cab."

The face under the derby reminded Jim of a bulldog, and one that had seen a few scrapes in his time at that. He was chomping on a short, unlit cigar.

"Come with me, Master Talbot, we need someplace less public to talk."

"But I need—"

The inspector started down the street before Jim could finish. He was moving so quickly that Jim had to run just to catch up and skip to keep abreast of him.

"But, sir, I need to get home. I'm past my time. My father will be worried and no doubt angry."

"I've interviewed the witnesses. I trust you delivered your packet to the Foreign Office."

"Yes sir, but—"

"You've made good time, there and back. Why did your horse start?"

"It was a popping noise of some kind, sir. May I ask where we're going?"

"Did you see where it came from, the popping noise?"

"No, sir, I just heard it. The horse jumped, and the gentleman fell."

"Did you see a man running through the crowd?"

"No, sir. I'm sorry, but where are we going?"

"Just around the corner here, there's a quiet room in a pub where we can chat. It won't take but a moment, and then you'll be on your way."

"I'm sorry, sir, Inspector, but I think I missed your name."

The inspector seemed momentarily distracted by the approach of a fashionable young lady who was having a heated discussion with a young gentleman companion.

"Pardon me for a moment, lad. This may be unpleasant."

As the arguing couple grew near the lady suddenly sprinted away from the young gentleman. Without looking ahead, she crashed directly into the inspector. He seemed prepared for the blow even though he was looking at Jim when it happened. He brushed her aside and spit his half-chewed cigar directly in her face at about the same time as her bottom smacked the sidewalk.

The young gentleman rushed in to assist the inspector from falling, a gallant act that seemed unnecessary given the small effect of the collision on the inspector. Coming at the inspector from the side on which Jim stood, however, the young gentleman managed to jab Jim in the ribs at the same time. The sharp blow was such that Jim fell back, only to find himself nearly on the ground and on top of a young boy who must have been right behind him.

"So sorry, let me help you up," the young boy blurted out to Jim.

Before Jim could get to his feet he saw the inspector flash by, bull-rushing the young gentleman and pinning him to a nearby building. With his left hand the inspector held the young gentleman's right wrist and his forearm was pressed hard against the young gentleman's chest.

"Don't you presume to do such a thing to me! Give me the watch," barked the inspector.

The young gentleman frantically felt for something around his waistband with his free hand.

"Looking for this?" A knife appeared from the inspector's right hand. He kept his forearm hard against the young gentleman's chest, but rotated his wrist to point the blade of the knife at his quarry's nose. "Don't presume, sir. Let loose of the watch."

Jim was on his feet. When he looked about, the young lady and the young boy were gone. The young gentleman was shaking as he opened his right hand to reveal a gold pocket watch. The inspector loosened his grip and took the watch from him.

"What shall I do with these, Inspector?"

Jim turned around to see where the question had come from. Standing in the road was a barrel-chested brute with arms the size of a man's legs. His thick neck was as wide as his head, which was topped with a workman's cap fringed with his curly auburn hair. His arms were extended from his side and parallel to the street. In one hand he held a small boy; in the other, the fashionably dressed young woman. He held each by their forearms, dangling them above the ground like a poulter displaying two larger turkeys.

"Thank you, Mick. Let the woman go. She's just the distraction. The boy can go too, once you've relieved him of the coins he took off Master Talbot. We have more important matters to tend to."

Jim felt his now empty pocket and was amazed to see a handful of coins, his coins, produced from the pants of the boy who had cushioned his fall. The boy and the young lady scampered off as soon as the brute released them, as did the young gentleman once the inspector let him go. All three scattered in different directions, like cockroaches when the lantern lights. Jim looked at the inspector with stunned amazement, trying to piece together what had just happened.

"He wasn't after my watch, lad. That was just a target of opportunity. The street is buzzing with talk of your little affair today. Rumors about a large sum of money paid to a young cab driver are bound to bring out the opportunists. There may be more about. My man Mick will hold your money for now. He can escort you home safely when we're done. Now, one more door on, follow me."

Jim followed into a lively pub and up a flight of stairs to a quieter second floor. The inspector sat at a table in one corner. Jim dutifully sat across from him, still shaken and more than a little confused.

A woman appeared from another room and made her way to their table. "Scotch, Inspector?"

"Yes, and a beer for the lad."

"Thank you, sir, but if Father were to smell alcohol—"

"Lad, you appear to me to need it." The inspector looked up at the woman and thumped the table with his stubby pointer finger twice in a spot in front of Jim.

"One scotch and one beer," acknowledged the woman.

"Are you certain you saw no one running through the street after your horse started?"

"Yes, sir. I was very concerned with the gentleman and his leg. I don't recall seeing much beyond him at the time."

"I see."

The inspector sat quietly staring at Jim. Why was he looking so coldly? Jim was relieved when the woman reappeared with a glass and a mug. The inspector placed a coin on the table, which she swept into her apron. He then raised his glass and pointed it at Jim.

"To your health."

"I beg your pardon, sir, but can you tell me what this is about? I really must be on my way home. I'm past my time, and my father will worry."

"Speaking of time, would you like a watch?" The inspector held out two gold pocket watches for Jim's inspection. "He may have taken one of mine, but I relieved him of two of his. They weren't his, anyway. Pick one. It's yours."

"Sir, these would be stolen watches, then?"

"I'm quite certain of that. He probably stole them from some gentlemen today and hadn't time to sell them off before I took them back. Which one would you like?"

"I can't, sir. They belong to someone else. That would be stealing."

"It's not like you stole them. He stole them, then I recovered them, and now I offer one to you. They appear quite valuable. Look, this one is gold and has a fine gold chain."

"It's not right, sir. It's not Christian. Perhaps you could find the owners and give them back. Thank you kindly for the offer. May I go now?"

"Very good, lad." The inspector took a drink. "I have a few more questions first."

13

The inspector seemed pleased for the first time. Odd, why wasn't he upset that his gift had been refused? Jim squirmed in his seat, wishing he'd never picked up the gentleman with the red packet.

"How long have you lived in London?"

"All my life."

"Do you know it well?"

"Like the back of my hand. I've been riding with my father since he bought his first horse cart. I could barely walk, he tells me. He's taught me every street and lane in the city."

"How did you get to the Foreign Office and back so quickly?"

"I ran."

"That doesn't completely answer my question. You surely spent some time waiting for an audience with Lord Lansdowne. That, added to the distance you had to cover and the crowds you had to navigate…you made excellent time."

"You have to know the mews, sir. They can save you considerable distance when you're on foot."

"I assume you saw Lord Lansdowne."

"Yes sir, as I was told."

"Describe him to me."

"I beg your pardon?"

"What does he look like?"

"He has a high forehead and long narrow face, brown hair but balding in front, sideburns, and a moustache that he waxes and twists at the end."

"What color are his eyes?"

"Blue."

"How old would you make him?"

"About sixty, I would think."

"The woman who ran into me on the street outside, what color were her gloves?"

"Light blue with white trim at the wrists."

"And her shoes?"

"Black."

"The policeman who directed you to me, did he have a mustache or no?"

"Yes, a bushy black one."

"And how tall would you make him to be?"

"Taller than you, perhaps six feet or more."

"Close your eyes."

"I'm sorry?"

"Close your eyes." The inspector paused from the rapid-fire questioning.

Jim felt increasingly anxious and further confused. He could hear the inspector take a sip of something. What were his options? He could get up and run, but that hulking Mick was still about, assuming he could outdo the lightning reflexes he'd seen the inspector employ. Besides, the brute still had his money.

"Now, lad, without peeking, what color are my eyes?"

"I'm not certain, sir."

"You're not certain?"

"I mean, they seem to change depending on the lighting or something. I think they're mostly gray, maybe green, but then they look light blue. I'm not sure. Your left eye, the one with the scar below it, has more brown, though."

"What was the first thing I said to you?"

"Come with me. We need someplace private to talk."

"Are you sure? Think on it again. *Exactly* what did I say?"

"You said, 'Come with me, Master Talbot, we need someplace less public to talk.'"

"The man who took my watch, what was he wearing on his head?"

"A derby, like yours, only cleaner."

"Yes, very good indeed, lad. You may open your eyes now." The inspector grinned and sat back in his chair. "I think you'll do."

"Sir, please, what is this all about? I'd very much like to go home."

"Master Talbot, I'm with Scotland Yard. I'd like to employ you. You've demonstrated the characteristics I need for the task at hand. No, please, don't interrupt. I know you've been through much today, so just listen.

"I'm on the trail of an assassin. I can use honest and reliable eyes in the street. I'd like to hire your cab for the next several weeks. I'll pay you full fare for each day while you are under my employment, with each week's payment made in advance. All you need do is ride through the city, as if on your way to pick up a fare, and keep your eyes and ears open."

"What am I to look for?"

"A man with a black box."

"I'm sorry. A black box?"

"Yes, a man carrying a black box, the box being about a third the size of a hat box, longer than it is wide. If you see a man with a box of that description, particularly in the vicinity of children, you must alert me immediately."

"And how will I do that, sir?"

"There's a checkered knit scarf under the seat of your cab. Is it yours?"

"Yes, it's useful on a cold day."

"No doubt. On such a cold day you must wear it with both ends in front. If you see the man or know where he might be, place one of the ends over your shoulder such that it dangles behind you. Upon doing so you should move your cab thusly: make a turn on

16

every fifth street you come upon, always in the same direction left or right, in accordance with the position of your scarf. If you intend to make left turns, place the scarf over your left shoulder. If you intend to make right turns, place the scarf over your right shoulder. Keep making turns at every fifth street in a consistent direction, left or right per the signal you've made, until someone flags you down and asks for a ride to Saint George's Dragon on Brick Lane."

"But there isn't a Saint George's Dragon on Brick Lane."

"Exactly, but whoever asks for such you should trust implicitly. Tell him what you know immediately, and follow his instructions to the letter."

"And what if the day isn't cold?"

"Then signal with your scarf by draping it over the back of your seat. Drape it on the left side for left turns and on the right for right turns."

Jim reached for his beer and took a long drink.

"This part is particularly important. You must be absolutely discreet. No one must know you're working for me or why, not even your father. That is a critical term of your employment and a condition that will keep you out of harm's way."

Jim took another long drink, downing nearly half the mug at once. He suddenly felt a little light-headed.

"Sir, I still don't know your name."

"Inspector Edmund Jenkins. Now, drink up, lad. We need to get you and your reward home."

CHAPTER 2
AN INTERNATIONAL AFFAIR

"MR. PRESIDENT, SORRY to interrupt. Mr. Thomas Mathis has requested to speak with you. Shall I tell him you're having dinner with your family?"

"Ah, Tom Mathis, ever the good newspaperman. No, send him in. Let's get another chair at the table. He's most certainly hungry. Newspapermen are always hungry, no matter what you feed them."

"Can I set a snake in his chair, Father?"

President Roosevelt smiled at his son with amusement. "I have a better idea. Go fetch that creature from the drawing room. That'll give him a fright."

Quentin Roosevelt bolted from the table while the other children giggled and smirked at each other.

"Teddy, really? Must you let the children torment every guest?"

"Edith, let them have a little fun. Tom won't mind. Those newspapermen are all good sports. No, here, put the chair next to me. Ethel, Kermit, scoot down some and make room. That's it, push the chair under the tablecloth. We'll give Quentin some cover."

Quentin returned, cradling something in his arms as he ducked below the tablecloth, conveniently held up by one of his brothers, and disappeared. Shortly thereafter President Roosevelt looked up to see a familiar man enter the room, ushered in by a black butler.

"Mr. President, I'm sorry to interrupt. You're eating dinner. Perhaps I should come back later."

"Nonsense, Tom." President Roosevelt rose from the table, extending both hands for a hearty shake. "Please, sit next to me. You remember my wife, Edith, and these are some of my children, Kermit, Ethel, Archibald." He paused, allowing each to nod politely in turn. "Ted is away this evening, but, good grief, Edith, where has Quentin gone?"

The children all looked down at their plates and attempted to suppress more giggles.

"A pleasure to meet all of you," said Thomas Mathis as he pulled his chair out from the table. "Good heavens! What kind of beast is this?" he exclaimed after jumping back from the table, thus setting off a roar of laughter.

"It's called a horned toad, Tom. Quite harmless, I assure you. Ah, and this"—the President looked down at the small boy clawing his way up from under the table and into his father's lap—"this would be my youngest, Quentin. Son, please remove the horned toad from Mr. Mathis's chair and return him to his cage. Now, Tom, please take a seat before more creatures find their way to it. You're just in time for the main course."

"A horned toad, you say? What is it, a frog, a lizard? Seems like a mixture of both? He's quite a fearsome-looking creature despite his size."

"I suppose he's a mixture between a toad and a lizard, closest thing to a small dragon I've ever seen. He was sent to me by my Rough Rider friends in New Mexico. Good men. I miss them all. You won't find men any more solid anywhere in the world."

"Tell him what it does when it's mad, Father."

"Oh, that. Quite curious, you see, if you make him mad, say thump him hard on the nose a few times, he'll spit blood out of his eyes at you. He's quite a courageous little beast when cornered."

"My, what an act of defiance, spitting blood out of one's eyes. Something I'd expect from you, Mr. President."

The President roared out a full-throated laugh as he rapped the table twice with his fists. "Now that would be a story, hey, Tom? 'President Roosevelt spits blood out of his eyes.' That would start tongues a-wagging. Now, what brings you out on a Sunday evening? You're not going to lecture me on that Moroccan crisis."

"You've heard about it, then? I had hoped I'd be the first to brief you."

"No, sorry, Tom, two of your competitors have already been here today before you. But that's all right. I'm sure you can give me additional details."

"My apologies for being tardy, Mr. President, I was in church this morning."

"Of course you were, good Episcopalian. The Lord should always come before the President. I think the other two were Catholic, weren't they, Edith? Perhaps they had special dispensation from the Pope?"

"Oh, stop, Teddy. The man comes to you with serious business and all you do is poke fun at him. Please forgive my husband, Mr. Mathis. He's as harmless as the horned toad and as silly as his children."

The President grinned broadly at the suggestion, leaning back in his chair and hooking the thumb of one hand on the front of his vest. "She's quite right, Tom. I'd never spit blood at the press. Let's talk business, then. What do you hear from Morocco? Pass the potatoes down to Mr. Mathis, Archie."

"Thank you. As you know, the Kaiser has really stuck his nose where it doesn't belong. He caught everyone off guard, the French, the Russians, even the British, by showing up in Tangier suddenly on his private yacht along with a German warship and proceeding to make quite a show of throwing his support to the Sultan of Morocco at the expense of the French. As you know, Germany has no substantive interest in Morocco, while to France it's the most important of countries. His purpose seems to be to disrupt the *Entente Cordiale*."

"What's an *Entente Cordiale*, Father?"

"Hush now, Archibald."

"That's all right, Edith, the boy's just curious. See, the French and British have been at odds for quite some time over who gets what piece of North Africa for their new colonies. They've almost come to blows themselves over the issue more than once. But in April of last year they signed this treaty called the *Entente Cordiale,* which said that Britain can have Egypt, and France is free to expand westward from Algeria to Morocco. I think the French are still smarting from the past confrontation thing with Britain, but the whole deal was cut without involving the Kaiser, and he thinks of himself as the biggest, most important man in Europe. Besides, he can't let the French and British start to cozy up to one another with treaties and such. He's much happier when they're at each other's throats.

"How did I do, Tom?" The President grinned again, turning his attention from his son to his guest.

"Quite well, sir. And now, the German Kaiser himself shows up in Morocco and announces that he considers the Sultan of Morocco as the ruler of a free and independent empire subject to no foreign control, meaning French control, and that he will deal directly with the Sultan on all issues of trade and commerce, implicitly threatening to use German military might to support the Sultan should the French continue to take over the country and make the Sultan a French puppet."

"What a ghastly man," exclaimed Ethel Roosevelt.

"The Kaiser's not so bad as he's made out. I think his chancellor, that von Bulow fellow, works him into a lather and then he does the most outlandish things. So, Tom, what do you think the Kaiser is up to?" asked the President before shoveling a forkful of chicken into his mouth.

"I think he expects the British to stand aside while he publicly spanks the French. The French can't afford another war with Germany. They'd be crushed, just like in 1870. Then, after he humiliates the French, they'll be so mad that the *Entente Cordiale* will be shredded in revenge."

"Do you think the British will stand aside then?"

"I don't know why they would want to intervene. They have no quarrel with Germany and no love of France. You look skeptical, Mr. President."

"Hmm, yes, I suppose I am. Take these two boys here, Archibald and Quentin, separated by three years, giving Archibald a three-year strength advantage on Quentin. Now, let's say Archibald has been shoving Quentin around for some time, much to the amusement of their even older and stronger brother, Kermit. But they've finally reached a truce, an entente, and have agreed to work out their differences. Along comes Kermit and punches Quentin in the nose, announcing that he's going to take away the things Quentin had bargained for with Archibald. So, Archie, what would you do about this new development involving your older brother picking on your younger brother?"

"I'd punch Kermit in the nose. Me and Quentin could take him."

"Quentin and I," interjected Mrs. Roosevelt.

"Quite right, young man, quite right. And that, Tom, is what I think the British might do, punch the Kaiser in the nose. Neither the British nor the French are strong enough to deter the Germans alone, but together, that's a different matter. I'm not sure the British can afford to have the French humiliated."

"If you're right, Mr. President, that could lead, dare I say, to a major war, the likes of which we've not seen in Europe in decades if not centuries, an international affair. The Germans don't take getting punched in the nose lightly, and when they start swinging they're likely to hit everyone in the room."

"A war!" chimed in Archibald. "Will you and the Rough Riders go too?"

"No, son, I'm too old to go charging up hills anymore. Besides, it would worry your mother to death. Thinking of the Rough Riders and Germans, Tom, do you know what Secretary Hay said to me about our near scrape with the Germans during the Spanish-American war? 'To the German mind there is something monstrous in the thought that a war should take place anywhere and they not profit from it.'"

"Yes, I quite agree. I recall Admiral Dewey's comment on the same subject. 'They have bad manners, are too pushing and ambitious. They'll overreach themselves someday.' Perhaps this is the day they've overreached."

The President chuckled and shook his head. "I should know better than to get into a quoting competition with you, Tom. You've quite a talent for remembering what was said. I suppose that comes in quite handy in your line of work. Overreach? Perhaps, we'll see. What do you think I should do about all this?"

"I think you should sit back and wait. It's all a little murky right now, and old man Europe may need our help at some point."

"Wise advice, Tom, wise advice, you can quote me on that. Would you pass me those rolls before Kermit eats them all?"

* * *

Lord Lansdowne was absorbed in reading the report set before him, momentarily oblivious to Sir Charles Hardinge, who sat quietly across the small table from him.

"Charles, this is all quite disturbing. Our best man in Germany is dead from a cause not determined. Two of our men in France are missing, and a third is found floating face down in a pond outside Paris. We haven't heard from our Russian contact in weeks, and our man inside the Austrian court has been expelled. It's as if someone were intentionally trying to blind us. How are we to conduct the foreign affairs of the Empire if we can't know what's going on in the world? I feel like we're sailing with a corpse in the cargo hold. I can smell it, but I can't find it."

"Yes, Henry, quite disturbing."

"Have we any news of the Morocco affair?"

"Thus far the French have not mobilized, at least not officially. They've canceled all military leave and are consolidating their fleet.

24

The Germans don't need to mobilize, as they can do it much faster than the French, but they are watching the French very closely."

"Understandable, the whole world is watching them very closely." Lansdowne stared down at the report again, but he'd seen enough to know he didn't want to read any further. "Have you ever met that French socialist, Jaures?" Hardinge shook his head in the negative. "Damnable man, but brilliant in some respects. Listen to what he wrote in a French socialist paper yesterday: 'Peace has been left to the whim of chance. But if war breaks out it will be vast and terrible. For the first time it will be universal, sucking in all the continents. Capitalism has widened the field of battle, and the entire planet will turn red with the blood of countless men.' We mustn't let that happen, Charles. We need to know what is happening and why."

"Henry, may I make a suggestion? We've also lost a few good men right here in London of late. And if all this is intentional, there must be a source of it here, perhaps internal to the Office. We are not equipped to deal with such catastrophe. We have no branch to investigate missing agents. Perhaps we could use some help outside of the Office. It might be useful to employ someone with a wholly different, more provincial, shall we say, perspective, someone from the outside."

"What are you proposing?"

"Perhaps we should employ Edmund Jenkins."

"Inspector Jenkins of Scotland Yard? A bit unconventional, wouldn't you say?"

"These are unconventional times, and we have unconventional problems. He's discreet, thorough, dogged in his pursuit, and, as best I can tell, totally incorruptible. I'd certainly rather have him working for us than against us."

"Dogged? Is that a good trait in our line of business? I wonder if a more subtle approach may be called for. The last thing I need is a police inspector triggering another international incident."

"He does exact justice swiftly and efficiently. The Yard uses him when no one else will do, when the problem seems otherwise impenetrable. The First Lord of the Admiralty retained him a few years ago to track down a suspected internal spy. Jenkins found him, very highly placed indeed. He also left a few dead men in his wake in doing so. The First Lord later told me the butcher's bill was well worth the price, the exercise having probably saved tens of thousands of seamen's lives in service of their country."

"An inspector from Scotland Yard is certainly a better idea than turning it over to the army, bungling fools. Talk about impenetrable. I don't know, let me think on it." Lansdowne sat back and closed his eyes. After a moment, he sat up and looked back at the papers on the table. "We need to know, Charles, we need to know how to stop it. This can't continue to spin out of control."

"Perhaps I should leave you to your thoughts."

"Yes, let me think on it, Charles, thank you."

Hardinge pushed back his chair, bowed slightly while rising, and turned for the door.

"Charles, you're right. Send for Jenkins."

* * *

Jim Talbot hoped he wouldn't have to keep up the circuit long. His news would be stale soon. After nearly three weeks of trawling the city he finally flashed his scarf, and he hoped it had caught someone's attention.

There was the fifth street, time for his second right turn. Suddenly a carriage drawn by two sweating horses pulled up beside his hansom cab. Steam rose from the horses' backs into the chilly London air. A familiar figure in a derby leapt out of the carriage and onto his cab, spitting out the stub of an unlit cigar in the process.

"Inspector, I didn't expect you personally."

"No time. Tell me, quickly."

"I was on the Outer Circle at the west-by-south side of Regent's Park when I saw a man in the park hand a black box to a young boy. I saw the boy fall down. The man retrieved the box, stowed it under his overcoat, and walked briskly away. I lost sight of the man for no more than a minute, but he emerged to the street and hailed a hansom cab in front of me."

"Could you hear where they were going?"

"Yes, King's Cross Station. I followed them onto Baker Street, and just south of the Allsop Place intersection I displayed my colors so as to alert you. Having to stay on my course of right turns at every fifth street, I'm afraid I lost them shortly thereafter."

"What was he wearing?"

"A top hat and long, black coat. I didn't see much else."

"Good work, lad. Our horses are spent. You can take me and the rest will follow." The inspector turned back to the coach and shouted, "Top hat and black long coat, King's Cross Station.

"Let's go, lad, as fast as she can."

She was a good and fast horse, quick to start and long running. In no time the coach with the inspector's cohorts was left behind. Jim felt the scarf over his right shoulder flap in the breeze as they raced through the city.

"Good work, lad! Keep her at it!" came the occasional call from the inspector.

As they pulled into the King's Cross station, the inspector jumped from the cab before it had lost half its speed. He hit the ground running, using the momentum to carry him forward. His legs appeared almost unable to keep up with his torso until the momentum bled off, thus allowing him to run more upright than headlong. Jim watched him disappear into the station.

Jim wondered how long the coach would be. They had to be a couple of minutes behind by now. He called out calmingly to his horse. "Good girl. You've done well today. Good girl."

The inspector was gone for a very short period when Jim saw the man they were after emerge at a run from the station. Jim tried to see his face as he ran past the cab, but he was just a blur.

The inspector emerged from the station a few seconds later, hot on the man's trail. As he neared Jim's cab, someone stepped out from the crowd and collided with the inspector, causing him to tumble to the ground.

Jim jumped impulsively down from his cab and took up the chase. If he could just keep the man with the black box in sight, perhaps the inspector would keep him in sight and eventually catch up with them both.

Down the road Jim ran. The man seemed to be pulling away. Jim realized they were headed toward the St. Pancras Station, which was a stone's throw from King's Cross. But the man didn't avail himself of the steps leading from the King's Cross side of the station. Instead, he followed the roadway along the brick wall above which sat the elevated front of St. Pancras. As the wall shortened and finally ended at the other side of the station, the man made a quick right turn into the main driveway and proceeded back the other direction up to the front entrance. So he was going to St. Pancras. He must have taken the long route just to put more distance between them. Jim pushed hard, but his legs could do no more than their present speed.

Jim made the turn just in time to see the man sprint into St. Pancras Station through the main entrance. Jim raced up the drive hoping that the inspector was near behind. Soon he was inside.

Inside the station people jostled about like swarming bees in a hive, but Jim made out a top hat bobbing above the crowd and heading for the platforms. Jim followed as best he could, still losing ground by the second.

Coming around a corner, he heard a conductor's whistle followed by the chug and hiss of a locomotive. When he arrived at the platform the train was pulling away from the station.

"Was he on that train?" Jim heard from behind. The inspector was soon beside him breathing hard but glancing about like a hawk trying to regain sight of his prey.

"I think so, sir. I followed him to this platform, but I didn't see him board."

Three other men came running up to join them, all breathing hard as well.

"You," the inspector shouted at one of them, "find out where that train is going and alert the next station."

"Shall we search the station?" asked one of the other men.

"Top to bottom. Meet me back here in thirty minutes if you don't see me before then. First, though, one of you report an incident at Regent's Park. Use the telephone in the station office. We may have a child in need of assistance. I want our men there before the press gets wind of it."

"Yes, Inspector."

"Master Talbot, you did a good turn today."

"Thank you, Inspector. He's very fast."

"Indeed, but you kept him in your sights and I kept you in mine. I flushed him out the front in the hopes of reinforcement, and sure enough, you rushed in to do the job. Master Talbot, I've not much time at the moment, so listen carefully. You've done your service well. Your anonymity was compromised today. Consequently, I no longer require your assistance. You can keep your advanced pay, through the end of this week. For your own safety you must keep everything you've seen and heard today in complete confidence. Do not try to contact me, and never mention my name or any man with a black box to anyone."

"But what am I to do now, sir?"

"Be a cab driver, just like thousands of others in this city. Now, if you'll excuse me, I have an assassin to catch."

* * *

29

Lord Lansdowne put the paper down with disgust. Rumors of war sell, but did they have to fan the flames so enthusiastically?

"Excuse me, Lord Lansdowne, may we interrupt?"

"Sir Charles, please come in. Sit down, you and your guest. I was just about to have some tea. May I pour you some as well?"

"Yes, one lump if you please. May I introduce Inspector Edmund Jenkins of Scotland Yard?"

"Inspector, thank you for coming. I've heard much about you over the years. I'm delighted to finally meet you. Please have a seat. How would you like your tea?"

"The pleasure is all mine, Lord Lansdowne. With a splash of scotch if available."

"Certainly, a splash of scotch. Tell me, Charles, is the inspector fully up to speed on our situation?"

"I believe so. We've spent a good deal of the morning discussing it. He has some interesting insight already that I thought we might share with you."

"Please go on."

"Inspector, perhaps it would be best for Lord Lansdowne to hear the direct testimony."

"By all means. I understand the Foreign Office has suffered a string of unfortunate deaths of important and capable men. Sir Hardinge has reviewed the cases with me, and I'm now familiar with the details as best they can be ascertained. I believe I have, by coincidence, stumbled upon a potential suspect, a person of great interest in the matter and to me."

Lord Lansdowne straightened in his chair, holding his cup suspended above its saucer. "I'm all ears, sir."

"I've spent the last several months on the trail of an assassin who seems to use a very peculiar tool in his trade. I've not yet determined the exact role it plays, but its presence in some relation to each crime scene has demonstrated a link between what would otherwise be random events. Namely, he carries a black box with him."

"You can't be serious, Inspector?" Lansdowne dropped his cup onto its saucer. "I read this morning about some man with a diabolical black box. Poppycock! Don't tell me you believe such fanciful stories."

"Not only do I believe them, but I have of late encouraged the press to publish the details. At first I worked to keep the press quiet, but my normal methods haven't brought the assassin to bay. So I've enlisted their support or, more accurately, the support of the people of London. I'm hoping to put him on the run and push him out of his element. I needed more hounds to flush him out, and now the entire city knows to look for a man with a black box."

"And what has this to do with the Foreign Office?"

Charles Hardinge put his hand on the inspector and turned to Lord Lansdowne. "Several of our dead colleagues were seen with a man with a black box immediately before their deaths."

Lansdowne looked down at his cup, taking a moment to chew on the last bit of news. "Continue, Inspector."

"I wish I had more details beyond the connection of the black box. I don't yet have a motive, a specific suspect, or a reason for any connection with the Foreign Office, but the detail of the black box cannot be ignored."

Lansdowne took a sip of tea, thinking that perhaps scotch would have been a better drink under the circumstances. "Have you come close to catching this man with his box?"

"Yes, twice. The first time he took a shot at me and disappeared into a crowded street. The second time we chased him to a train platform, but the train pulled away from the station before we could get on board."

"Couldn't you intercept him at the next stop?"

"The entire train was searched, but he wasn't found."

"And how do you explain that?"

"Perhaps he was never on the train, or he simply blended in. In any event, if we've come close before, we'll do it again. Eventually his luck will run out."

"Sooner rather than later, I hope. But the press, won't that just cause him to change his methods?"

"Perhaps. It might also cause him to leave the city. If he does, he'll be leaving familiar ground and be less likely to blend in."

"And if he does leave London, where do you suspect he'll go?"

"He needs a major city. It's easier to stay anonymous when you can melt into the crowd. If he stays in England, I suppose cities like Manchester, Leicester, or Liverpool might do. He might jump a ship, in which case he'd head for the likes of Paris, Berlin, Vienna, Rome, or maybe even across the pond, to New York."

Lansdowne flashed a skeptical frown at Sir Charles. "New York? Good God, just what we need, involvement of the Americans."

CHAPTER 3
THE BOX

DOCTOR SAMUEL CUNNINGHAM raced his spidery fingers across the patient, pausing here to take a pulse, springing next to feel the forehead, momentarily breaking from the task at hand to rake back his mop of red hair and adjust his stethoscope. He continued his methodical examination of Miss Molly Bell, all within the silent observation of Molly's plump, hovering mother and her equally plump nanny, the former nervously jerking and jiggling with every change of focus in the doctor's examination, the latter peering attentively from the corner of Molly's bedroom.

Satisfied that he had checked all that could be checked, the doctor gazed intently at the little girl with the short brown hair who lay as still as she was able on her bed, a frozen statue staring back at him with wide, questioning eyes.

Molly was his most beloved patient in all of New York. It was hard not to get sentimental about the young ones, and it was easy to be especially sentimental about Molly. She fought her frequent childhood bouts of asthma with cheer and optimism.

"Don't...cry...Mother...it's...not as bad...as last...time," he'd heard her whisper between wheezing gasps for air. Not even her asthma, though, seemed to dampen her joy of life. Her scraped knees and elbows bore witness to her love of romping about the outdoors with her imaginary friends, her bobbed hair and sturdy clothing a testament to her mother's acceptance of the inevitable dirt, leaves, and other flotsam of nature that Molly would bring home after a good day of adventure in the park.

"Fit as a fiddle," he pronounced with a grin. "No trace of fluid in the lungs or any blockage. You've done well again, my little Molly."

"Praise God," exclaimed Mrs. Bell as she jiggled her arms above her head and looked skyward, as if she'd see the Almighty somewhere through the ceiling. "Praise God! This has been such a week. First with all this talk about some crisis in Europe, and then Molly starts wheezing again. With my husband having served in the Rough Riders with Colonel Roosevelt, I've been worried half to death that he'll find himself in some faraway war. He's away enough as it is without having to run off to some godforsaken battlefield, putting his life on the line for who knows what. It's all too much for one week. Thank God, and thank you, Doctor.

"Mrs. Brown, run and get the good doctor some tea and cake. You will stay for tea and cake, won't you? You've been so good to our Molly. I really insist."

"Thank you, Mrs. Bell, but I must be off. I have two other patients to tend to this morning." Refusing Mrs. Bell's offer of tea and cake was hard indeed. He had known her to be such warm company, not just to her daughter's devoted doctor, but to all those fortunate friends who called to keep her company while her husband was off on his frequent business trips. He lowered his voice and tilted his head toward his patient. "I made sure your Molly was the first."

"Oh, Doctor, you're so kind. I don't know what Molly and I would do without you. Mrs. Brown, please fetch the doctor's hat and coat. We mustn't keep him from his rounds. Please make some time to stay with us next visit, Doctor. I insist."

"Doctor Cunningham, may I go to the park tomorrow? You said no trace! I do feel fit as a fiddle! I absolutely must go to the park tomorrow! I haven't hunted for dragons in the park in weeks. They miss me, you know, my dragons."

The doctor squatted and gently touched his patient's shoulder. "Listen to me, young lady. You stay in bed today, eat what I have instructed Mrs. Brown to make for you, get a good night's sleep, and if your mother finds you as fit tomorrow as I find you today, you may go for a walk to the moon and back with your dragons if you like."

"Oh, you can't walk to the moon, and there are no dragons up there, either. But I'll be in the park tomorrow. You'll see!"

"Your coat and hat, Doctor."

"Thank you, Mrs. Brown. Please make sure Molly follows the routine I've prescribed, and let me know immediately if that cough comes back. Good day, ladies."

It was a short walk to his next appointment, and his long, bouncing strides covered the ground quickly such that he began to gain on the familiar form of an older gentleman ahead of him on the sidewalk, slightly stooped and moving with a noticeable limp, his thick, white hair poking out from under his hat. The doctor soon caught up with the older man and pulled in beside him, shortening his gait so as to maintain a position at the man's shoulder, as though he'd been there all along.

"Sam, my lad, how are you?"

"Quite well, Doctor Glass, just making the rounds in your neighborhood today."

"Ah, been to see the Bell girl, then?"

"Yes, she's recovering from another bout. I thought she might have a pneumonia complication this time, but apparently not. She seems quite well today."

"Nasty stuff. How old is the girl now?"

"She'll be nine shortly. Such a sweet girl, a wonderful imagination. She dreams up the most amazing stories, all filled with fantastic creatures, dragons, monsters, animals speaking to each other as intelligently as you and I. I see greatness in her future, perhaps a noted author, or passionate leader of some cause, assuming she makes it to adulthood."

"You just get her through a few more years, those young lungs will grow strong enough to put you out of a job. Perhaps before then I can convince you to reconsider the terrible professional mistake you've made. What a waste, Sam, family doctor and all. You're the best student I ever had. You should be working at the research hospital with me. I could use a bright mind like yours. We could all use a bright mind like yours. You're only in your late twenties, right? What, twenty-eight, twenty-nine? Now, there is plenty of time to right this ship and get on with a proper career."

"Thirty. Yes, yes, Doctor Glass, I know. Thank you as always for the kind words. As I've said before, though, I feel *this* is my calling. I can make a difference for children like Miss Molly Bell. And if she someday achieves what I envision she can, won't that be a greater contribution to society than I could ever make at the hospital?"

Doctor Glass started to speak again, but Doctor Cunningham raised his hand in protest. "Please, Doctor Glass, I know. I'll never get rich being a family doctor. But I have no wants, no needs unaddressed."

"Perhaps, Sam...ever the idealist. Well, if you won't let me twist your arm today, then you'll join me for supper after the seminar this afternoon. You are going to the seminar?"

"But of course, I wouldn't miss it. What a great opportunity, three of our colleagues from London. I look forward to hearing all about how much further along they are than their bumpkin colonial cousins across the Atlantic."

Doctor Glass laughed heartily. "Indeed. I hear they'll be speaking about a most curious new disease they have just identified involving children in London. I look forward to you solving the mystery for them. Then, you will come to dine with me? I promise, not a mention of the terrible mistake, your incredibly bad judgment, or the ruinous result of the path you have chosen. Not a word, I promise."

"Yes, Doctor, I'd be delighted."

* * *

Doctor Cunningham arrived for the seminar just as it was starting. The room was nearly full, so he took a seat two rows back from Doctor Glass. As he expected, the first part of the seminar was not particularly interesting. British doctors could be so condescending. After all, they were on the leading edge of everything, and Americans could so desperately use their learned insight. The only saving grace for the entire New York medical profession was that Doctor Glass had studied in London. These gentlemen, however, were London men, born and bred.

The last speaker got up with a grave countenance lacking from the previous presenters, and, after surveying his audience with a headmaster's glare, addressed the group. "Gentlemen, I bring you a mystery, a troubling mystery. We in London are losing children, at a statistically significant rate, to some as yet undetermined disease.

"These are the operative facts, facts that you may have read about in recent press accounts. Children, typically between ages five and fourteen, are succumbing to some sudden seizure, most often in public locations. Hyde Park has seen more of these cases than other such places. But it is, as you may know, a large and busy park, much more impressive than your Central Park, I might add.

"In any event, the children are perfectly healthy, as far as we can determine, and at the next moment they faint, fall into a coma, and never recover. They waste away until, typically after thirty days or so, their young bodies shut down and they expire.

"We believe the first cases appeared early last year, but we can't be sure, as there have been no linking symptoms other than those I just described. We also believe we have identified over fifty cases since then, but there may be more. It's hard to tell in a city of our size. Yes, Doctor Glass, a question?"

"Any fever, strange coloration, or difficulty breathing?"

"Neither before nor after. All indications are perfectly normal, other than the coma. We have autopsied over thirty children thus far, and can find no toxicological or physical abnormalities. Their young bodies starve to death, as we can keep them hydrated but cannot sufficiently feed them to save them from their fate. The numbers are small enough now, but our inability to identify either a cause or a cure has become quite alarming."

The presenter went on to discuss individual cases, demonstrating with specificity the general points he made at the beginning. Doctor Cunningham listened patiently, and at an appropriate point raised his hand, which seemed politely, though coolly, recognized.

"What about the environmental conditions of the children and of the locations where the attacks first manifest themselves?"

"No pattern we can detect. The children come from different backgrounds. Other than being evidently healthy prior to the onset of the symptoms described, we can find no common trait. The attacks do generally occur in public, as I mentioned before, which has led us to wonder if there isn't some quick-acting viral agent that they're encountering. Then, of course, there's the fantastic story recently stoked by the tawdry side of our press, but we attribute any supposedly credible witness accounts along these lines to the power of suggestion or, perhaps, lively imaginations fed by, well…"

Doctor Cunningham sat up straight in his chair. "Go on, Doctor, please."

The presenter paused for a moment, looking more than a little irritated. "According to reports from some of our, shall we say, more sensational newspapers, some witnesses of the initial collapse of some of these children report that, immediately beforehand, the child is approached by a man with a small black box. The man talks to the child and then presents the black box to the child. The child is then observed peering into one end of the black box, as if it were a kaleidoscope. You do know what a kaleidoscope is, Doctor? Well, yes, of course. The child then collapses, according to the narrative, and enters the coma we have discussed."

Doctor Cunningham ignored the sudden outbreak of mumbling in the crowd and focused intently on the speaker.

"Please, gentlemen, if I may continue. We have consulted the leading child psychologists, and they unanimously refute the theory that the children are seeing something so incredibly terrible that it induces a coma. I suppose it is possible that such a man, or several men meeting this description, could be carrying some yet-to-be-discovered contagious disease, but the immediacy of the attacks and the lack of any toxicology to support such theory leads us to the conclusion that this mysterious man with the black box is a flight of fancy, probably concocted as the story *du jour* designed to sell more papers. We find these stories as credible as the stories of werewolves that run side-by-side invading London. We prefer to deal with verifiable facts, symptoms, and cures, not ghosts and goblins."

"Of course, Doctor, I did not mean to suggest otherwise. Thank you."

"Quite right, Doctor. I only hope that this remains our problem. So far we have heard of no cases outside of London. I trust any of you will let us know immediately if you require our assistance here in America."

"God forbid," muttered Doctor Cunningham to himself. "God forbid."

* * *

Doctor Cunningham took another bite of bread, set the roll down on his dining table, and turned the folded newspaper over to the next page. He continued munching on his noonday snack, half of his attention on the newspaper while the other half went back to the various patients he'd seen that morning during his Saturday rounds, with occasional reflections on the strange seminar he'd attended the day before.

The most interesting news was all from abroad. The front page and several thereafter were dedicated to the latest from the Moroccan crisis. The French had not yet mobilized, but the semi-official German press had been hinting for weeks that war was coming, putting the French understandably on edge. The French press seemed quite conciliatory and urged its government to find some solution short of war. The British press had become uniformly anti-German, with several sources claiming that if war were declared the French could count on the British Empire coming to their aid. No one was sure where the Russians stood on any of this, nor of the attitude of the powers with the most regional interests, the Spanish and Italians. There were rumors that both the Germans and British had approached President Roosevelt for support; rumors the President had thus far declined to address.

He soon found himself drawn to an article on page six on a completely different topic, an article on the very mysterious disease discussed the day before at the seminar. All thought of the morning rounds was pushed from his mind as he focused on the curious tale related in the black print before him.

The article, summarizing reports from several London papers, was, indeed, sensational. Children in London were dropping like flies, each falling into a coma only to die a month later. The London public was alarmed, but thus far there had been no official recognition from the government of any particular problem. Newspapers in London had warned their readers to keep their children inside or under close supervision until the medical community had identified the cause. Reports were recounted linking a man with a black box to many of the victims. Some witnesses reported seeing a child peering into one end of a small black box given to them by the man immediately prior to the child losing consciousness.

Here the story enlarged from what was reported at the seminar. The man with the black box was also appearing in accounts of the sudden deaths of adults. Reports were coming into Scotland Yard of cases linking immediate seizures and death with adults peering into the box. Scotland Yard wouldn't comment on the veracity of the tales of a man with a black box being involved with any death of either an adult or a child. However, Scotland Yard had requested that anyone with information about the man or his black box contact the inspector in charge of these cases, Inspector Edmund Jenkins.

The article ended ominously with speculation of some terrible scene held within the black box, a scene so unimaginably horrible that upon observation it shocked adults to death immediately and stunned the more innocent children into a coma. The best professional minds in London were investigating.

Doctor Cunningham was so lost in the article that he hardly noticed the knock at the front door and the excited exchange coming from the front of the house.

"I beg your pardon, Doctor. I told her you were not to be disturbed at your lunch. But she insisted that she must see you immediately," announced his housekeeper with exasperation. She was a short, humorless woman with a round, flat face and pale, placid eyes. She didn't often show emotion other than exasperation, but her agitation was more than usually demonstrated at the moment.

"Who insists?"

"Why, Mrs. Brown, the nanny at the Bell house, she's most hysterical and cannot be reasoned with. I'm sorry, Doctor, I—"

Doctor Cunningham threw down the paper and bolted for the front room, leaving the housekeeper in mid-sentence. He was soon confronted by a panting and red-faced Mrs. Brown, who had made her way inside the house.

"What is it, Mrs. Brown? Is it Molly? Another attack?"

"I don't know, Doctor. Mrs. Bell told me to run and fetch you as fast as my legs would carry. She was fine this morning. Now we can't rouse her at all." Mrs. Brown gulped for air between words, her face flush and sweaty.

"What of her breathing?"

"She was fine, and now I can't wake her. I told Mrs. Bell not to let her go to the park. I told her, Doctor, but Molly was so insistent. She was just fine. I did everything you told me to."

"Mrs. Brown, please, what of her breathing? What is the rate?"

"She breathes fine, Doctor. Nice and steady, no cough, no wheeze, as strong as you could ever want, but she just won't answer. She just won't answer!"

"What happened? Mrs. Brown, please, calm yourself."

"I don't know. One minute she's playing, and the next she faints and won't answer. She's playing like normal, talking with a man in the park. The next minute she falls to the ground. She just drops the man's black box and falls down. And now we can't wake her, Doctor!"

* * *

"Why New York, Jenkins? Out of your jurisdiction, wouldn't you agree?"

Inspector Jenkins rubbed his round, balding head with his short, stocky fingers. "Lord Lansdowne, I've given it much thought. If you'll allow me, I'd like to detail the facts that have brought me to this decision."

"By all means, please. Care for a cigar?" Lansdowne extended a small cigar box toward the inspector.

"Why, yes, I'd quite enjoy one, thank you." The inspector pulled a cigar from the box and slid it past his nose, taking in a deep breath. "Havana?"

Lansdowne smiled and nodded, producing a lighter. "Yes, compliments of President Roosevelt. To the victor go the spoils. Here, allow me."

The inspector placed the cigar in his mouth and leaned toward the flickering flame, taking in three puffs before pulling away. "Yes, quite good." He paused as he took a long draw into his mouth, exhaling slowly. "Quite good. You taste one of these, and it almost makes sense for the Americans to go to war over that little island."

"I suppose the President says something similar about the English when he drinks the scotch I send him. Do you smoke Cuban cigars often?"

"I don't smoke any cigars often. I find smoking clouds my senses. No, but I do chew on them when I can. For a Havana, though, I'll risk the smoke in my eyes." He took another long satisfying draw. "Back to the detail. Last week I received an urgent cable from a Doctor Cunningham in New York. One of his patients, a young girl, had fainted after looking into a black box presented by a stranger. She was in a coma, but otherwise her symptoms were unremarkable. The doctor requested any assistance that the Yard could provide in determining the cause of her affliction."

"Most peculiar," replied Lansdowne. "A man with a black box outside London? You've flushed him, then?"

"Yes, I think so. Of course there've been no recent cases reported here. I'd hoped that the matter had died down. Perhaps with the recent press attention parents are more aware of hygiene, surroundings, or something. Even the reports of adults succumbing to instant death related to some black box have stopped. It's difficult to ascertain a pattern in a city as big as London, but there has been a certain lull in the reports of such mysterious happenings."

"No doubt due to your persistent digging in the matter, Inspector."

"Hmm, substantial doubt on that account, I think. However, I have considered the possibility that whoever he is, he may have gone to ground for a while now that we are focused on the black box concept as something more than mere fantasy spurred on by lurid press reports."

"Interesting. Are you certain now that this isn't all just fantasy?"

"I've seen so much of that in my career, monsters of every imaginable description lurking in the darkest corners of the city. This is different, though. This seems to have purpose, of what exactly I'm not sure, but purpose nonetheless. And, I still think, a purpose related to your engagement of me. The deaths of your agents here in London were no coincidence.

"The news of the black box has surely reached New York by now. I'd hoped that the decline in reported incidents in London was perhaps the beginning of the end of this mystery. Having received Doctor Cunningham's plea, however, I had to determine if the contagion, monster, or whatever it is had crossed the pond." Inspector Jenkins paused just long enough to take another draw on his cigar.

"I visited the various shipping lines and inspected the logs of recent transatlantic passages. The logs of one passenger ship in question caught my attention. During the voyage two men and one woman were found dead on board. The cause of death for each was unidentified, but was presumed to be heart attack or some other sudden seizure. Yet, after some additional investigation, it appeared that none of the three were in poor health before the trip.

"The ship in question had departed for New York just nine days before I received the doctor's request for aid. No new deaths of interest had occurred in London for the two weeks preceding the doctor's request. The coincidence is too much to ignore. This man, if he exists, may have left London and now be in New York."

"Good heavens, shall we alert the Americans?"

"I'd like to avoid any publicity in New York. I don't have the resources in America that I have here, and I think it important that my arrival in America be known to as few as possible. If, however, you can impress, discreetly, upon the American government the importance of my visit, it may become useful later to call upon them if I find myself in a tight spot with a need for assistance."

"Consider it done. We exchange more than just cigars and scotch with President Roosevelt."

CHAPTER 4
REDEMPTION

"AH, MY GUEST has arrived. I'm so glad you've come. Relieved, in fact. Please sit." Doctor Cunningham motioned Inspector Jenkins to a seat in his front room. "Please fetch our guest some tea. You do take tea, sir?"

"Yes, thank you, with a splash of scotch if available."

"I'm sorry, no. We do have American whiskey, for medicinal purposes, you understand. I don't drink the stuff, but I'm told it's quite good."

"That will do. A splash of whiskey then, thank you."

"Tea with a splash of whiskey," parroted the housekeeper as she left the room, closing the door behind her.

Doctor Cunningham took a moment to take the measure of his guest. The inspector was of average height, but with broad, strong shoulders and arms that were proportionally longer than his torso would justify. His face looked like an English bulldog with thick eyelids and the occasional random scar, the latter evidence no doubt of a life involving the not infrequent use of his compact fists. Tanned skin and rough hands gave the impression of a man who did his job away from his desk. He had a quiet and relaxed demeanor, tranquil in fact, as he made himself comfortable in the chair nearest the door.

"I trust your trip was uneventful. Thank you for coming. I'm quite at a loss, and any help you can give me and my patient would be appreciated."

"No need to thank me, Doctor. It's my job. You're the best lead I have at the moment. Tell me, how is your patient?"

Doctor Cunningham sensed that the inspector had already taken measure of him as well, but had not in the slightest revealed his own conclusions. "Most perplexing, most perplexing and, quite frankly, frustrating."

"Molly is her name, isn't it? Molly Bell, if I recall." The inspector's tone was steady, low, and matter of fact.

"Yes, Molly Bell, age nine as of two days ago. She's suffered from asthma all her life, and had just recovered from another bout. I saw her less than two weeks ago, healthy as I've ever seen her. Her breathing was normal, no signs of asthma or any other issues. I permitted her to go to the park the next day when, well, you know the details." Doctor Cunningham bent his head and paused, as he mentally fortified himself to continue.

"She entered a coma and has not recovered since. Her condition worsens daily. I can keep her hydrated, but I can't give her sustenance. She's starving to death, Inspector, and I can't do a damned thing about it."

"Any return of the asthma?"

"No, she breathes well, although she seems restless at times, as if she's having nightmares. Not a sound out of her, though, not even a whimper."

"Yes, quite typical. I am sorry, Doctor, I can't help you on the medical side. I've come for a different purpose. The man she saw before she lost consciousness, the man with the black box, what can you tell me about him?" The inspector demonstrated for the first time a perceptible change in facial expression, with his right eyebrow rising slightly after the question had been asked.

"Your tea, sir," interrupted the housekeeper as she bustled into the room.

"Thank you, please put it on the end table. I would like some privacy with my guest, if you please." Doctor Cunningham waited a moment after the door had closed to continue. "I don't know that there's much more to say. She was seen holding a black box that a man had given her in the park. She peered into the box, and fell to the ground. She's been in a coma since."

"Any description of this man?"

"Nothing stuck out to her nanny. He was just a man, an ordinary man. I suspect the shock of seeing Molly fall has erased any specific memory she had of him."

"Did anyone notify the police?"

"Molly's mother did, but there's nothing much they can do about a man in the park with a black box. The only reason I contacted you was because you were mentioned in a newspaper article I had read that very morning about such a man in London."

"The article in the *Times*?"

"Yes, I read it every day, front to back. That article struck me as unusual, coming from the *Times*. Perhaps you'd see something like that in the *Herald*, but the *Times*? It further caught my attention because I had attended a seminar the evening before which included a brief and dismissive discussion of a man with a black box somehow related to the same mysterious affliction which now seems to be affecting Molly. I could never have imagined I'd be faced with my own case. I still can't quite believe the whole man with a black box idea. Is he real?"

"Who else in your circles knows who I am, Doctor?" The inspector took a sip of tea, never diverting his gaze from Doctor Cunningham.

"Doctor Glass, a senior colleague of mine, and I passed on your request for anonymity to him as soon as I got your cable. Other than that, just my fiancée."

"Miss Scott, Mary Scott?"

Doctor Cunningham was startled. He didn't recall ever mentioning Mary to the inspector. "Yes, Ms. Mary Scott. We are to be married in four weeks, but perhaps you know that already, too. In any event, she has been sworn to secrecy."

"'Miz'?"

"Yes, she prefers that title, until we're married. Perhaps you've heard of recent proposals for use of the term? She's rather independently minded."

"A suffragette?"

"Indeed, Mary is quite active in the movement, with my full support, I might add. We've treated woman like a subhuman species far too long."

"Can she be trusted, Doctor? I mean no offense. It has been my experience that women tend to enjoy gossip as a general rule, that's all."

"She's not the general type. In fact, this may sound strange, but she has the habit more of a man when it comes to maintaining confidences than any woman I've ever met. Come to think of it, she's less likely to gossip than most men I've met as well. That characteristic is important to me, as you might imagine."

"Would she ever keep a secret from you?"

"I confess that thought has never occurred to me. We're very close. She's my sounding board and I hers." He paused to consider the issue. "I suppose she'd keep something from me if she felt that to do otherwise would somehow hurt or endanger me. I trust her to make that judgment."

"And Doctor Glass, what can you tell me about him?"

"He's a respected member of our profession. I mentored under him as a younger man. He's one of the founders of a prestigious medical research facility here in New York. He studied in London and is well respected there as well, as I have learned. He specializes in understanding physical pain and treatments for it. As you would expect of a doctor, I've found him most reliable in the past with confidential information."

"Good, that will all do, although I'd prefer neither of them know more than what you've already told them. I'll get straight to the point. Doctor, I know you were hoping for my help, but it is I who need your help. I don't have the resources here in America such as I have in London. I need to relate some confidential information to you, and then I need you to assist me in certain particulars. We do have a common interest. I don't know if my work here can save your Miss Molly, but finding out more about any possible man with a black box, I'm convinced, is the only route to saving her of which I'm aware. Can I count on you in all respects?"

"I'm willing to try anything to save Molly. Yes, please continue."

"Excellent. Now that I have your commitment, I beg you'll forgive me for asking you a few additional questions first. I understand this may seem rather strange."

"Please, ask away. I understand. You don't know me yet."

"My hat was placed on the hat stand behind you. Without looking, what is it?"

"A black derby, rather faded and dusty, if you'll forgive me for saying so."

"Do I smoke tobacco?"

"You don't smell of tobacco, but your teeth give you away. I suspect you chew tobacco of some sort."

"What was the first thing I said to you walking into this room?"

He had to stop momentarily on this one. "It had to do with wanting scotch in your tea."

"Now a riddle. Listen carefully, as I won't repeat myself. Jack and Jill must determine George's birthday by month and day. They are both told it is one of the following: May 14, 15, 19; June 16, 17, 18; July 14, 16; August 14, 15, 17. One of the eleven days I just mentioned is George's birthday. Jill is then separately told the specific number of the day that is George's birthday, but nothing more. Jack is then separately told the specific month of George's birthday, but nothing more. Jack next says, 'I don't know George's birthday, but neither does Jill.' Jill then says, 'I didn't know George's birthday, but I know it now.' Jack lastly says, 'I now know his birthday too.' What is George's birthday?"

Doctor Cunningham sat back and smiled. "July 16."

"And how long do you think it took you to determine that answer?"

"The first time? That riddle was in the *Times* last weekend. It took me several minutes, I must confess. My Mary, Ms. Scott, solved it almost immediately. But it took me at least five minutes. Is that fast enough, Inspector?"

"Speed was not the test, Doctor." The inspector leaned in and, after a sip of tea, lowered his tone. "To answer your earlier question, I have reason to believe that there *is* a man with a black box, and that he's no longer in London, but here, in New York. I don't know if he is an assassin, the carrier of some unknown and highly communicable disease, or keeper of some diabolical machine in this black box. The fact remains that he has been linked, over and over again, many times, by reliable witnesses, to the immediate deaths of adults, and the eventual deaths of children."

"Dear God." The doctor leaned back and took a deep breath in contemplation. "What description do these witnesses give?"

"That point is in itself peculiar. All the witnesses report that he's quite 'normal,' 'average,' 'nothing unusual,' or that nothing at all stands out. They can't seem to describe a face or even his dress, only that he was just a normal man. You can't sketch a suspect's features with that kind of persistent non-description."

"No doubt, like a disease with no symptoms but death."

"Hm, I suppose." The inspector took another sip. "I need you to look into certain recent deaths in New York and, I'm afraid, some that have yet to occur." The inspector produced papers from his pocket and passed them to the doctor. "These are all recent and sudden deaths, all adults, reported in your local papers or that I have learned about through various sources. I need you to investigate them. See if you can determine a cause of death. Find out any facts you can about the circumstances, witnesses, background on the decedent. Discreetly inquire about any man with a black box who can be linked to any of them. I'll continue to provide you with this information while I follow up on other leads that I'm working on."

"Yes, I see."

"Doctor, forgive me, but I must emphasize how critical it is that you be discreet. This man with the black box must not get the sense that I'm about. I was close several times in London, and that's perhaps why he's here now."

"Killing New Yorkers, instead of Londoners. Perhaps you shouldn't have flushed him into our country."

"If this man is in fact a killer, he must be stopped, regardless of whom he's killing."

"Yes, you're right, sorry."

"Perhaps I made a mistake by getting the press involved in London—doing so certainly fueled the speculation, but I needed leads. This time I'd like to keep this quiet as long as possible. You can reach me"—the inspector scribbled on a pad of paper—"at this address. If anyone should inquire, I am an acquaintance here on holiday."

The inspector took a last sip and set down his cup. "I do love this city of yours, very vibrant, very innocent. One gets the sense that there is nothing that can't be accomplished."

"I hope your man with the black box doesn't feel the same way. I'd just as soon not have so many clippings to look after."

The inspector smiled and stood to leave. "Good day, Doctor. We'll be in touch, then."

"Before you go, what was the test then? The silly quiz from the newspaper?"

"Honesty, sir. Trustworthiness must be determined quickly in my line of work. Quite frequently my life depends on it."

* * *

Molly had lost her grip on time. She could tell she was moving through it, but there were no minutes, no hours, no days, no sun coming up and going down, but just the pain of constantly increasing hunger, a sucking grip in her stomach that never let go.

At least she had her new friends. They were difficult to look at, initially, with their faces a mixture of animal and human features, something like a blend of a cat and a child, and they flashed sharp, long teeth when they smiled. They were all more or less her size, but she looked down on them when she stood because they stooped when they walked on their skinny legs, as if they were dogs that had learned to walk upright. They had tails, too, like the lions she had seen in the zoo, but shorter. Their bodies were mostly without hair, except for a line of rough hair that started on their tails, followed their spines, and ran to the tops of their heads.

The way they talked to her, she thought they must be children like her. They were very friendly, offering her water to quench her thirst and keeping her company. They were all hungry, too. They all talked about hoping to eat soon and walked around clutching at their stomachs. They evidently ate frequently, but were still often quite hungry.

She didn't need them to tell her she was in a different place, a different world, at least a place like none she had seen before. They told her she was lucky. She would obtain eternal life here, which they explained meant she would never die. Molly just wanted to go home to her mother. They tried to console her. She would never go home, though, they said. They were her family now.

* * *

"Sam, what's wrong? You haven't touched your food nor said so much as two words all evening." Mary Scott reached across the table and gently rested her hand on her fiancé's wrist.

"Sorry, it's all just such depressing stuff, sifting through obituaries, visiting grieving relatives, poking at dead bodies."

She looked at Sam tenderly, his head bent low on his slender neck, his shock of red hair all but covering his right eye. He had never seemed so sad to her before. The boyish face wore lines of fatigue and bags hung under his bright green eyes. He looked ten years older, which placed him about the age he really was, when she thought about it. She had tried to keep the conversation light, but slipped up when she saw how little he had eaten.

"Sam, you're doing everything you can."

"I know. I know. I never realized there were so many deaths in this city. So many people no one cares about. I checked on a young lady yesterday, a lady of ill repute, shall we say. Quite young, she couldn't have been out of her teens. No name, no relatives, no friends, just a hard profession, a profession that killed her. It's all so sad. At one time she had a mother, you know. Somewhere she had a father, too. She may have brothers and sisters. No one knows. No one cares." Doctor Cunningham put his head in his hands and wrapped his long, elegant fingers about his skull. Surgeon's fingers, that's what Doctor Glass called them, Mary heard him say once.

"*You* care. You can't take on the woes of the whole city though, Sam. You're doing all you can."

"But it's not good enough! Do you know what Molly weighs now? She's starving to death. Why can't I stop it? Why does she have to die, the most imaginative little mind I've ever known? Why, Mary? Why does she have to die?" He began to cry softly as he hid his face in his hands.

She'd never seen him cry before, not even after losing a patient. Poor, dear Sam. If only she could do something to ease his burden. "Darling, you're so tired. You've been working incredibly hard. Tell the inspector you need a rest. Let's take a holiday to Atlantic City. You need some rest. You deserve some rest."

"Mary, I'm sorry. I've been so obsessed about this. You deserve a fiancé, and instead you get a crusader."

He stretched his long arm across the table to touch her cheek. She took his hand and pressed it against her face.

"I must continue the work, I'm sorry. I can't let her die with any stone unturned. The inspector is so determined. He pops up at the strangest hours with the strangest requests, wants me to educate him on all sorts of medical issues. I've never met such a…well, such a determined man. He approaches his task with a fierceness that is unsettling. If ever I should disappear, my Mary, I should only hope the inspector is on the case."

"No, Sam, I've met a more determined man." She pulled his hand from her cheek and kissed it lightly. "If ever I am terribly ill, I hope I'm blessed with you as my doctor."

Mary stared adoringly into her fiancé's eyes, which drew a transformative smile in response.

"You know, my dear Mary, you once told me that God, by his nature, communicates with man continually, but not always with words. He does so with glorious sunsets, with gentle breezes scented by flowers, with bubbling brooks, and by the cries of gulls over splashing surf. He also speaks in the faces and voices of the ones we love. I always think of that when you look at me with that sparkle in your eyes. It makes me feel like God is speaking to me, and I so much love what He has to say."

"Amen. I love you, Sam Cunningham. Now, eat. You can't help Molly if you don't feed yourself."

* * *

Molly's friends were in an excited frenzy. They were going to eat! They were all so hungry. Molly had never seen them eat before. "You're not ready yet," they would say when they went to a meal. But today they would show her. Today they would show her the way to eternal life. Today they would eat their fill and rejoice.

"I'm so hungry. Can't I eat, too? I want to eat."

They all laughed and smiled, flashing sharp teeth dripping with saliva. "You're not ready yet. Just watch. You're not ready yet to eat. Just watch, and learn."

Molly's protests were cut short by the screaming of a girl. Her friends were clinging to the girl, holding her down. The girl screamed and shrieked, but she couldn't break free from the grasp of dozens and dozens of clawed hands. Molly's friends were a swirling, excited mob, spinning and jumping around the girl. Or was she a young lady?

Molly tried to get a closer look. She was young, but not a girl. She wore makeup, with lots of rouge on her cheeks. Her clothes were torn and her black stockings were ripped. She kept screaming and fighting to free herself, but it was hopeless. There were too many of them.

"What are you doing? Let her go. She hasn't done anything to us. Let her go!"

Molly's pleas were drowned out by the high-pitched howling of the mob. They became more and more excited, each one screeching and jumping. Soon the noise of the mob drowned out not just Molly's pleas but the screaming of the young lady as well. Then there was lunging, then blood. One last piercing shriek rose above the howls. Molly struggled to make her way through the mob.

As she pushed closer she began to see over the top of the pile that was wriggling above the young lady. Then she started to make out individuals among the crowd. They were bloody, familiar faces, heads thrust at a body on the ground, mouths ripping at her arms, legs, and face. They were eating *her*! *She* was the meal! Molly put her hands over her eyes, but couldn't stop the racking dry heaves taking over her hollow stomach.

"Don't cry. Don't you see? We have redeemed her. We have saved her for eternity, and in return we live forever. You, too, will eat and worship the feast. You will join us. You will be eternal. You will redeem those who need redeeming. You will stop the hunger. You will be one of us. You will eat!"

"Never," she sobbed. "Never. I'd rather starve to death. What is this dream? I don't understand. Mother, please wake me from this dream. I want to go home!"

"We know, we understand. It's all right. You'll change your mind. Don't cry. We all felt just like you feel. You must eat. You will learn to worship the feast. You will eat. Then you'll understand. Then you'll join us."

* * *

"Interesting." The inspector broke the silence of Doctor Cunningham's study as he thumbed through the notes the doctor had prepared for him. "Interesting."

"Yes?" replied the doctor. In his experience, the inspector rarely found anything interesting unless it had significance. The man had an amazing ability to sift through the most mundane facts and quickly spot the important evidence buried therein. "What do you see, Inspector?"

"Oh, sorry. Tell me, how is Molly? Any improvement?" asked the inspector without looking up from the papers.

Doctor Cunningham sensed that he was purposely changing the subject. Perhaps he was still processing the interesting facts. "Worse every day, she's wasting away. Her body is running out of the nourishment required to sustain her. She still tosses and turns occasionally, as if in a bad dream. Quite peculiar, all that, which we don't normally see in a coma. She won't last much longer, I'm afraid."

"Quite sorry, Doctor." The inspector still had not looked up. After a few more seconds he set the papers down. "Do you recall Mr. Charles Hoffman?"

"Are you *really* 'quite sorry'? You don't show it. Is this so damned clinical to you? These are *people* dying in New York, and you find it 'interesting'!" Doctor Cunningham glared at the inspector for a moment and then dropped his chin to his chest, taking a deep breath. "I'm sorry, that was uncalled for."

"Apology accepted. Mr. Hoffman, if you please, Doctor, do you recall?"

"Yes, of course, the business genius fallen from grace. Embezzlement, a mistress, attempts to bribe a judge, it sounds like he had city government in his back pocket until recently."

"You couldn't determine the cause of death when you autopsied him, correct?"

"No, I couldn't. He was forty-five years of age and in good health. There was no evident damage to the heart. All his organs appeared normal. There was no sign of any foul play or any natural cause of death evident. He died at his desk, or more precisely, he died at the chessboard he kept in his office."

"What else?"

"Well, other than what I wrote down, he was a snappy dresser. He died wearing a fine Italian suit and a red bow tie."

"Did you talk to his secretary?"

"No, as reflected in my notes, I spoke only with his family. Upon inquiry, I couldn't find his secretary. She's no longer employed, I believe."

"That's correct, Doctor. But I've found her. Mr. Hoffman had good taste in more than clothing, I might add. Unlike the suit, she's English, and rather distractingly attractive. In fact, I doubt few men could resist her advances for long." The inspector paused for a moment as if lost in thought. "I pray that neither you nor I are ever put to the test. At any rate, she recalls the day that 'her Charles' passed away. She found him dead in his office shortly after his last appointment of the day. An appointment, Doctor, with a man, a nondescript man, with a black box. That, sir, I find interesting."

* * *

Molly's hunger was unbearably intense. She struggled to think of anything other than the pain in her stomach. She had grown almost numb to the feedings that her friends continued to make her watch. She didn't want to watch, but they insisted she must. The victims always screamed for help and mercy. Her friends were never satisfied for long.

It seemed, however, that some victims satisfied them more than others. The more the victim needed to be "redeemed," the more her friends seemed happy and satisfied. The victims were from all walks of life, men, women; they were all different in some way or the other, except they were all adults. There were more women with rosy cheeks, lots of makeup, and black stockings. There was the business man with the red bow tie. He must have needed lots of "redeeming."

She didn't want to eat any of them, despite her hunger. It was just as well, she was told. Her first feast would be of a different sort. She needed a worthy meal, a meal that would provide them with very little sustenance, but would change her forever. Her meal would need no redeeming. Her meal would be her chance at eternal life. She needed a special, transformative meal.

"I don't want a transformative meal, whatever that means. I want to go home," she would say.

"We understand, but you have no choice. The pain will only grow and grow. You must free yourself from the hunger, and eating is the only way." They explained that she must be set free from her present form. She would join them, become one of them. A worthy meal would do all this and set her free. She would live eternally and help them redeem others. Her meal would move on to another world, but she would stay here with her friends, forever. All she needed was to accept what her body was telling her to do, eat. Forget everything else, just listen to the urge and do it. The time would come when a special meal would be brought just for her. Then she would understand. Then she would eat and join them, forever.

Molly was shaken back to the moment and away from her thoughts of hunger by the howls of her friends. Another meal must be coming. As the group got closer, though, there was no screaming victim, just a man, an old man. He was not screaming. In fact, he didn't even seem to resist. He just followed where he was led. And he was led straight to Molly.

"It's here!" they exclaimed. "Your meal, Molly. He is worthy. He can transform you. Set him free, Molly. Set yourself free, Molly! Eat! Eat!"

Molly felt the hunger growing and pushing her body forward toward the man. Her mouth was watering. She shook with a wild and morbid anticipation. She forgot who she was, where she was. All she felt was hunger and the desire to quench it.

She looked at the man's face. He had sad eyes. He looked back at her in a way that went straight through her. She looked down to avoid his gaze and focused instead on his neck. His neck—

"Oh no, no, no, he's a priest! I can't, please stop! I can't."

"Molly, you must. Let go. You must be free. He will do little for us. He doesn't need our redeeming. You must eat. He can help only you."

"I can't." She looked back up at the old priest. Suddenly it all came rushing back, who she was, where she was. "Please let me die. Please, Father, I just want to die!"

Tears began to well up in the old priest's eyes just before the mob turned on him. They ate him like the others.

"Not much of a meal," they said, matter-of-factly, when they were done. "You should have eaten him. You have no choice. There will just be another, and then another, until you join us. You have no choice, Molly. None of us had a choice. Please trust us. You'll understand once you join us. Let go. You must learn to worship the feast. You must eat."

CHAPTER 5
THE SUMMONS

DOCTOR CUNNINGHAM SAT up in his chair and rubbed his stubbly face with his hands. He checked his watch to find that it was still late afternoon. He had needed the catnap, but also needed to get back to work. There were so many deaths in the city, so much hay, so few needles, so little time. He just had to keep looking. Molly was near the end, he thought. Her pulse had slowed. Her breathing was shallow. She couldn't have much left to sustain her.

Was he chasing a ghost? Was it all real? A man with a black box, children entering comas, adults dropping dead for no apparent reason; none of it made sense. Hopefully the inspector would have some news.

He heard a knock at the front door followed by the muffled scurrying of his housekeeper. Then there was a voice, a man's voice. He could faintly make out a short conversation followed by the sound of the door shutting. Strange, the inspector was not expected for another half hour. He was usually quite punctual unless he was running late due to an unexpected lead he had to follow, but never early.

"Excuse me, Doctor. A gentleman delivered this note and asked that I give it to you."

"A gentleman? Who did he say he was?"

"He didn't, sir. He didn't answer me, he just told me you would want to see what's in this envelope." The housekeeper handed it over.

"What did he look like?"

"Sorry, sir?" she replied, seeming befuddled by the question.

"This gentleman, what did he look like? What was he wearing? How old did he look?"

Each new question just seemed to pose more of a puzzle than the last. She paused for a moment, and then looked at the floor as she fumbled for words. "I, I'm not sure, sir. I'm sorry, I was focusing on what he was saying, and I just don't recall."

He turned his attention to the envelope, which contained a note. As he read, he gripped the note tighter with both hands.

"Doctor, what is it? You look as white as a ghost. May I bring you some water, or perhaps a cup of tea?"

"A summons. I must be on my way." He stuffed the note back in the envelope and grabbed his coat. "My friend from London will be arriving shortly. Please give him this envelope, and tell him I've left. He'll understand."

* * *

Inspector Jenkins shuffled his notes, trying to organize them before his visit with Doctor Cunningham. He had so many leads. The manpower the Yard provided in London was sorely missed indeed. He would focus on the Manhattan dock area this evening, with addresses of interest at Fulton, Fletcher, Pine, Wall, Pearl, and one in particular that he would case for a while on John Street.

The hansom cab pulled up in front of the doctor's house, and Jenkins emerged with both hands filled with notes to be reviewed, his mouth chomping on the stub of a cigar. "Please wait for me. I'll be only twenty minutes or so, and I'll need you this evening."

The driver nodded as the inspector trotted to the door, where he was greeted by the housekeeper.

"I'm sorry, sir, the doctor left in quite a hurry just thirty minutes ago."

"Did he say where he was going?"

"No, sir, he asked me to give you this note. He said you would understand. It will tell you where he's going, sir."

Jenkins examined her face as she held the note out to him. "Did he indicate that you could read the note?"

"No, sir, just to give it to you," she replied, diverting her eyes from the inspector.

"Well, since you've read it to yourself already, perhaps you'll be so kind as to read it to me."

She took a deep breath and then slowly exhaled as her shoulders seemed to curl in toward her chest and slumping head. "Yes, sir," she responded as she removed the note from the envelope. She looked down at the note and cleared her throat.

"I have a black box. Come immediately and alone, or you will never see it. Seventeen John Street."

"Is that all it says?"

"Yes, sir."

"And how did the doctor get this note?"

"Just a minute before he left a gentleman delivered it to the house. I gave the note to the doctor as the gentleman requested."

"What did this gentleman look like?"

"I don't know, sir. He just looked like a…a gentleman."

The inspector spit out the cigar, turned, and ran for the cab. "Seventeen John Street, as fast as you can."

* * *

The cab driver gave Doctor Cunningham an anxious look. "Seventeen John Street, sir. Are you sure this is the address?"

"Yes, thank you." He paid the cab driver and bade him goodbye.

He paused to survey his surroundings. Shabby, he thought, would be a generous description of the outside of the address. He crept up the steps to the front door. At the top of the stairs he paused, took a deep breath, and said a quick prayer for Molly.

"Come in, please," came a muffled, yet deep-throated answer to his knocking on the door.

The doctor entered and shut the door behind him. A tremor ran up his back. He clenched his teeth to hold himself steady. At first he couldn't see anyone else in the room, which was dimly lit by two small lanterns. It was dank, smelly, and sparsely furnished. As his eyes adjusted to the scene, the outline of a man emerged from the back of the room.

"Come in. Please come in, Doctor. I've been expecting you. Please, we don't have much time."

Doctor Cunningham walked cautiously toward a long table in the middle of the room, and was immediately drawn to the single object resting upon it: a small, black box. It came into focus sharply, unlike the man in the back of the room. He remained an elusive image, strangely unfocused.

"Yes, there it is, Doctor, the black box. It doesn't look like much, does it? You and the inspector have spent so much time and effort trying to find it, and here I offer it to you on a platter, so to speak."

"You know the inspector?"

"Inspector Jenkins? I know of him. We've never had the pleasure of meeting, although we've just missed each other many times. Like two ships in the night, both running without lights but only one visible to the other. Someday, it's inevitable. I look forward to it immensely. Knowing him, that is."

Doctor Cunningham focused hard on the man. He seemed so normal, so ordinary. He tried to discern features, facial proportions, anything to help him remember. Was this why no one could describe the man, or was something playing with his mind?

"Don't you want to know what it is, Doctor, how it works, what it does? Surely you're curious after all this time. As a man of science you don't believe all these fanciful stories the inspector has been feeding you, adults dying and all that, from just looking into a box? He's such an imaginative man. I suppose that's a prerequisite in his profession. But you, you're a medical man. You deal in cold, hard facts. Before you is a black box, simply that. Nothing magic here, Doctor. But what is it? What does it do? Pick it up. Look at it. What are you waiting for? This is what you've been looking for, for weeks, is it not?"

Doctor Cunningham slowly reached for the box. He picked it up with both hands, keeping it at arm's length as he turned it over to look at every surface. It was just a black box, rectangular in shape, about five inches wide, six inches tall, and nine inches long, he estimated. It didn't seem to weigh much, as if it was made from thin strips of wood, yet it was quite solid in construction. In fact, he couldn't discern how it was constructed. It looked like one solid piece, but he could sense that it was hollow. The only other feature of note was a small hole, something less than one inch in diameter, in the middle of one of the ends of the rectangular shape.

"Yes, you can look inside. That would answer all your questions, wouldn't it?"

Doctor Cunningham hesitated, staring at the box while still keeping it at arm's length. Was it truly lethal? It looked so harmless.

"It won't bite you. It's just a box. But I'll tell you something that I think you already know. Your patient, Molly..."

At the name, Doctor Cunningham jerked his head toward the stranger as he fought back a rage that welled in his chest.

"Ah, yes, I *have* met Molly. I do know *her*. Delightful young lady, quite extraordinary, in fact. You see, only you can save her. You know that, deep down inside. And to save her, you must solve the mystery of that box you hold. To save her you have to, well, you have to look inside, don't you?

"Doctor, I offer you this opportunity but for a short time. Molly's time is short, too, as you know. And only you can save her now. Look inside the box, Doctor. Don't be afraid. It's merely a box."

He sensed the man was right about one thing. Something deep within told him he had to look into the box, for Molly's sake, despite the screaming inside his head that said, *"No! Never look in that box!"* He trembled as he held the box in front of him, the mysterious hole just inches from his face.

"Doctor, as I've said repeatedly, we have little time. I have no doubt your inspector will be along soon, and Molly needs you now. You must either look in the box now or you'll never have the chance again."

Doctor Cunningham tried to focus on the man again. What were his options? His head was swimming in thought but nothing was clear.

"Doctor!" The man produced a revolver from under his coat. "Your options were quite limited and your time is up. You may choose to look in the box, or I shall dispatch you from this world and take it back from you. If you look into the box, your curiosity will be satisfied, you will understand what is happening with your Molly, and I will not harm you further. If you don't do so in the next five seconds, I will pull this trigger. On both points you have my word, on which you may most assuredly rely." The man pulled back the hammer on the revolver with a convincing click and pointed it at Doctor Cunningham's heart.

Doctor Sam Cunningham slowly lifted the box to his face and looked inside.

* * *

Her friends were all abuzz. Another meal had arrived. Another meal just for Molly had arrived. Now she could eat and learn to worship the feast. Now she would become one of them and be free forever and live forever. This time she would eat. They all seemed so certain and so happy, joyful at the thought of one more of them. Glad to soon be rid of the reminder of what they once were, human.

Molly caught glimpses of a man struggling with the mob. Clawed hands covered every inch of his body, it seemed, including his mouth, as he struggled to speak, and his eyes as he struggled to see.

Her hunger pains were more intense than she had ever experienced before. Her mouth watered with the thought of tasting flesh and quenching the flame in her stomach. She must eat. They were right. She couldn't stand it anymore. A tingle of excitement ran up her spine. Her teeth felt sharper than she remembered. She felt so alive. She would live forever. All she had to do was eat, and forget. She would set this man free.

She moved purposefully toward her meal. She felt drool running down her chin as she ran her tongue across her sharp and pointed teeth. She felt no hesitation now, no remorse, no self, just a dull, throbbing force pushing her forward, a warm pounding in her head.

As she moved within lunging distance of the man the crowd began to give way and a hand slipped from his face. Now she could see his eyes as she paused very briefly before taking the first tantalizing bite. She looked into his remarkable, familiar, bright green eyes.

"Doctor Cunningham!" she shrieked. She felt dizzy. Her mouth propelled her forward but something deeper inside, something in her core, tugged in the other direction, a quiet, persistent pull gaining in strength.

The hunger was intense. Her mouth was opening. Her friends began to shout with joy in such volume that the universe seemed to shake. Molly screamed skyward, and then her head lunged forward, but she flung her arm in the way.

Deep into her own flesh she sank her sharpened teeth. Ripping at the skin, she pulled her head back, leaving a gaping wound, a wound in her own arm. All her friends screamed as if in terrible pain. Then there was a bright flash, followed by darkness and silence.

* * *

Inspector Jenkins instructed the driver to stay put. Catlike, he deftly mounted the porch in front of the building and surveyed the scene. He touched the hinge on the door and examined the rusty dust that smeared his fingers. In the fading sunset he squatted and examined the scuff marks on the porch floor with the help of the lantern he had removed from the hansom cab. Standing, he felt the door and pressed his ear to the cold wood. He heard nothing but his own slow breathing. Everything pointed to someone having entered recently, but there was no evidence of anyone exiting.

He pulled a revolver from his jacket and held it low by his hip in his right hand. No time to find an alternate entrance. The room would probably be dark, so he closed his right eye and counted slowly and silently to sixty, in case he needed one adjusted eye to fight in a blackened room with a shot-out lantern. He squatted again and held the lantern high above his head at the level one would expect his head to be if he were standing. He swung open the door with his right hand while holding his revolver.

The door creaked. He peered inside, leading with the lantern, now opening his right eye. He forced his breathing into a slow, steady pace, fighting contrary to the hard thumping of his heart.

He saw no one, but he remained squatting with the lantern over his head and in front of his body as he looked about the room. Two dim lanterns on either side at the back of the room cast a weak light about the dingy place. The cool evening air from the open door seemed to breathe a much needed freshness into the building. He slowly stood, moving the lantern away from his body but keeping it at the same level such that it was still slightly ahead of him and at about the level of his head once he was standing.

He moved cautiously toward a table at the center of the space, continuously swiveling his head left and right, searching the room for any movement. On the table sat a black box. He picked it up and turned it round in his hands. In one end was a small hole. The opposite end was blown out, as if the box had exploded. He peered into the open end and saw nothing inside. It was just an empty box.

A moan from under the table made him reflexively point his revolver at the sound. He redirected the lantern and quickly dropped back to the ground. Keeping the drawn pistol behind the lantern but pointed straight ahead, he cast the light under the table.

"Doctor Cunningham, are you all right?"

* * *

"She's waking again, Doctor!" exclaimed Mrs. Bell in a hushed but excited tone. She paused from stroking her daughter's hair and tenderly brushed the back of her hand on Molly's cheek.

Doctor Cunningham looked up from the bandage he was inspecting on her arm to see Molly open her eyes and blink several times. She looked about her pink bedroom with a confused expression and then smiled at the doctor.

"Good morning, young lady. You've had quite a nap."

"Where am I?"

"You're home, Molly. I was just examining your improving condition. Mrs. Brown, fetch her some warm milk if you please. Easy, young lady, just relax."

"But I had the strangest dream, Doctor. No, it was a nightmare. It...too awful to talk about. Except the end, then it was wonderful," she said as the light began to come back into her inquisitive eyes. "I'm so hungry, though," she whispered.

"Here's your milk, darling," announced Mrs. Brown.

Molly drank slowly, gaining a little more color with every swallow. She peered over the glass at the familiar face of her doctor.

"Now, now, that's it. Take your time and then you can rest some more. No need to talk now. I want you to drink all that milk and then just rest. You can have some bread a little later."

"With lemonade, Doctor? You were there, I think, in my dream, right before the wonderful part. I can have lemonade, right?"

"Yes, I think that will do nicely, Molly. You drink all that milk, and in two hours, it's bread first and then one glass of lemonade, doctor's orders. Mrs. Bell, I'll be back this evening. I still have wedding plans to attend to. Please send word if you need me."

"Thank you so much, Doctor. God be praised, you've brought back my little Molly." Mrs. Bell raised her face to heaven and then grasped the doctor's hand as tears began to well in her eyes.

"There, there, I think she brought herself back to us."

Mrs. Bell let go of his hand to gently brush a strand of hair off her daughter's face. "It's all so strange. We heard her scream and came in to find her biting her arm. Then she looked up at the ceiling with wide open eyes and started chatting away in the most indecipherable gibberish. We gave her some milk, and she went to sleep. It makes no sense. What happened to her, Doctor?"

He opened his mouth, and then felt himself searching for what it was that he intended to say. "I'm not sure, Mrs. Bell, I'm just not sure."

* * *

Inspector Jenkins looked out at the busy harbor, focusing on no ship in particular. Such energy and optimism this young city held. It sparkled, like the sun dancing off the water. Still, it would be good to return to musty old London. Four weeks in New York was quite long enough.

He pulled out a watch from his waistcoat and glanced at the time. He should be along any minute, based on the inbound ship's schedule. Sure enough, before the watch was stowed, he heard the familiar lilt.

"Inspector, you're a sight for my sore Irish eyes. Nuttin' but green swells and fish for four days, it's good to be on solid ground again."

"Mick, I'm glad you've answered my summons, because now I can leave this country safe in the knowledge that you're on the job."

"Business in a moment, sir, for I've brought you a present."

"Indeed?"

Mick pulled a flask from his pants pocket. "Yes, a present from Ireland to you."

The inspector took the flask and yanked out the cork. He pulled the open top close to his nose.

"Ah Mick, *poitin*, bless your soul."

"From my uncle's farm, it is. He makes the best in the County Cork. They all say it's so. None of that rushin' about, he takes his time, he does."

After the sniff Jenkins took a nip, savoring the smooth liquid in his mouth before letting the warmth slide down his throat.

"As good as any whiskey I've ever had. Your uncle's a good man. Bless him too."

"You'll be needin' it on the way home. The swill they serve on these boats—"

"Yes, I've noticed. Thank you, Mick, I couldn't have asked for a better gift."

"Now for business, sir. What job might it be that you need Mick to be doin'?"

"Job one, disappear in this city. I don't want anyone suspecting you're here."

"Done and done, sir. This is New York, remember. Just another big dumb Irishman, I am."

"Job two, I need you to look after some of the natives. Take this." He handed Mick an envelope. "The details are all spelled out. Learn them by heart and then—"

"Yes, I know, destroy it. I'm not as new to this game as you make me out now, sir. You do me no justice. Have I ever let you down before?"

"No, and you best not this time. The stakes are very high."

"That's exactly the way I like my stakes, nice and high. No point in wagerin' if the odds aren't long. Don't you lose a wink a sleep. There won't be a flea slippin' by Mick in this Irish town. Now sir, a bird with one wing can't fly."

"Quite right...to your health." The inspector took another swig and passed the flask to Mick.

"Here's to women's kisses, and to *poitín*, amber clear; not as sweet as a woman's kiss, but a darn sight more sincere."

CHAPTER 6
THE NEW PARTNER

"AFTER ALL, MY good fellow, rank does have its privileges." James Aston grinned as he sat back in the plush leather chair in his new office. His long legs were propped cavalierly on the top of his impressive oak desk. "Perhaps someday, you too will rise to the top of the heap. Of course, you'll need a substantial dose of good luck, since you lack the wit, charm, handsome features, drive, and intelligence of the newest partner of Manchester's, no *England's*, best patent firm, our beloved Clark and White."

"Ah, yes, you forgot to mention his incredible modesty, and all accomplished before toasting in his twenty-eighth birthday. How honored I must be to have been so long acquainted with such a fine mate as you. You inspire me, James. You inspire me. Or should I now call you Mr. Aston?" Fred Miller grinned back at his best friend of over six years as he reveled in the image of the young man with the wavy blond hair, button nose, and boyish face, looking quite the imposter in his newfound surroundings. James was entitled to the gloating, he thought. He had worked like a man possessed. He had repaid the partnership of Manchester's finest patent agency with impressive skill and long hours of devoted service. Now he had been justly rewarded, and Fred was glad for it all, even if he had long pursued the same prize without yet achieving it.

"No, no, no, don't be silly. I think a simple 'sir' will do just fine. As in, 'Yes, sir, what is your bidding today, sir?' No need for formalities, Master Miller." James plopped his feet to the floor, stood, and took an exaggerated bow with his lanky frame bent nearly in two, looking as if he was trying to touch the floor with the top of his head.

"Bravo," cheered Fred with gusto as he rose, clapping rapidly in a staccato beat. "Bravo, young victor with the world at his feet. And to think, just last week you were a lowly associate of the firm, like me. I'm gone to London but a fortnight, and upon my return you are transformed. Bravo!"

James joined Fred in laughter, guffawing loudly.

"In earnest, my friend, let me buy you a pint and toast your health and happiness before you return home to that handsome wife of yours," offered Fred as he looked up at his friend who stood a full head above him. "All the London bravado about going to war with the Germans has left me yearning for a modest Manchester pub. You simply can't go anywhere in that city without someone slapping you on the back and asking if you're ready to kick the Kaiser in his seat."

"Perhaps another day, thank you. Matilda was not feeling well this morning. Her stomach seemed quite out of sorts. I'm afraid a night out with you, old boy, would not be taken in good humor."

"Yes, I hear being with child can result in such maladies. I've no firsthand experience in the matter, mind you. Well, the offer remains for you to accept. We must raise a few to celebrate. If not tonight, then the next may do." Fred paused to survey the new office. "I see a prominent placement of the chessboard, and an opening move, pawn to king four. Are you playing yourself, or has someone risen to the challenge?"

"No, I think it is an anonymous challenger, but I'm not sure. When I arrived this morning I found that move on the board. I've been trying all day to think of who might have moved the piece in what appears a challenge to play. It clearly isn't you."

"What, you think that after hundreds of ignominious defeats I would shy away from playing you again? What makes you so sure that I'm not your mysterious challenger?"

"Other than the obvious fact that you arrived in Manchester but a few hours ago, there is also the fact that you always open with pawn to queen four. You quake so at the idea of open territory in front of your king, thus you always, and predictably, open the file in front of your hapless queen, which I typically relieve you of around move twenty. So impetuous in life and yet so cautious at the game. No, if in fact this is a mysterious challenger, he most certainly is not you!"

Fred laughed and grinned again. "Move twenty, you do me no credit, sir! Besides, one must protect the queen, too, old boy. She is the most valuable piece on the board, as in life, I might add."

"She's but another piece to me. Too many players handicap themselves with the fear of losing her. Me, I use her as bait. Before you know it, I've traded her away for two rooks and a pawn, and the game is all but won."

"Well, whoever challenges you now, I'm sure he'll get the same thrashing you've delivered to every member of this firm and several of its clients over the years. It's a shame you never let one of us win. Perhaps you'd find more takers if the odds didn't seem so stacked at the outset."

"Not in my nature, I'm afraid. I go for the kill, mysterious challenger or dear friend. It makes no difference to me. I'll figure out who this is, even if he doesn't show his face."

"You really think you can tell who you're playing by the moves they make?"

"Chess is a window to the mind."

"Yes, but drink is a window to the soul. All the more reason to join me for one!"

James didn't answer and appeared suddenly lost in thought as he stared at the chessboard.

"You call me cautious, how then does Mr. Clark play, and what of Mr. White?"

"Mr. Clark, well, he's all bluff and blunder. He likes to think he can play with the best, and he superficially knows the right moves, having been coached extensively at the club. He opens well, but then flails about before he retreats into his shell. Occasionally he'll try the most absurd move in the hopes that it will turn out to be brilliant, as if he thinks the key lies just out of his grasp, and he need only try again and again, wildly, until the whole mystery of the game suddenly comes into focus, thus allowing his superior intellect to triumph over an obviously more practiced but less intelligent foe."

"And Mr. White?"

"Ah, Mr. White, an opponent of entirely a different character. You must be patient with Mr. White. He is a cautious player, to be sure, but he will hurt you if you let him. I think him nearly my equal if you give him enough time to think through his next move. He doesn't play well when pressed, but give him his space to think, and he can be quite dangerous. He likes to simplify the game by attrition, and then works for some small advantage that he can drive home in the end. Not a brilliant player, but quite solid fundamentals. I very much enjoy playing him, and I think he enjoys the challenge." James paused and looked toward the chessboard again. "Whoever this mysterious player may be, yes, I'll figure out who he is by the nature of his play. That much I promise you."

"Well, best of luck then, not that you'll need it. Speaking of mysterious, who was that distractively attractive young woman I saw about the office earlier today? Is she the new staff you were to hire?" Fred leaned into his friend, eagerly anticipating a response on this new topic.

"Oh, you mean Mrs. Jones. Sorry, you haven't been introduced yet? Attractive, you say? Hadn't noticed."

"Away but a few short nights and my best friend has gone blind, apparently. Shall I describe her then? Perhaps I'll help you to see her in your mind's eye."

"No, I've seen her. Let's see, long black hair, ivory white skin, large brown eyes, attractive figure, closer to my height than yours, how am I doing for a blind man?"

"And you said you hadn't noticed. You left off the long neck, the wide mouth turned down at the corners, the aquiline nose, and we won't mention the generous, well-defined bust and narrow waist for decency's sake. So, she is the new hire?" Fred leaned further in toward James, putting his hands on his desk. "What's her first name, then? What's her story? Come now, you may be married but I, your best friend in all the Empire, am yet a bachelor. You interviewed and hired her. Now, tell the details to your poor unmarried friend."

"Not a bad description for someone you've never met. Playing me the fool again, I see."

"No, no, not at all. I was with a client when I saw her about the office, but I could hardly disengage soon enough before she had disappeared. Damned clients. I surmised who she must be and endeavored to gain intelligence from you, my dear friend, before I might have the pleasure of seeing her again and introducing myself. So, come now, details, please!"

"To start, she's married, not that I should presume that would matter to you."

Fred grinned even broader and stretched even closer toward his friend. "Details, Mr. Aston, details."

"As I said, she's married. Her husband is an invalid lieutenant who lost one leg and one arm in the Boer War. Poor fellow, his pension is not sufficient at the moment, and she was seeking employment when she learned of the temporary interpreter position for which I was responsible. She has no children, is thirty-three years old, and seems to be of good background and upbringing. She is fluent in French, Spanish, and her German is passable with a smattering of Russian to boot. She fits the bill nicely for the project we had in mind."

"And her name?"

"I told you, Mrs. —"

"No, you fool, her first name!"

James paused long enough to flash a disapproving glare. "Angela, Angela Jones."

Fred was unfazed by the reproach. He rocked back slightly, rubbed his chin with his broad hand while glancing skyward, and then looked back at his friend. "Perfect. Angela. Of course, thank you. Well, I'll be off. Sure you won't join me for just one toast, my dear friend?"

"I've never known you to stop at one toast, my dearest friend. No, Mrs. Aston is expecting her hero, and her hero she shall have." James turned back to the chessboard once more. "Yes, I'll smoke you out, whoever you are. Let's see what you do with knight to queen's bishop three. Will you defend your pawn, or will you come out and fight?"

"Well enough, I'm sure you'll solve the mystery in good time. Until tomorrow, then, good day, Mr. Aston, sir."

"Good day, Master Miller, until tomorrow."

* * *

"Gentlemen, next item. I was informed this morning that the Paris stock exchange is in a state of panic. I presume this is in response to the recent strident articles in the German papers *Kreuzzeitung* and *Matin*. What else do we know?" Lord Lansdowne addressed the question to all the men in the room, but looked straight at Sir Charles Hardinge in particular, who took the cue.

"Yes, the rhetoric was particularly strident. The French view *Kreuzzeitung* and *Matin* as mouthpieces for Prince von Bulow, and thus the official position of the German government. As of yet, though, the Germans have not mobilized and von Bulow has issued a statement indicating that Germany has no plans or desire for war. Our best guess is that the Germans are rattling their sabers a little harder in order to push the French to an international conference, where the Germans hope to embarrass them before the world."

"Are the French still holding firm against that conference idea?"

"Yes, but the pressure is building for the sacking of Minister Delcassé. With Delcassé gone, the French will have no one strong enough to resist the German pressure. I expect a capitulation to the conference proposal would follow shortly."

"Agreed. If he goes, we lose our best ally in the French government. The rest of the bunch are spineless." Lansdowne let out an audible sigh as he began tapping the table with his index finger. "All right, do we have *any* promising news today?"

"I think so. We've acquired something interesting from the American front, the text of a recent letter sent by President Roosevelt to his legislative confidant, Senator Lodge." Hardinge reached below the table and produced an envelope from which he pulled a piece of paper. "May I?"

"By all means, please."

"I'll skip to the relevant portions."

It always amuses me to find that the English think that I am under the influence of the Kaiser. The heavy-witted creatures do not understand that nothing would persuade me to follow the lead of or enter into close alliance with a man who is so jumpy, so little capable of continuity of action, and therefore, so little capable of being loyal to his friends and steadfastly hostile to an enemy. Undoubtedly with Russia weakened Germany feels it can be fairly insolent within the borders of Europe. I intend to do my best to keep on good terms with Germany, as with all other nations, and so far as I can to keep them on good terms with one another; and I shall be friendly to the Kaiser as I am friendly to everyone. But as for his having any special influence with me, the thought is absurd.

Hardinge looked up at Lansdowne with a wry grin.

"Most interesting, I suppose the only place in the world where we have any agents left of any proficiency is Washington. I'd say he has the Kaiser fairly well pegged, and perhaps us as well." Lansdowne stared at his now still finger resting on the table and then looked up to address the group. "Perhaps this gives us some room to maneuver. If the Germans rattle swords to unsettle the French, I think it's time we flex our muscle a little to give them resolve. The Admiralty has been champing at the bit. We now know where America stands. Roosevelt will push harder for peace if he sees us all glaring at each other. Perhaps that will derail this conference idea. Let me give it more thought."

Lansdowne looked down again for a moment, rolling the news from America around in his head. "Fine, gentlemen. I shan't keep you longer. Charles, I would like a brief word with you, if you don't mind."

With several salutations of "Good day, Lord Lansdowne," the room cleared but for the two men.

"Care for a drink, Charles? This port is excellent."

"Yes, thank you, I believe I would. How was your evening with the German ambassador and his entourage last night?"

"Tolerable. We were all best of friends. They do try my patience."

"Dinner and a concert, as I recall?"

"Yes, they were quite excited to hear Strauss's *Ein Heldenleben.* 'A Hero's Life,' I believe, in translation?"

"Yes, that's right. He wrote it about himself, quite modestly, I'm sure. The Germans, I've heard, think the piece brilliant. Did you find it so?"

"Humph." Lansdowne took a sip of the ruby-colored liquid, savoring the tangy sweetness in his mouth. "Brilliant, perhaps, but musical? He's no Brahms, that's for certain. Although I must confess that Brahms puts me to sleep, now that I think about it. No sleeping through Strauss, clanging and banging with trumpets blaring and the strings screeching, I was relieved when it was over. The Germans, on the other hand, were quite animated during the whole of it. The war section, loud and chaotic, moved them immensely, with lots of fist-pumping and feet-stomping. At one point some of them were shouting joyously, but I needn't have been embarrassed. The good orchestra drowned them out. Then, just when you think the piece will become peaceful in the hero's retirement, off we go with more spasms of chaos that brought the ambassador to his feet in excitement."

"Such an excitable race, particularly when the cannons sound. I sometimes think they were bred for war."

"Unfortunately, Charles, I think they suffer from the same belief. We must always remember that. It's force they understand, not nuanced arguments. They have no tolerance for a two-sided discussion." Lansdowne paused again to stick his nose in the small glass, taking a satisfying sniff before another sip of the port. "I understand Inspector Jenkins has returned from America."

"Yes, he believes the man with the black box is back in England."

"I still find it all quite fantastic, a black box that kills. I'll be much relieved when he gets to the bottom of this, and I trust he'll do it soon?" Lansdowne stared at his glass, turning it slowly in his hand.

"Henry, what is it?"

"The ruby color, like a mixture of blood and iodine straight off the hospital floor. It haunts me, Charles. I can hear it, the noise. I hear it in the distance, a hollow rumble already, violence working itself up. The sound of war...the sound of steady drumming like a noise in a dream. I keep asking myself, how much longer, how much longer can we push back this tide? Each crisis seems larger than the last. Will this be the one? It's not capitalism to blame as that socialist, Jaures, believes. It's humanity, humanity itself is clamoring for its own destruction. Germany, Russia, France, Austria, Italy, this great kingdom, we all march on so inevitably. The people clamor for it." Lansdowne paused and looked up at the ceiling behind Hardinge. "We need answers, not theories, not a shadowy figure with a mysterious box."

Lansdowne paused again, now looking Hardinge straight in the eyes. "Do you fully trust Jenkins?"

"Implicitly, Henry. He's never let us down before."

"I don't know. He consistently gives the appearance of being forthcoming with me, but I sense he knows so much more."

"Perhaps he does, that's his job, after all. But I do think we can trust him. We've got to. Nothing else seems to be working. I think we have to trust him."

81

"God help us if you're wrong. More port?"

* * *

Quite puzzling. James Aston had expected to figure out who the mysterious player was by turn ten. But here he was, eighteen office days later, turn eighteen, and he still had not a clue.

He stared at the board intently. Thus far there was no hint to go by. The game was developing traditionally enough with both sides jockeying for control of the center and developing their pieces. The king had not yet castled in his protective cove, so Fred was ruled out. There had been no aggressive and foolish foray yet, so it didn't appear to be Mr. Clark. There was no purposeful attrition yet either, so Mr. White could be ruled out. He'd tried a couple of simple traps that a novice would jump at, but this player was too experienced for such trickery. That fact ruled out every other person he had ever played who would have access to his office on a regular basis.

It was too early to tell just how strong this player was, but so far he had matched James play for play. It was as if he was playing himself. Funny thought, playing one's self. Surely such a game would end in a draw every time. "All right, then, let's see if you can take some heat," James muttered as he thrust a knight deep into his opponent's territory.

"Ahem."

James, startled out of his fixation on the board, quickly turned to see who had politely cleared her throat at the doorway to his office.

"Ah, Mrs. Jones, I didn't know you were still here. Quite late, isn't it?"

"Sorry, Mr. Aston, I heard someone in your office and didn't expect to see you here, either. May I interrupt now that I've found you? I've a question about one of these documents."

"Oh, why yes, please, come in."

James watched intently as Mrs. Jones made her way straight toward him. His heart raced as he fought back the urge to moisten his lips. He pondered how with every encounter with Mrs. Jones it became increasingly harder for him to maintain his composure. Fred was right. She was incredibly handsome.

As she drew near he couldn't help but catch a quick glimpse of her lips. She had the most sensuous mouth of any woman he had ever seen. It was difficult to look at her face at close range. Her eyes seemed to look right into his soul, a place a married man could ill afford to share with another woman.

"It's this paper from the French institute that you gave me yesterday." Her voice was rich and soothing.

James stared transfixed at her exposed neck as she read a passage to him in French from the document. Her accent was perfect and lyrical, just as well-read French should be.

"You see, that makes no sense when referencing the graph below."

James tried to focus on the paper held in her hands. As he moved closer he could discern clearly now the scent that always accompanied her. It was intoxicating. In his mind he had tried to describe it, to put a name to it. Nothing but "woman" seemed to fit. She smelled of woman. It was a musky, slightly pungent and sweet smell. He never could tell if it was her or some exotic perfume that she was wearing, but it drove him to distraction. He felt his heart beating faster and palms begin to sweat.

"Ah, yes, I see. Well..." James stepped back and looked awkwardly at his desk. "I'll need to study this to be sure. Leave it with me, and I'll take a closer look at it in the morning. Now, if you will excuse me, Mrs. Jones, I must be on my way home."

"Certainly, Mr. Aston, as you wish." She moved closer and handed him the paper. She paused for a moment, turning squarely toward him. "Mr. Aston, is there *anything* else I can do for you this evening?"

He was momentarily taken aback by the question, maybe not so much by the question as by the answer his brain was straining not to give. "No, quite all right, thank you, Mrs. Jones."

She stood looking at him for what was surely just a moment, but seemed like a blissful eternity. He felt like a trapped animal being eyed by a taunting wolf, but he thrilled at being the prey. She was so beautiful. It was hard not to look at her, as much as he wished he wouldn't, or rather, knew he shouldn't.

"Well, shall I move first, then?"

He dropped his jaw as he tried not to stammer. "I, I beg your pardon, Mrs. Jones?" His face felt hot and his breathing became erratic. Time seemed to slow to a crawl.

"Yes, I note that you moved your knight. Shall I counter now, or would you like me to do it later?" She smiled as she casually pointed at the chessboard.

The import of the second question was even more stunning than what he had interpreted from the first. He openly gaped at her as he struggled to find a response.

"Oh, I'm sorry, I thought you knew. You don't mind playing me, do you? I picked it up from my father. You see, Mother died when I was but eleven, and Father sent for me to join him in India. He was a senior agent for the Company. We played chess long into the night. It was his passion, and it became mine because it was his. He always told me that chess was a window into the mind. He used it as a tool to evaluate business associates. I just love to play.

"I'm told you're quite good, Mr. Aston. I hope I don't disappoint you, as I haven't played in such a long time. I couldn't resist when I saw the board in your office all set up and just begging to be touched, just begging to be played. You don't mind, do you, if we play?"

"Well, of course not. I had no idea you knew chess. I'm just, well, I'm just—"

"Surprised, yes, I can see. I'm sorry for being so presumptuous. I should have asked." She looked ashamed and started to turn to leave.

"Nonsense, I'm delighted to know you play. I'm enjoying our game immensely."

Her smile widened, showing just a hint of the white teeth beneath. "Well, then, this should do." She picked up one of her bishops, sliding it into a strong and threatening position, ignoring the knight deep within her ranks. "I'll check in with you tomorrow. Goodnight, Mr. Aston."

James watched her as she strolled out of the room, savoring the view until she was completely out of sight. He looked at the board, and then slowly sank to the floor where he sat in stunned contemplation.

CHAPTER 7
MATE

"PLEASE, GENTLEMEN, SIT down," President Roosevelt announced as he stormed into the White House Press Room, interrupting the casual banter of the half dozen men spread about. "No need to stand on my accord. I'll get right to the point. I've but a few minutes before I meet with my cabinet, but I didn't want to keep you waiting.

"I'm sure you all want to know my position on the recent resignation of the French foreign minister, Delcassé. I read your papers this morning, and there was a lot of unnecessary and silly speculation. I have officially sent my condolences. Delcassé has served his country well, and I wish him the best in his retirement. No, I'm not pleased to see him go, as some of you have suggested. He's a good man who has steadfastly sought what is best for his country. I hope the same can be said of me when I retire.

"Now, what else do you need to know? Yes, Thomas, no need to raise your hand, just spit it out."

"Mr. President, what do you make of the rumors that Delcassé was sacrificed by the French government in order to appease the Germans?"

"I think that question would be best raised with the French government. As you know, I consider myself and our great country on friendly terms with all the European powers. I am confident they will eventually settle their differences, and I stand ready to offer my assistance in the cause of international understanding and peace."

"And what of the surprise British Navy maneuvers in the Baltic?"

President Roosevelt flashed his signature toothy smile, but focused a steely gaze at the reporter. "Perhaps I should have made you raise your hand on that one, Tom. I suppose you *all* know about the Baltic maneuvers?"

"I shouldn't speak for the other papers, but I believe so, Mr. President. Our understanding is that the British fleet has made a surprise appearance in the Baltic, not far from the home port of the German fleet. The German fleet has been put on war footing, but the British claim it's just a peaceful exercise in international waters. Do you know what they're up to, Mr. President, and what is your official reaction to this provocation?"

President Roosevelt allowed his demeanor to soften while maintaining his smile. "I'll be damned, gentlemen. The United States press corps is second to none, second to none. I salute you. I do believe you find out information faster and in more detail than our poor understaffed government will ever be able to match. I wish I could afford such excellent intelligence. The power of the market at work, marvelous, simply marvelous.

"I don't know that I call it a provocation, Tom. The British say it's just a peaceful maneuver, and I don't have any reason to believe otherwise. The Germans are concerned that the British may sneak in and sink their fleet at anchorage, and I understand that concern. The British have a knack for doing just such a thing when they think they're threatened. Just ask the Danes about the attack at Copenhagen in 1807. But this isn't 1807. Last I checked, Napoleon is still dead, and I don't believe the British feel threatened by any new Napoleon who might use the German fleet like they thought Napoleon would the Danish fleet. I'm sure this will all die down in due course, as soon as His Majesty's fleet starts to run a little low on coal and returns to home port." He pulled a pocket watch out of his vest and glanced down to check the time. "Now, if you'll excuse me, gentlemen, as I'm sure you can appreciate, I have a few matters to attend to."

* * *

"Slow down, old boy. I'm sure they have an ample supply. No need to try to drink Manchester dry all at once." Fred looked on quizzically as his friend downed yet another beer.

"Yes, sorry, I suppose I've had a few."

James stared blankly at his empty mug, seeming quite sad to Fred.

"Relax, I'll down the next two while you watch me enjoy them. It won't catch me up, but at least we'll be nearer equals."

Fred tried to cheer him with a wide grin, but James continued gazing at his mug without response.

"What is it, James? You seem quite pensive tonight, not like you at all."

"Oh, nothing the matter at all. I was just lost in thought for a moment."

"Well, yes, rather what I meant by 'pensive,' you understand." Fred wryly raised a brow and then tried once again to draw out the normally chipper James. "Thinking of your next move, I suppose? Is she any challenge? You've been playing for what, a month now?"

"What, oh, you mean Mrs. Jones. Yes, she plays quite well. She's given me one of the best challenges I've faced in quite some time. In fact, at least at this slow pace, she's as good as the better players at the club."

"You think she couldn't play well if pressed for time?"

"Most certainly! It is well established that women don't play chess well to begin with, much less under the stress of a face-to-face game under the pressure of the clock. She must think through her moves all day long. She only makes one a day, you know."

"As do you."

"Yes, but I don't need all day to think through my next move. She does."

"You must be right. After all, the board is in your office." Fred tried smiling again, but got the same non-reaction from his friend. "Can she beat you, given this slow pace?"

James finally laughed. "Another," he shouted above the murmur of the pub at the man behind the counter. "No, I can handle her under any condition. It's just a matter of time. She'll over-think the situation while I slowly build a strategic advantage. Then I'll squeeze her into submission."

"I'll drink to that." It was Fred's turn to laugh as he raised his glass. "Here's to squeezing Mrs. Jones into submission. Sounds like good fun!"

James waved his hand with a look of disgust. "Is that all you ever think of? Oh, why do I even ask?"

Another mug appeared in front of James, and he quickly downed a long draught. "Of course, there is the wager." James's face suddenly took on a serious complexion.

Fred stopped mid-drink. He could tell his friend was letting on to something that he'd been trying not to. "Wager?"

"Yes, nothing really, Mrs. Jones suggested that we should play for a wager. At the time I saw no harm in it. I still see no harm in it." James paused and stared at his mug again. "It's just a wager on the game, nothing more."

"What is the wager?"

"If she wins I must grant her request, and if I win she must grant mine."

"So, what is her request and what is yours?"

"Neither has been specified yet."

Fred took a slow drink, put his mug on the counter, and looked at his friend in silence. James was holding his beer in his right hand with the back of his hand facing Fred. Fred glanced at the familiar two small moles that had resided on his friend's right hand for as long as he'd known him. They were roughly an inch apart, just above and to both sides of the knuckle of his middle finger, such that when James put his right fist flush on a table the two moles formed two eyes to the knuckle's nose. Over the years he had noted that the moles tended to change color from mild pink to bright red under two circumstances: when James was under stress and when James was drunk. Those two little eyes looked angrily red this evening.

"Well, that is interesting. So, what will be your request, then?"

"It doesn't matter, in a sense. When I win, I'll graciously grant her the request that she would have asserted, and all will be well."

"Which is?"

"A permanent position, of course, what else would she want? She desperately wants her position to be made permanent, you know. I've already decided that it should be made so. Thus, when I win, my request will be that she accept the offer she would have requested that I offer to…you understand what I mean. I'll have done nothing that I didn't intend to do, and she'll be happy even in defeat."

"Brilliant! Here's to happiness in defeat!" Fred raised his glass again to his increasingly inebriated friend, but James seemed too preoccupied to return the toast. Fred put his mug back on the counter.

"Are you sure about all this? Perhaps you should call off this game."

"No, no, of course not, I'll be fine." James peered at Fred with moist eyes. His mouth was turned down in a sad frown. "It's hard, Fred, the stress of being a partner. And then there's…Matilda and I haven't shared a bed in months. I don't know who'll be the happier when this damned pregnancy runs its course. Life seemed simpler before. I don't know, I just…" James grabbed his mug and downed its contents. "I'd best be off. The next thing you know I'll be confessing deep respect for all your many flaws!"

James was smiling again as he got up from his stool and straightened out his long frame with a slight wobble.

"Yes, and they are many indeed." Fred put a supporting hand on his friend's arm upon seeing James reach for the bar to steady himself. "Matilda will deliver the child soon. Things will brighten on all fronts, I'm sure."

James sighed and then smiled again. "Yes, you're quite right. Thank you, Fred! I'll see you in the morning."

"Are you sure there's nothing else, James?"

"Yes, no, I mean, I'm fine, Fred, thank you." He hesitated briefly. "Well, all right, something I've wanted to ask you."

"Please."

"You fancy yourself a student of the Bible, yes?"

"Only because my mother, God rest her soul, beat it into me. Why?"

"Why did God forgive King David?"

"What an odd question! You've clearly imbibed too much this evening."

"No, in earnest, why? That Bathsheba mess was unconscionable."

"The simple answer is because he confessed his sin to Nathan, and thus to God, in Second Samuel."

James looked bewildered. "Then what is the not simple answer?"

"I think it shows that God's grace is infinite, once we recognize and accept that our sin is sin against God, not just against our neighbors. His capacity to forgive is without bounds."

"Thank you, Fred, I think I just needed to hear that. Good evening."

"James, I'm no Nathan, by any reckoning, but always know I'm here to listen."

"I know, Fred, thank you. Good evening."

"Good evening, and give my regards to Matilda."

* * *

"You wanted to see me, Mr. White?"

"Ah, James, please come in." Mr. White pointed at a chair near his desk. "Please have a seat."

James noted a serious countenance in Mr. White. Gone was the usual impish grin on that round face under the balding dome. The wispy white hair at his temples framed a serious look, one of concern, perhaps? He was a small man, but his presence always seemed to James to fill the room, particularly when that room was his own office.

"How is Matilda? Doing well, I trust?"

"She's quite well, thank you. The doctor has ordered her to bed until the child is born, but she'll be fine, I'm quite certain."

"Yes, I'm sure she will. I understand her father has been called up by the Admiralty, something about activating reserve forces. I hope he's not gone long."

"I, as well. She's quite attached to her father. I know she'll be anxious until his return."

"This confounded Moroccan thing; the Germans may have gone too far this time. James, I'll come to the point. Your familiarity with Mrs. Jones as of late troubles me. What are your intentions with this woman?"

"Intentions? I'm not sure I follow, sir?"

Mr. White paused for a moment, seeming to gauge the response. "You must decide if she is to be made a permanent employee or let go. What are your intentions?"

"Oh, yes, well, she has done a superb job with all the translations I have assigned to her. She has a quick grasp of the technical details of the project. And I have found her to be competent, thorough, and diligent. My intentions are to offer her a full-time position."

"Yes, I assumed as much."

Mr. White maintained a steady gaze at James that made him feel a bit squeamish.

"What do you know of this woman, Mrs. Jones?"

Her name suddenly played like a gonging bell in his head. James paused for a moment to recover his senses. "She comes from a good family. She's married to an invalid lieutenant of our own First Manchesters. He was wounded in the siege of Ladysmith.

They have no children, but it seems his pension is not sufficient for their household."

"Lieutenant in the First, you say?" Mr. White raised one eyebrow and put his hand to his chin. "Strange, I'm not familiar with a Lieutenant Jones. I thought I knew all of the Manchester officers. I'll have to inquire of the Colonel when I see him next."

"Sir, you made reference to a familiarity causing you concern. Might I inquire about the nature of this concern?"

Mr. White dropped his hand to his desk and focused squarely at James, again seeming to take his measure.

"You're playing a chess game with her, correct?"

James nodded in response.

Mr. White lowered his voice and responded with slow deliberation. "Need I remind you that you are a partner in this firm as well as a married man?"

"Sir! Indeed, it's nothing but a chess game. What are you suggesting?" James straightened his spine and glared back at the smaller man. James had seen Mr. White pressed aggressively in a number of different settings. He was a man not easily ruffled, and he didn't seem to be the least ruffled now.

"Mr. Aston," he replied in an even lower, measured tone, "I'm aware of your wager."

James sank back in his chair. "Fred," he muttered under his breath.

"Most inappropriate, sir. Partners do not make wagers with their employees. Married men do not play chess with women who are not their wives."

Mr. White paused while his admonition sank in.

"You are my partner now, James. I can no longer instruct you on your conduct. I can, however, strongly suggest you reevaluate your course and make corrections yourself. Your relationship with Mrs. Jones is unseemly, improper, and could have negative repercussions for this firm. I request that you attend to that point.

I'm here, as always, to advise you should you need my guidance or assistance."

James stared off in space, his head spinning, feeling too small to answer.

"James, life is not a game. There are consequences to our actions. You have achieved so much, and lead quite an enviable life. You enjoy financial success. You are respected in the community. You are about to start the most magnificent journey of raising a family with your charming wife. Sometimes little stumbles lead to hard falls. You seem to me on the verge of a stumble. I want, I hope, you will avoid it."

James steeled himself with anger by forcing himself to focus on the older man having questioned his ability to manage the situation. "Thank you, Mr. White. I'm sorry if I've disappointed you. Is there anything else, sir?"

Again, there was a long pause. "No, James, there is nothing else. Thank you for stopping in to see me."

"You're quite welcome, Mr. White. A pleasure as always. Good day."

* * *

James was incredulous. How could it be? He was down a pawn and pressed on all points of the board. He'd been forced to play quite defensively for the last several moves, which was something he was not accustomed to doing. He had to get back on the offensive and make his opponent react as opposed to being forced to react to her moves. Then he might be able to leverage the knight-for-bishop trade he made early in the game. Bishops were much more powerful once the board started to clear. He hadn't normally focused on that calculation, and actually made the trade more to maintain momentum, but now it was his best advantage.

He must be patient. Or was there a way to make Mrs. Jones become impatient? "She can't be this good when rushed," he muttered. The hours she must put in at home with some duplicate board, perhaps inquiring of…

Of course, that was it! He wasn't playing Mrs. Jones at all! He must be playing her husband, or at least some combination of the two. Clearly the two of them spent hours studying a duplicate board in their home. He could see it now, as the two tried move combination after combination until coming up with the final solution for the next day's move. The couple must be desperate for her to win and press her wish for a permanent position. Well, the ruse was up.

He felt much better, much stronger. He studied the board intently. She played so aggressively with her queen. Perhaps he could trap her before the force of her extra pawn came to bear.

"Excuse me, Mr. Aston, but I was just leaving and wanted to know if you needed me to come in tomorrow. It is Saturday, and I had mentioned last week about the matter I must attend to in Leicester. Did I interrupt? I'm sorry."

James broke his focus from the board and looked up at Mrs. Jones standing in his doorway. It always struck him how beautiful she was, and always more so than the last time he saw her.

"No, not at all, Mrs. Jones, please, come in."

"I'm so sorry, I had meant to ask you earlier today, but—"

"Not at all, please do come in. I was just about to move, there, how's that? What do you think? Perhaps you'd like to counter since you won't be able to move tomorrow?"

Mrs. Jones sauntered to a position in front of the board just to the right of James, focusing on the pieces the whole way. He suddenly felt and smelled her presence, a rush of sensations. His heart raced as he took in a long breath, holding it as if enjoying the bouquet of some excellent wine. She was intoxicating. He felt his knees starting to buckle. He stiffened his right arm, fighting the urge just to touch her, to slowly put his right hand on the small of her back.

"Ah, here, then." She looked up and smiled as she moved her queen forward, once again pressing toward the back row of her opponent.

James blinked and fought to focus back on the board. He was right. She can't play when pressed for time and without her husband's advice! Now was his chance.

"Well, I see, perhaps, yes, this should do just fine." James moved his rook out as bait.

"Mr. Aston, I know it's late and I'm keeping you. Perhaps we could discuss my request for tomorrow off, and then I'll let you get back to your work."

"Oh, no, you aren't keeping me at all. I have a late dinner scheduled at the club this evening, and I'm just marking time. Tomorrow, well, of course, by all means, take the day off. Would you care to study the board before you leave?"

"Thank you, Mr. Aston."

Mrs. Jones reached out and again aggressively moved her queen, now in pursuit of the exposed rook. She glanced up, possibly catching the grin starting to form on his face, which he quickly suppressed.

"Mr. Aston, perhaps we should finish the game now. We're so close to a resolution, it seems a shame to prolong it any longer. I don't mind staying a little longer since you're merely marking time."

"Excellent idea, Mrs. Jones, let's do." He feigned studying the board, knowing what move he would make. He mustn't seem too eager, though, she might get wind of the trap and retreat. He rubbed his chin, and then slowly extended his arm to grasp the rook. He tapped it on the board several times, as if trying to slip a Gordian knot. Then he set the trap.

"Why, Mr. Aston, I'm afraid you've left me your rook."

James watched her as she looked quite perplexed at the board with her head tilted slightly forward. Soon he lost himself in her exposed neck. She was wearing her hair up, fastened in a bun on top with little wisps escaping here and there, lying like black feathers on her white skin. He felt a sudden urge to hold her. He bit the inside of his left cheek in an effort to focus on reality. She had moved but was still studying the board. He slowly turned his head back to see what course she had taken. Now it was inevitable. Two more moves and the queen was his. There was nothing she could do to stop him.

He moved quickly now with no pretense of studying the board. She moved quickly too, as if knowing the end was in sight and that nothing could change her fate.

"So sorry, Mrs. Jones, I'm afraid your queen has run her course. Check." The trap had been executed flawlessly. His bishop waited to swoop in for the kill, its field of fire cleared by the movement of his knight, which now threatened her king, thus forcing her to move the king and leave the queen to her fate.

She let out a long sigh. The smell of her breath nearly yanked his heart from its moorings. It smelled of vanilla and sweet milk. She was so close to him now that the heat of her body warmed his right arm, which again he stiffened against the urge to caress her. His head swam against the powerful tide of her presence next to him.

"Yes, Mr. Aston, well done." She moved her king to safety, and he swept in with his bishop for his prize.

Undeterred, she pressed on, casually moving her knight about the board while James pressed down on her king. Then, after several moves, he suddenly stopped his arm in mid-air, leaving it hanging over the board. He stood frozen in silent shock. His right hand hovered over the board with two bright red moles staring back at him.

He played the next two moves in his head over and over again. Always the same result no matter what combinations he countered with. He couldn't believe it. He was trapped. The game was hers, and there was nothing he could do about it. What had happened? Then he played back the previous several moves in his head. He had been so distracted by the chase for her queen that he missed the subtler, longer-developing counter trap. She must have seen his trap from the beginning and developed the intricate response that now gave her the game. It was incredible. He'd never seen such depth of play in his life. His shoulders slumped and he finally dropped his hand with its two angry, red eyes to his side. Then he reached up again and laid his king on its side.

"Well, you've won."

"I believe I get to say 'mate,' Mr. Aston."

"Of course. Sorry. Well, then, with regard to our bet, what is your request, Mrs. Jones?" James stared at the board, still in shock from the quick turn of events.

"Yes, 'mate,' surely you've seen it coming, perhaps you've even guessed my answer. I said 'mate,'" she responded with an amused smile, holding the last word as if it were a final note of a song.

"Indeed, it was mine as well, but you've clearly outplayed me." He sighed and looked into her eyes. "So, what is your request? You've won fairly and squarely, and I am prepared to settle our wager."

"Why, Mr. Aston"—she threw her head back and laughed—"do you intentionally misunderstand me, or are you daft? I said—"

"Mrs. Jones," he interrupted, "if it is about your position, I am perfectly prepared—"

"My position may be whatever you'd like, but you made a promise to *me*," she said forcefully as she moved closer, looking him squarely in the face. "And I expect you to keep it."

James physically held his ground, but he felt the room retreating. Her breath caressed his face. He could taste her mouth in the air, the vanilla notes coming through with alarming clarity. All his senses sharpened to her frighteningly close presence, yet his whole body felt warm and relaxed. Her eyes fixed his with a power he couldn't look away from.

"Let me state it more plainly, then." Her voice was low and deliberate.

She pressed her hips to his. The heat of her body held him motionless, suspended. He couldn't speak. He couldn't retreat.

"Kiss me, James."

* * *

"Come in, please, Inspector. Please have a seat."

Inspector Jenkins watched Mr. White as he stood up from behind his desk and motioned to an open seat in his office.

"I'm delighted to meet you, and may I introduce one of my associates, Fred Miller. I hope you don't mind if he joins us. These past few days have been a whirlwind of questioning by the police, and I think it will save all of us time if you interview us both together."

"Pleased to meet you, Inspector Jenkins."

The inspector nodded in acknowledgment at Fred Miller, who stood and bowed slightly. Jenkins lingered momentarily to take his sounding of Mr. Miller. He was a short, stocky man with bushy black eyebrows that rose and fell as he changed his focus from one object to another while glancing nervously about with dark, almond-shaped eyes that sparkled even in his apparent state of anxiety. His wide mouth showed a slight pattern of creases at the corners indicative of frequent smiling and little experience with frowning.

"Before we begin, may I offer you some tea, sir?"

"Yes, thank you, Mr. White, with a splash of scotch if available."

"Most certainly, I always maintain a bottle at the ready." Mr. White removed a key from a vest pocket and unlocked a small cabinet behind his desk. "I must admit, Inspector, that I remain quite puzzled by your visit. Both Mr. Miller and I gave long interviews to our most competent local magistrate. This firm has certainly suffered a string of unfortunate tragedies, but why the involvement of Scotland Yard? Can you shed some light on our situation?"

Jenkins watched Mr. White move about his office casually as he distributed the tea and then returned to his desk, all done with no hint of emotion. The inspector took his time in answering, first stirring and then taking a sip of steaming liquid. The earthy aroma of the scotch filled his nose, matching the peat notes he expected from the bottle that was poured. Mr. White was a man who was going to be hard to read. There was a façade there, pleasant and cordial at the surface, but what lay beneath was difficult to see. Not a man to play poker against.

"Yes, if you'll indulge me for a moment, I'd like to review the facts surrounding these tragedies."

The inspector took another sip, but still garnered no new information from his continued surveillance of Mr. White.

"As I understand it, your partner, Mr. Clark, died suddenly at his desk a fortnight ago. The same can be said for your draftsman, one Irving Bolton, the day before. There were no witnesses to either event, although they both happened during the workday with others present in the office. There is no evidence of foul play in either case and no discernible cause of death. Both men had been healthy with no apparent medical issues. Further, your youngest partner, James Aston, has been missing since the night before Mr. Bolton's death, having never arrived at a dinner he was scheduled to attend at his club."

"Inspector, you have recited the facts correctly, but still not answered my question. Why are you here? Men die every day. Men do strange things and don't return home for days, particularly when under the stress of a pregnant wife at home and new demands at work. While this has been a tragic time for our firm, these strike me simply as coincidences of unrelated, albeit awful, events. But perhaps you can enlighten us about some deeper connection."

The inspector took another sip of tea, savoring the warming scotch aroma, then set the cup on a nearby table. "First, please let me continue to test my understanding of the facts. You are also missing another employee, albeit a temporary one, a Mrs. Angela Jones. She failed to report to work the day after Mr. Clark died." Ah, at last, a small reaction. The mention of Mrs. Jones had brought a small glint of anger to Mr. White's eyes.

"Yes, Mrs. Jones, if that is in fact her name."

"Exactly, Mr. White, if that is in fact her name. Certainly nothing else in her résumé can be confirmed. Finally, as to the disappearance of Mr. Aston, we have not a clue, no note to his wife, not a word to his best friend, Mr. Miller here. One must assume that he is either dead as well or doesn't want to be found."

"Yes, Inspector, and I find both of those possibilities very unpleasant."

"Indeed." The inspector picked up his cup again and took another sip, glancing at Mr. Miller, who sat forward in his chair looking like an earnest and sad puppy trying to comprehend the incomprehensible.

"So, why am I here? Your intuition serves you well, sir. I do see a connection in these events, and I must, to some degree, take you into my confidence if I'm to have any hope of fully understanding this connection." Setting his cup down again, the inspector reached into a bag he had carried with him into the room and produced a roll of paper. "Mr. White, I'm not particularly familiar with your profession, patents. Can you tell me what these are?"

Mr. White carefully unrolled the papers and made a quick examination.

"They are drawings, Mr. Jenkins, patent drawings. The magistrate collected them from Mr. Bolton's office on his first visit after Mr. Clark's death. I can see from the legend that they were drawn by Mr. Bolton on the day of his death."

"I gathered as much, thank you, but what of the code at the bottom left of the legend? What information can we ascertain from that?"

"That would be an internal accounting. It indicates that the drawings were done at the request of Mr. Clark for one of his clients."

"I see, and who would the client be?"

Mr. White looked the inspector in the eye, holding his gaze but revealing nothing in the form of changed expression.

"Until their patents issue, the identity of our clients is a confidential matter."

Jenkins maintained eye contact with Mr. White. The room was silent but for the ticking of a clock. He sensed Fred Miller squirming slightly in his seat. The inspector let the tension build a little longer, and then looked away and picked up his cup to take another sip.

"Mr. White, I, too, frequently deal in confidences in my line of work. Two members of your firm are dead, and two are missing. I mentioned that I would need to take you into my confidence. Very well, I'll play my cards. I believe Mr. Bolton and Mr. Clark were murdered."

Still no reaction was forthcoming from Mr. White, which the inspector had anticipated. As he sipped his tea again and surveyed Mr. Miller, though, Jenkins noted no reaction from that quarter either, which he found quite revealing. "Can you tell me what Mr. Bolton is depicting in those drawings?"

Mr. White looked at the drawings again, this time appearing to focus his attention for a few moments.

"A box."

"A box, you say? Yes, I could see as much. Can you tell me what it is with any more particularity?"

"I'm not being coy, Mr. Jenkins. The drawings depict a rectangular-shaped box. There is a small hole in one end, but otherwise there are no distinguishing features. If I knew what it did, I would not tell you. But in all candor, I'm not familiar with this invention, its purpose, or how it works. As I said, this was done on behalf of a client of Mr. Clark, not of mine."

"I see, the very client whose identity shall remain unrevealed for the moment. Well"—the inspector shifted in his chair, giving him peripheral views of both the other men while looking directly at neither—"let me hazard a guess. I believe Mr. Clark's client was related in some respect to Mrs. Jones. Perhaps the client was Mrs. Jones herself, or she merely acted as an agent for the ultimate client."

His gambit paid off. Neither gentleman answered in response to his assertion, but Mr. Miller's resumed fidgeting gave Jenkins the confirmation he was looking for.

"Assuming for a moment that you are correct, what are you suggesting, that Mrs. Jones is a murderess?" asked Mr. White in a quiet, polite voice.

"I'm not suggesting Mrs. Jones, or whatever her name may be, is a murderer. I'm asserting that directly. I'm merely trying to determine the roles of others. I'd like to know why she picked Mr. Clark to be her agent on a patent matter, thus giving her more intimate access to that man.

"Mr. White, I do understand your concern about confidentiality in this matter. If I were in your shoes, I would take the same position. You live in a world dependent on reputation and discretion. You have partners to whom you owe the utmost loyalty in life and, certainly as to their reputations, even after they have gone on to receive their final judgment.

"Yours is a world of nuanced ethical dilemmas. Mine, on the other hand, is black and white. I have at least two murders to solve. The guilty must be identified and caught." Jenkins emptied his cup and set it on the table.

"More tea, Inspector?" offered Fred.

"Why yes, please, thank you."

The inspector casually watched Fred as he retrieved the pot and poured him a cup finished off with another splash of scotch, the sound of which plopping into the cup seemed to linger in the momentary silence that followed.

"I have credible witnesses who have identified Mr. Clark as being in the company of Mrs. Jones under circumstances from which one could draw conclusions that would not reflect well on either of them. Thank you, Mr. Miller." He retrieved his cup for another sip while waiting for the effect of that bombshell to settle in. "Tell me, Mr. White, where is the box that is depicted in those drawings?"

Mr. White looked blankly at the inspector. He waited until Fred sat down and then turned his gaze at his young associate, giving him a slight nod when Fred looked up at him.

"Mrs. Jones took it with her when she left the office the day Mr. Clark died," answered Fred.

At that, Mr. White rose from behind his desk and approached the inspector.

"Mr. Jenkins, I regret that I have an appointment that requires that I cut our visit short. I want to assure you that I remain at your disposal and will cooperate with your investigation as best I can. I leave you for now in the company of my able associate. He is at your disposal, and eagerly so, I might add. I'm confident he can answer your remaining questions and perhaps provide you with some additional assistance, assistance that I, I trust you appreciate, cannot provide."

Jenkins rose from his chair as Mr. White extended his hand. The handshake was firm and long. Mr. White dropped his façade as he faced the inspector with a look of earnest respect. He then spoke slowly and deliberately.

"Sir, identify *all* the guilty and catch them. I wish you Godspeed in this endeavor."

Jenkins gave him an understanding nod. When the door closed behind Mr. White, he turned to face Fred Miller.

"Now, Mr. Miller, let's start with you telling me what you know of Mrs. Jones."

CHAPTER 8
CONFESSION

"BLESS ME, FOR I have sinned."

The familiar female voice, low and taunting, immediately caused the Reverend Peter Hobson of Saint Martin's Church of the Church of England in Leicester to straighten his back and take in a deep breath, as if preparing for a physical blow that would come out of the darkness of the confessional booth. He responded mechanically, stunned by the sensation of being a trapped animal waiting to be dispatched by the calculating hunter aiming at him from the other side of the screen. "The Lord be in your heart and upon your lips that you may truly and humbly confess your sins. In the name of the Father, and of the Son, and of the Holy Spirit. Amen."

The "amen" response was in unison, as it should be, but the penitent drew out the word such that it started and finished well beyond the bounds articulated by Father Hobson, seeming to mock the pronouncement.

Now the torture began. "I confess to God Almighty, the Father, the Son, and the Holy Ghost that I have sinned in thought, word, and deed, through my own grievous fault; wherefore I pray God to have mercy on me. And especially I have sinned in these ways..." Then the pause, always the pause, before the painful details emerged. The preamble was stated more like boasting than a confession, but the details were always related with earnest precision.

Father Hobson listened with as much detachment as he could muster. It was more than a single priest could bear. At first he thought the woman with the sultry voice must be insane. Her sins were so fantastic and otherworldly. Yet, discreetly, he had investigated her claims, and they always bore some truth. She even predicted events before they happened, things like deaths, missing persons, and children going into comas, not with enough detail for one to prevent such tragedies, but with enough detail to confirm them later. Then she would explain her role and responsibility for these tragedies as if she were some skilled, sadistic surgeon wreaking havoc on her hapless earthly patients. As her story, her confession, unfolded, the stone floor of Saint Martin's seemed to pitch and undulate, as if Father Hobson was cast adrift on a swelling sea. Feeling dizzy and sweaty, he clutched at the wall of the booth for a physical anchor to the real world.

Occasionally he strained to make out any recognizable feature of the woman through the lattice portal to the other side of the confessional, but he discerned nothing through the screen except a shape, black hair, and fair skin; that and the outline of a beautiful mouth. The scent was always the same, though, addictively intoxicating. It was a scent that simultaneously repelled and attracted, certainly much more of the latter than the former. It was the musky and sweet scent of an unbathed woman, a scent that would haunt him long after the sessions were over and even well into the night as he lay restless on his bed fighting the urge to surrender to her imagined form.

Then there was the perfume of her breath filling his side of the confessional. She seemed to tease him with it, blowing breathy sentences with her lips close to the screen. Next she would turn away, leaving him gasping for her return, as he moved his nose closer and closer to his side of the screen, listening for the velvety voice and pining to taste her breath again. Just when he could no longer resist the rising urge to beg her to speak closer, the perfume would return on the breeze of a word wafted onto his nearby face, nearly causing him to faint with aching relief. Her scent and the taste of her breath were imprinted on his mind, inescapable, always haunting him.

He hated the reaction her memory excited in him. At night, alone in his room, he had resorted to clinging to the headboard of his small bed with both hands in order to resist the urge to answer her horrifying siren song. He had lately found himself occasionally losing that lonely battle of his imagination, and would seek refuge the next morning in Paul's Letter to the Romans. "For we know that the law is spiritual: but I am carnal, sold under sin. For that which I do I allow not: for what I would, that do I not; but what I hate, that do I..."

Why and how she always found *him* for confession was the least of the mystery she presented. Why and how she cast such a spell on him was the most perplexing thing. How could he be so temped, so obsessed, by one so evil?

He could no longer face this beast alone. He mustn't reveal her confided secrets; no young priest should break that commitment without consultation. He must seek guidance. After much prayerful consideration, he resolved to enlist the help of the person he most trusted and respected in the entire diocese, in fact in all of England, the Reverend Philbin Tate.

"For these and many other sins which I cannot now remember, I pray God to have mercy on me. I humbly beg forgiveness of God and his Church, and ask *you* for guidance and absolution."

Again, the taunting tone, but thankfully the end was near.

With what little strength remained he made his mechanical reply. "Our Lord Jesus Christ, who hath left power in his Church to absolve all sinners who truly repent and believe in him, of his great mercy forgive thee thine offenses: And by his authority committed to me, I absolve thee from all thy sins, in the name of the Father, and of the Son, and of the Holy Ghost. Amen."

Father Hobson had survived the assault once more, at least until he once again found himself alone in his bed, clutching desperately at the headboard, her scent, voice, the smell of her breath, and imagined form wrestling him to submission.

* * *

Father Philbin Tate sat placidly, giving Father Hobson the impression that his mentor was in no hurry for his troubled companion to speak. Father Hobson knew he looked tired and aged beyond his twenty-five years. In the mirror that morning his normally sparkling eyes appeared haggard and glassy. Still, he held his small but solidly built frame erect, though he allowed his long arms to rest listlessly in his lap.

"Father Tate, I don't know where to start. Thank you for taking time for our appointment on such short notice. I know your duties about the church have kept you quite busy of late."

"Not too busy for you, Peter, I'm blessed to do it. The administrative parts of my calling can wait. Relax. You should begin where you're most comfortable. We can then move to where you want to go. Tell me, what leaves you troubled so?"

Father Hobson took a deep breath. The words of the older priest were a tremendous comfort. Father Tate had that way about him. His soft-spoken humility seemed to so perfectly match his round and kind face which was framed by a wreath of thick, peppered hair that wrapped from ear to ear around his otherwise bald pate. He had big, round eyes that drew in the world around him, always accompanied by his half smile that seemed to say, "It's all right, I see and understand." It was no wonder the bishop and the rector trusted him with so many delicate assignments.

Father Hobson looked straight into those trusted eyes. "Do you believe in the possibility of a devil incarnate?"

"You mean literally, in human form amongst us?" Father Tate seemed taken aback by the nature of the question.

Father Hobson took another deep breath. "Yes, precisely. Well, no, I'm only talking hypothetically here. But your thoughts on this issue could help me sort out an analogous point."

"Mankind certainly experiences extreme evil at the hands of certain cruel individuals. Many believe that such is evidence of the devil incarnate. But I tend to think that the better interpretation is that the devil might act through these people to serve his purposes."

"Father Tate, you've heard many private confessions, I know, in your long service to this congregation. It goes without saying that your support of bringing back this rite to the Church has resulted in many converts to the Anglo-Catholic movement, me being one, most certainly. But have you—" Father Hobson stopped in mid-sentence and took a moment to steady and collect himself.

Father Tate quickly filled the silence. "It is a service to the congregation, is it not? That's a lovely way to put it, Peter. Yes, I am a strong believer in reinstatement of the rites of private penance. I wish there were more priests like you who agreed. Anglicans should have the same opportunities for private confession as our Roman Catholic brothers. In the meantime we'll have to get by with our ad-hoc approach, and I do appreciate your support." He paused and looked with curiosity at the younger priest. "I hope my Anglo-Catholic agitations won't endanger our blessed Saint Martin's pursuit of cathedral status. How lovely that would be, Leicester's own cathedral. The bishop is truly a tolerant man. I pray he won't hold my views against us." Father Tate paused again as if waiting for an answer. "You've not come to talk of Church politics, though. What troubles you so? How can I help?"

"I'm not sure you can." Again Father Hobson sat silently for a moment before continuing. "Have you ever heard a confession that was so evil that you suspected the work of the devil as, perhaps, the only plausible explanation that wouldn't otherwise shake your faith in mankind? I mean, where you truly questioned how such evil could be...could be of this world?"

This time it was Father Tate who seemed to gather his thoughts before speaking. "Like every priest, I have on occasion forgiven what others might consider unforgivable. One could expect as much serving this industrial city for as long as I have. I've tried not to struggle too much with the motive behind such acts of cruelty. There is, truly, much evil in the world. Some of it hardly bears an earthly explanation." Father Tate bent toward the young priest as his voice lowered to almost a whisper. "We, on the other hand, are only human. We are soldiers of Christ, that is true, but we are distinctly human."

Father Tate leaned back in his chair and crossed his arms as if waiting for the statement to sink in.

"Peter, what is it that troubles you so? I've never seen you so distraught. Please, how can I help you?"

Father Hobson put his face in his hands, then looked up at the gentle eyes. "I have been taking the confession of a woman recently. Somehow, she always finds me, regardless of the time I'm serving or whether other priests are available. I'll be prepared to leave the confessional after having just heard someone else, and there she is. Her confessions have ripped me to the core. I've no explanation for her motives or who she is, but she is evil, if that word has any meaning. In fact, I'm not sure just 'evil' does her full credit. And yet..." He paused, swallowed hard, and wiped his hand across his eyes. "As much as she repels me, she also haunts my mind at night, stirring desires that I can't abide." He put his hands over his face again and he began to quietly sob. "I, I don't understand it, any of it."

"Ah, a physical attraction. That's nothing new, Peter. You're not just a priest, you're a young man in his prime."

"No, I've been attracted to women before. I'll even admit to certain intimacies before I took my vows. It's more than that. She has something, some power that she exerts against me. Something that overcomes everything else I hold dear."

"All women have a tremendous power over men, just very few know they have it and even less how to use it. That they are the weaker sex is a myth in my opinion. Men force women to their will with brute force. Women force us to their will by our own desires. Perhaps you've encountered that rare woman who knows fully how to wield her power."

"No, Father, I tell you it's more than that. She's more than that. There's evil at work here, and I'm not sure what to do."

"Father Hobson, we, you and I, are sinners. We can't help it, we are humans. We must beg forgiveness every day for our 'thoughts, words, and deeds.' Would you like me to take *your* confession? Perhaps that would be a start."

Father Hobson looked up as relief washed through him. "Bless me, for I have sinned."

* * *

"Excellent meal, don't you think, Peter?"

"Quite, excellent meal indeed, and excellent idea to dine out this evening. Thank you for inviting me along, Father Tate."

"My pleasure, I thought it might do you good to have a change of scenery."

Father Hobson lifted his mug in reply and then surveyed the Leicester pub, soaking in the sense of comfort it instilled in him. The room was beginning to thin now, but the tobacco smoke still hung heavily from the low ceiling. The chatter and banter from the other patrons filled the room with a human warmth that had certainly contributed to his improved mood.

"Back to your earlier comment, Peter, are you saying that you now follow the rationale that the existence of evil depends on the perspective of the individual?"

"No, sorry, I haven't expressed myself very well." Father Hobson took another drink of his beer. "Starting with the proposition, generally speaking of course as there is an exception to every rule, but starting with the proposition that there are two basic human perspectives on the nature of evil, one perspective is that evil exists, will always exist, and must be identified and treated as such and will never be understood."

"Yes, what I like to call the black and white perspective."

"Yes, exactly, Father Tate, I've heard you refer to it as such before. Then the other perspective is that evil is merely a term we use to describe human behavior and, at the bottom of every so-called 'evil' act, there is a quite plausible explanation. We just need to look long enough or work hard enough to identify it."

"Ah, what I like to call the shades of gray perspective."

"Yes, which I suppose might then correlate with a religious definition of evil as a lack of good in varying degrees. Well, maybe

113

not, exactly, but all I'm saying is that it seems to me that most people tend to adopt one of these two perspectives as their everyday view of evil and act accordingly."

"I love these discussions." Father Tate paused to take a drink. "We priests have been having them for centuries. Keeps the mind focused. The nature of evil…I think I could give a year's worth of sermons on that one." He took another swig from his mug. "Don't you agree, though, that the shades of gray perspective is the correct Christian approach? We are all sinners, thus none of us could be truly evil. We just commit evil acts. In many cases it's a cycle that must be broken. It can't be broken if it's not recognized as such and forgiven."

"I'm not so sure anymore." Father Hobson glanced down at the dark wooden table. "Jesus didn't forgive the devil, he wrestled with him."

The older priest leaned forward on his elbow while still holding his mug above the table. "But Jesus teaches us to love our neighbor, and to forgive the trespasses of others. You can't presume to have authority to wrestle with the devil."

"Assuming that, though, can I presume to have authority to forgive the devil? I'm trying to understand…"

"Ah, but now you must be black and white, otherwise there is no devil, only shades of gray in human behavior. I accept your general point, though, about the two perspectives." Father Tate leaned back, took a long pull from his mug, and set it on the table with a thud announcing an empty vessel well drunk. "And you, Peter, what is your perspective? Are you black and white, or shades of gray?"

"If I understand you, I suppose I've been shades of gray all my life, until…" Father Hobson took another drink and lightly set his empty mug on the table.

"Another round, if you please, of this most excellent ale!" called Father Tate toward the bar. A tall man with long bushy sideburns grunted back at him in acknowledgment. "Until you began taking her confession."

"Yes." Father Hobson stared blankly across the room.

"Well, let's test the other perspective then on this example, shall we? You know nothing of this lady's past, so she can be a clean slate on which we draw our own hypothetical conclusions. What if I were to tell you that I know all about this woman's background?"

Father Hobson turned his head slightly in order to look squarely at his tablemate.

"Her mother was a prostitute. Through no fault of her own, this innocent child of God was brought into the world without a father at home. The comings and goings of strange men were as familiar to her growing up as was the humiliation of daily hunger and living in filth. One night when she was still too young to understand, but quite old enough to remember, one of her mother's clients beat her mother senseless right before her eyes. The child tried to make him stop, but he beat her as well, breaking one of her arms. He not only killed her mother, but mutilated her body with a knife, leaving her in a bloody heap in their small one-room home. Another of her mother's clients discovered the shocked little girl two days later. Her only description of the killer was of a strange bull tattoo with fierce red eyes on the man's chest.

"Skipping ahead and glossing over other painful events, she was later taken in by an aunt, whose drunkard husband raped the girl for years. Eventually she followed in her mother's footsteps, suffering the occasional beating from her own clients. One fateful night she brought a client back to her room, an elderly gentleman. As the man removed his shirt she saw a familiar tattoo of a bull with red eyes. Something deep inside her raged forth. She attacked him right there in her room with a butcher knife. She stabbed him numerous times and then mutilated his body. That was the beginning. She did much more thereafter."

"Two beers." The man with the bushy sideburns plunked down two fresh mugs, collected the empties, and grunted as he turned back toward the bar.

Father Tate took a long drink as Father Hobson stared at him in stunned contemplation.

"Well, what say you, Peter? Is this shades of gray or black and white?"

"Do you truly know this woman?"

"Oh, the story, well, let's just say it's a compilation of things I've heard myself in the confessional booth. Confessions that I didn't want to forgive, confessions that haunted me well into the night, confessions that made me struggle with the concepts of God, and Jesus, and man, and good, and the lack thereof, evil." Father Tate's tone had turned serious. He stopped and took another long, hard drink.

"I'm sorry. I suppose it has been rather selfish of me to assume that only I—"

"Nonsense, Peter, you haven't been selfish at all. *I'm* quite sorry." Father Tate looked up and smiled. "I've thrown a wet blanket on our evening. Please forgive me. Here, let's drink to our health. Here's to those of us who see the evil of the world firsthand, and live to drink and eat and share the company of friends. And no more talk of evil this evening. We can wrestle with that issue, and the devil, another day. Cheers."

"Cheers."

* * *

"Father Hobson, please sit down. It's so good to see you today." Father Tate motioned the younger priest to a chair at his small dining table. "I'm sorry I was unavailable yesterday. All this war chatter has nervous parishioners coming out of the woodwork. They're all so brave in public, with 'kill the Hun' and 'spank the Kaiser.' Then the mothers and fathers come to me and confess their fear of losing their children. Such blind hypocrisy…but enough of that. How have you been?"

"Much the same, I'm afraid, much the same." Father Hobson let out a weary sigh as he sank to the chair across the table from his host.

"Did she find you again today?"

"Yes, and yesterday as well. It's a relentless assault. I can't fathom the purpose. I can't see why I am the object of her game, if a game it is. I've tried to be more understanding, remembering your story the other night. But it's insanity, and"—Father Hobson paused, took in a deep breath, and blew it quickly back out—"she's driving me insane."

"You've been very brave with all this, my lad. You've done well by confessing your feelings to me, and I hope the exercise has done you good."

"Oh, most definitely, Father. I could not have withstood this for so long without your help. She relates the most disturbing things, things that have already happened for which she seems to infer some credit, and things yet to come. The frightening thing is that the near-term future events always, to her evident delight, always happen as she predicts. It's, well, 'unsettling' would be a mild description."

"Hmm." The older priest lifted a wine glass and took a slow sip. "We've talked at length about your feelings of guilt based on an unusual attraction to this woman. I believe that is coloring your reaction to all this. I doubt that conclusion surprises you. I've done a lot of praying and thinking on this point. This is an unusual case, and I hope you'll understand my unusual approach to the matter. I've taken an interest, confidentially and discreetly to be sure, in observing the occasional penitent coming and going from your confessional station. And I believe I've seen this woman."

Father Hobson sat up straight. His heart raced at the thought of a third-party description. "Go on, please."

"Rather handsome, I must confess. She has black hair, large brown eyes, a fair and fine complexion, aquiline nose, full mouth, and quite attractive figure."

Father Hobson closed his eyes and felt himself physically shudder.

"I take it that description comes close to your imagination?"

It took a moment for Father Hobson to gather himself. He responded meekly, "Yes, remarkable, yes, I see her clearly, as if she is standing before me. Yet, I've never seen her, fully, but only in my mind's eye. I feel like I know her intimately. I know the touch of her skin. I know the smell of her hair. I know the taste of her kiss."

"Father Hobson, please collect yourself. Here, a glass of wine with me if you please."

Father Tate poured a glass of dark red wine for his guest and then another for himself. With a shaking hand that he could not steady, Father Hobson grasped his glass and took a long drink.

"Peter, I know this is quite personal, but it helps me understand. What I mean to ask is, what would you do if confronted with this woman in the flesh? What if one night she was not an apparition, but real, at your bedside?"

"I...I would, I wish I could say I would..." He tried to steady himself, looking around the room searching for some moral anchor. "Truth be told, Father, and I am ashamed to admit, I don't think I could resist her. I would sin. I shudder to think of it, but I believe I've fallen that far. I can't explain it. She has tried to turn me to her purpose, and I feel, perhaps, turned. I hope I'm wrong in this. I would resist with all my soul, but, I...I don't know."

"Peter." Father Tate leaned forward and placed a hand on Father Hobson's shoulder. "You are stronger than you think, and you are not alone. Have patience and all shall be resolved in a light that you may not now understand. Ours is a complex world that we do not always comprehend in the moment. We all, each of us, have angels and demons that battle for our souls. The key is knowing how to recognize which is which. Things are not always as we first perceive. I know that all will be revealed to you in time. And you can rest assured that you may always rely on me."

"Thank you, Father, you bring me great relief. I pray that your faith in me and my future is well founded. I must confess, I have my doubts."

"It is, Peter, have no doubt. My faith is unshakeable. And soon, so shall yours be."

* * *

"What is it, Henry? I came as soon as I was able."

Lord Lansdowne looked up from the papers in his lap at the alarmed face of Sir Charles Hardinge.

"Charles, thank you for coming at this late hour. Please have a seat."

"I was at the club when you tracked me down. I knew it must be important to ask me back to the office well after dark."

"I'm afraid it is. The French have buckled. I received word this evening that they have acceded to the German demand for an international conference to resolve the Moroccan affair. Without Delcassé they've no stomach for any pressure from the Germans, particularly with the Americans urging them to accept the conference. The Germans will go into the conference with the Austrian delegation in their hip pocket. If they can convince the Italians and Spanish to join them in their position, the French will have no one but us to back them, and thus far that has shown to be insufficient. They'll be isolated, humiliated, and then they'll blame us."

"What about the Americans?"

"There's the wild card, Charles. I must confess I underestimated their influence in the matter. What happens in the conference may well come down to what the Americans view as a reasonable result. Any more insight from our American agent? It would be quite useful if we knew what the Americans were thinking."

"Not on this issue, no. Roosevelt plays it down the middle in the American press. They adore him, and he's quite good at getting them to do his bidding. He recently gave them their own room in the White House. The 'Press Room' he calls it. Where his mind truly is at the moment, I can only speculate."

"He's unpredictable, which makes him dangerous." Lansdowne reached for a glass and took a contemplative sip of brandy. "I'm sorry, how incredibly thoughtless of me, Charles. May I offer you a drink? I'm afraid I have quite a head start on you already."

"Yes, whatever you're drinking will do nicely. How are the prospects of the election looking?"

"Not good at all. Balfour has botched this one. I expect that this time next month you'll be working for a new Secretary as part of the Liberal cabinet. I'm afraid I won't be here to see this through. I do take comfort in knowing you will."

"Thank you for the compliment, but elections are such fickle things. You may be surprised."

"I doubt it. I suppose I'll go back to the House of Lords and do battle there. Perhaps I'll ask for a commission in the army once the war breaks out." Lansdowne took another sip. "You know, I have a good idea who your next Secretary might be."

"Henry, really, this isn't a very pleasant topic."

"No, in earnest, I think you should know. I believe Sir Edward Grey will soon be sitting in this chair. He'll need you. He's a good chap, but short on experience. You know he's never even been to Germany. I don't think he has the slightest idea how to communicate with them. That can be dangerous. He can't use that subtle gentlemen's discourse he learned at Oxford. The Kaiser only understands simple, straightforward propositions. You've got to speak to him like a child. 'You do that, and I will do this,' none of this suggesting and double meaning solicitor-speak. Grey will need you to help him with that."

"If I find myself in that position, I will do my best."

"I won't miss it." Lansdowne stared into his glass. "Not like Canada. That was the best assignment of my life. You should see the Rockies, Charles. Magnificent. I've never felt closer to God than walking along a mountain stream, reading the water in hunt of the day's catch. It's indescribable, the crystal clear river, the bright sky, the smell of pine, and all the while the music of the water and the birds, the wind whistling in the trees."

"It sounds marvelous."

"When I was there I made it a point to visit with the natives whenever possible. I felt it my duty as Governor General. One day I was in the camp of one of the western tribes. They had a renowned medicine man who, so they believed, could tell the future. When I met him he took my hands, turned them both palm up, and began to study them with great interest. After a few minutes he looked up and with reverence made his pronouncement. The tribe elders all reacted approvingly, nodding their heads and smiling. Not knowing his language I naturally turned to my interpreter for assistance. He looked at me with a blank face. 'Governor, he said that someday you will be important enough that others will fish for you.'" Lansdowne paused and smiled while looking at his glass.

"Perhaps he was right. I never fished when I was the Viceroy of India. Perhaps that's what he meant." He took a long sip and held the stinging liquid in his mouth before letting it slowly slide down, leaving a trail of warmth all the way into his chest. "Yes, Charles, you really must see Canada. One more thing about Grey, you'll need to be very delicate about explaining the Inspector Jenkins engagement. He'll be predisposed against it. Jenkins is unconventional, rough around the edges, and retained by a Tory. As a Liberal from Oxford, Grey is more likely to do business with the devil himself."

CHAPTER 9
BAIT AND SWITCH

"YOU CAN'T BE serious!" Father Tate showed a rare flash of anger, certainly rare in Father Hobson's experience. "You have an absolute vow of confidentiality. I understand this is an extreme case. But extreme cases can't justify breaking your vows! Think of what you're saying!"

"Father Tate, I respect your opinion immensely. Please, I have given this point enormous consideration and much prayer. This evil must be stopped. I needn't disclose any specific confidences beyond conjecture, nothing direct. But this is an extreme case. I know it's hard to fathom, I barely fathom it myself, but there is something much bigger at work here, something that must be stopped."

"And therefore it is *you* who will make the judgment on what to disclose and what not to disclose to stop it. You cannot presume such authority! I can see now that my insistence that you continue to take this woman's confessions was a mistake. You must stop immediately. Give yourself time to think clearly. In the name of God, Scotland Yard? Of all courses of action, you mustn't! You cannot! Why do you force me to take this matter to the bishop? He will likely defrock you."

"Father, please, I do not take this decision lightly. You don't know all that I've heard, all the terrible things I've heard. There is a plan that she's a part of, a plan that she reveals only in disturbing glimpses. She's trying to turn me to her cause, and I can't resist any longer. If I'm turned, then will others be. All the while, those who can't be turned are killed, or 'redeemed,' as she puts it. It's all like a dark, vile river...no, an ocean flooding forth on humanity, men, even reasonable and intelligent men committing acts of unspeakable brutality. She talks in riddles and strange disjointed thoughts sometimes: concentration camps in our Boer War; acts of assassination and terrorism; a future filled with death and destruction on a scale that the world has never seen; innocent men, women, and children killed by the millions; our own London a burned and smoldering rubble from fire falling from the sky; Armageddon in a blinding explosion of light. Insane, I know, but there is something to it all. There's something in this chain that must be broken. It mustn't be inevitable. It can't be inevitable. I have to try, Father."

"Peter, you're speaking nonsense. You'll be deposed!"

"Then I must resign from the Church. I have no choice."

"Please, Peter, don't be so rash. Take a holiday, immediately. I will report to the bishop your state of exhaustion. You must rethink your position."

"I have rethought my position. Your daily counsel has done me good. I have regained my strength, at least enough of it to know I must act while I'm still strong enough to do so. Please inform the bishop of my decision. I can't wait until he gets back from his present absence. I'm not strong enough to wait."

"Father Peter, he will be gone but another ten days. Do this for me, take a holiday and consider your actions. If you don't return in ten days, I will assume you have betrayed your vow and will so report to the bishop. But please, consider your actions first."

"I will consider it. I can promise no more than that. I had thought of going to York for a few days. Perhaps some contemplation there will do me good." Father Hobson extended his hand, which Father Tate quickly grasped with both of his.

"Consider it, Peter. Yes, do. I'll be here when you return and will tell no one of this matter until then. You *must* think further upon this. Think upon all we have discussed. I beg of you, put your trust in what I've told you. All will be revealed in time, but you mustn't take this matter outside the Church. I beg of you. Peter, before you go, think on this. I must know, and you must hear your answer. When you listen, when you listen to the quiet voice of God, that contemplative voice that comes softly to us in our still meditations, what does He say on this matter? Have you asked Him?"

"Yes, Father, I have, many times, and the answer always comes back the same. Strange that it should be so specific, and perhaps that's part of what compels me so. It's a name, just a name: Inspector Edmund Jenkins."

* * *

"Ye Olde Watling, very curious," Inspector Jenkins muttered as he strode briskly along a familiar London street toward his destination. He could frequently tell in advance the nature of a meeting and of the people he was to meet by the selection of the meeting place. Pubs, almost always pubs. He supposed it was quite natural from their perspective. If you have to meet an inspector from Scotland Yard, you might as well do it on familiar turf with reliable aides at hand.

There were quite a few pubs in London where he would have approached an anonymous meeting with much more trepidation and certainly not alone. Dark, evil dens they were, frequented by brutish men who would just as soon stab a man as give him the time of day. But Ye Olde Watling? Who would choose that meeting place, as tame as the nearby St. Paul's Cathedral? In fact, he was as likely to run across a bishop in Ye Olde Watling as anyone else.

A tingle up his spine demanded his attention. To what? Then he heard it consciously, the same walking pattern from behind him as several streets before. It was a light step that changed speeds with the changing topography of the buildings along the street. He was being followed.

He continued his brisk walk and kept his head forward. A sudden change would alert the tailing party. Then the topography gave him what he needed. The buildings along the street up until the next intersection presented no doorways or quick exits that could provide cover in the event he turned around to see who was following. Consequently, his pursuer would have to hang back until Jenkins cleared this section of buildings and then catch up with him. If he turned at the next intersection, the pursuer would have to catch up quickly or risk losing sight of him all together.

125

Now all that was needed was a doorway around the corner, and the trap could be set. If memory served, the doorway was there.

He turned abruptly at the corner. Once he was out of the line of sight of his pursuer he sprinted to the doorway, which was just where he remembered. He turned to face the street and flattened himself against the door. There was just enough room to hide himself from anyone who came racing around the corner after him. He pulled his revolver and waited.

He didn't have to wait long. The familiar pattern of steps was just around the corner and approaching fast. As a figure began to pass the doorway Jenkins grabbed the nearest shoulder and pulled, spinning a man to face the door as Jenkins swung around behind him and pinned him there. With his forearm jammed in the back of his pursuer's neck, Jenkins pressed his revolver to the pursuer's temple and pulled back the hammer.

"Please, don't shoot!"

"Jim Talbot! What in heaven's name are you doing?"

"Please, Inspector, don't shoot. It's me, Master Talbot."

"Good grief, of course I won't shoot. Now turn around and tell me what the devil this is all about."

"I'm sorry, Inspector. I wanted to see if I could follow you."

"It's self-evident that you were following me, but why?"

"I wanted to prove to you I could do it, sir. I wanted to show you I could follow you without you noticing."

"Well, you failed in that regard. Caught after only five hundred yards, not a good showing at all."

"It was seven hundred, sir. I'm sorry."

"Master Talbot, calm yourself. What did you hope to accomplish by proving you could follow me?"

"It's my day off, sir. I've been thinking, I mean, I've thought about it a great deal, how much I desire to work for Scotland Yard. I'm good at things like this, following people and seeing things. I've followed policemen and gentlemen for miles without any of them noticing me at all. I can be useful to Scotland Yard. When I saw you across the street half a mile back I resolved to follow you and—"

"And ask me for a job at Scotland Yard."

"Yes, sir. I know I'd be up for it. You could teach me how to follow people even better, so that not even you would know. I'm sorry, sir. I meant no harm."

"You nearly got yourself killed, lad. In addition, you specifically ignored my instructions."

"Yes, sir, I'm sorry. But I reasoned those instructions were for my benefit, such that no harm would come to me. I don't care about that. I mean, I'm not afraid. I want to help. I kept the rest of your instructions. No one knows about you or the man with the black box. I've told no one, not even my father."

"Master Talbot, look at me. I can't overlook this transgression. Someone who works at Scotland Yard must obey orders to the letter. Do you understand?"

"Yes, sir."

"To do otherwise can place others at risk as well. This was a serious transgression. Consequently, I'm officially placing you on probation for two years."

"Probation, sir?"

"Yes, probation. You must refrain from any detective work for a period of two years from this date; no following policemen, gentlemen, or inspectors. Further, you may not have any contact with me or anyone from Scotland Yard during this two-year period. Mark this date, and if two years hence you've served your term of probation without violation, then you may present yourself to me at Scotland Yard for a proper testing of your capabilities and suitability to serve. Do you understand?"

"Yes, sir! Thank you, sir. I promise I'll keep to the terms of my probation."

"Just to be clear, this arrangement is secret as well. Only you and I will know about this probation. If you serve it out properly, I will forget this transgression ever occurred and evaluate your application on equal footing with any other applicant."

"Yes, sir. Thank you, sir. I know you won't be disappointed. I'll be the best applicant you've ever seen!"

"Two years from today, Master Talbot. Now, be on your way, quickly. Don't look back."

Jenkins suppressed a grin as he watched Talbot run down the street. Half a mile? The lad was good.

Jenkins went back to his course, pondering again the absurdity of his destination as a location for a clandestine meeting. Perhaps his contact would say grace before confessing his role in some evil scheme.

Soon Ye Olde Watling hove into view. Dispense with standard precautions? No, mustn't get sloppy.

He quickly cased the exterior of the pub, seeing nothing peculiar. He then went down a side street and entered through the back door. He knew all the entrances to the London pubs, a knowledge born of professional necessity. He would enter the pub from an unexpected direction, giving him the ability to clear his escape route in advance if one were needed later, and to check for hidden accomplices.

As he emerged into the main room, he was just to the side of the bar with a clear view of the front door and the men then in the pub, about a dozen or so. It looked like a usual and sedate crowd for Ye Olde Watling. He soon spotted a younger man sitting erect with his back to the bar and looking intently at the front door. This must be his man, and from behind he recognized a familiar form.

"Mr. Miller, why the coy games?" he inquired of the suspect. But when the man turned to face him he saw that, while the resemblance was striking, this was not his familiar acquaintance, but rather a young priest.

"I'm sorry?" replied the priest.

128

"Apology's all mine, Father. I mistook you for someone else I know. I believe you're looking for me, though. I'm Inspector Jenkins of the Yard." He extended his right hand, taking the normal precaution of watching to see if anything was produced by the priest's hand coming from his pants pocket, but nothing but a strong, warm grip followed.

"Delighted, sir, my name is Father Peter Hobson. Is there somewhere quiet where we can talk?"

"There's a suitable corner booth upstairs. Please, after you, Father."

* * *

The two priests sat quietly eating their meals, facing each other across the small table in Father Tate's residence.

"I am disappointed, Peter, but not surprised. I have not informed the bishop yet. He will surely defrock you for the confidence you've shown in this inspector. I'm afraid there is no turning back now. More wine? Try this one. I think you'll be pleased." Father Tate extended a newly poured glass.

"Thank you, Father. You always sup with the most delightful wines. I'm most grateful that you still chose to receive me as a friend." Father Hobson swirled the dark red liquid before taking a long and appreciative sip from the offered glass. He held the smooth red nectar in his mouth, swishing it about before letting it flow down his throat. "Yes, delightful indeed."

"But of course, I will miss you, my lad. I'm glad you saw fit to confide in me this last time."

"Thank you. I feel quite at peace now, actually. Would you believe me if I told you that God spoke to me last night? Not directly, I mean, but through one of his favorite messengers." Father Hobson could tell his companion was a bit perplexed. "I went to the symphony last evening. It was Mozart's *Requiem*, a beautiful piece throughout. But when the soloists sang the Benedictus, God spoke to me. He opened my mind to him, and he gave me peace. I don't know how else to explain it. He gave me peace."

"Interesting. They say Mozart didn't write much of the *Requiem*. It was completed by one of his assistants, you know."

"Yes, I've been told, and perhaps you can hear it in the pedestrian nature of some parts, particularly some of the transitions, but the soloist section of the Benedictus? No, Father, that was pure Mozart. I'm sure of it."

"Well, I'm glad of it then. And I'm glad you've come here tonight. It means a great deal to me. I'm curious on one issue, though. This all began when you asked me about the possibility, in the abstract, of course, of a devil incarnate. Do you recall that conversation?"

"Yes, of course."

"Have you told the inspector your theories in this regard?"

"That, and more, I'm afraid. It's good that I'll no longer be a priest. I've not been a good one. I suppose I was never cut out for it."

"Oh, to the contrary." Father Tate let out a laugh. "If you only knew. That's your failing. You see, you are the perfect priest. That was the attraction."

"I'm sorry, I don't follow?"

"Peter, does the inspector know that you've come to see me this last time?"

"No, I merely told him I had to wrap up my affairs and would return to London in a few days' time."

"Good, well enough. I presume he doesn't know of your discussions with me about this affair?"

"But of course. He knows nothing of our discussions. Why would I tell him about confiding in you?"

"I didn't mean to offend. Please don't let my impertinent questions distract you from enjoying this delightful wine.

Returning to our philosophical discussion, if one were to presume that the devil was incarnate and among us, would he seek apostles?"

Father Hobson took another sip of wine while he pondered this changed line of thought. "I hadn't considered it in those terms, but yes, I believe he would. Accomplices, I would call them, but yes, apostles will do, I think."

"Let's refer to them as apostles for now. Assuming further that such apostles are among us, what type of persons do you think this devil of yours would recruit?"

Father Hobson took another long drink of wine and another longer pause to answer. The response was forming slowly in his head, and it took a while to collect it. "I suppose they would be very intelligent, unscrupulous, perhaps having fallen quite far from grace, but, well, quite indistinguishable, yes, that's the word, indistinguishable from the rest of us."

"Hm, makes sense, but why the last point, Peter?"

"The devil works in darkness. To reveal his plans too fully would undermine his goals."

"Ah, I quite agree, but what of his goals? What does the devil want? To what end do his apostles work?"

Father Hobson was beginning feel a bit hazy. He decided he would ease up on the wine for the moment. "I wish I knew, Father. It all seems so, so senseless. I mean, assuming we are applying the abstract to the situation at hand, there seems to be a plan, a plan to eliminate and turn various, specific people, both young and old. I know it may sound dramatic, but I feel...this does sound strange...I feel there is a desired result, the destruction of humanity. But why? None of it makes sense to me."

"Ah, but it wasn't until well after the resurrection that many of the disciples of Jesus could make sense of their Lord's purpose. Perhaps these disciples of the darker lord suffer the same ignorance, but sense, and are drawn to, something they cannot yet fully comprehend, some awesome purpose."

Father Hobson started to feel alarmingly light-headed. He felt compelled to choose and sort his words carefully before speaking so as not to slur his response. "Father Tate, you sound as if you speak in defense of these imagined apostles and my theoretical, my theoretical devil."

Father Tate looked down at the table and smiled. He took a drink from his own wine glass, noticeably savoring the aftertaste long after he had swallowed.

"Peter," he said as he looked up with a purple-stained grin, "how are you feeling at the moment?"

"Strangely cold and, and light-headed. I'm sorry. I may need to call the evening to an early, to an early—"

"Indeed, if you only knew. By the way, I *do* believe in some of your flights of fantasy with this mysterious woman of yours. I too see evidence of the dark ocean of which you speak, washing, flooding over humanity. But you can't stop it. No one can stop it. One either helps or gets out of the way."

Father Hobson saw the room gradually start to turn. He closed his eyes. When he reopened them he focused hard on Father Tate, bringing the slowly spinning room to a momentary halt.

"Father Hobson, do you know what was my father's profession?"

"No, I don't believe you've ever...ever mentioned, mentioned...it." He struggled to get the words out. His body shivered, and he felt sweat beads forming on his forehead.

"Why, the same as that of my older brother, the same to which I was apprenticed until my brother's miraculous recovery from a long and presumed to be fatal illness. You see, I was trained at first not for the priesthood, but as an apothecary. Oh, no need to reply, Peter, your tongue will no longer answer. The time has passed.

"Very useful trade, apothecary, and my father had some interesting and well-placed clients. Some of these clients' needs included, shall we say, 'convenient' ways for friendships to end, permanently, and discreetly.

"Feeling cold, are we? Yes, you had quite a wine tonight, a special concoction I made up just for you. It's very convenient indeed, tasteless and impossible to detect in red wine. It's attacking your nervous system now. Yes? Having difficulty breathing? Don't look so stunned. You're dying, Peter, and you can't even move to save yourself. Your last memories in this world will be of me speaking to you. Oh, and another useful feature of this particular concoction is that you will die with your eyes wide open. Why, yes, I've seen it happen myself. You'll be looking at the world as you now know it right up to the end!"

Father Tate stopped, poured himself another glass of wine, and looked back sympathetically at his speechless tablemate.

"Quite fortuitous, that you've fallen into my lap like this. You surprised me by showing yourself this evening back in Leicester. Sad, though, she would have had you eventually, one way or the other. She had you turned. You know it. Don't fret. No man can resist her advances for long. You certainly would have found her, shall we say, 'earthly' method much more enjoyable than the fate about to befall you. But then, you did the unexpected. You broke your vows for what you perceived to be a higher purpose. Such a shame, Peter, I would have thoroughly enjoyed working with you. You most certainly would have enjoyed being turned. Now she's looking to kill you instead of seduce you. What a shame. Whether you die by my hands or hers, though, it matters not. I'll just have to tell her she can stop looking for you. She's very good, you know, one of the best, no, *the* best, a rock on which to build."

Father Tate reached under the table and placed something, Father Hobson couldn't make out what, in his lap. The room resumed its slow spin as he fought to focus on every word.

"In a way, I envy you, Peter. I believe that you are about to see a purpose, a divine goal, clearly and without doubt. You have been tested, and, depending on whose shoes you wear, you've either failed miserably or passed with flying colors. Now, before your mind stops working, you shall peer into this lovely, simple black box."

* * *

Fred Miller sat patiently in the confessional booth at York Minster peering out through the latticework at the back of his stall toward the Cathedral doors. York, a lovely little town, much prettier than Manchester. Had they missed their chance? The window of opportunity, if there was one at all, would close quickly. In the meantime, he would wait.

It was early afternoon, and the Cathedral was lightly visited, and the newly placed confessional not at all. The Cathedral door opened only occasionally. He'd stopped getting excited each time it did, having watched it for over two hours.

He noticed the door opening again. A tall, poised woman with dark hair carrying a large handbag sauntered in. She moved purposefully to the confessional stall. He held his breath. His heart was pounding. She took the penitent's seat and faced the screen.

"Father Peter, so good to see you again. I know you missed me, so I was delighted to learn about your reassignment to York Minster and its experiment with private confession. So progressive, don't you think? I thought I'd congratulate you, a welcoming party of sorts, an old and familiar friend from your previous diocese. Are you glad that I've come?"

She paused, but he let the silence hang in the air.

"Surprised? You weren't running away from me, were you? Surely you didn't think that I would let you slip away?"

She pressed her mouth close to the screen and breathed her words directly into the priest's compartment.

"You did miss me, didn't you? You've thought of me often. Tell me it's so."

Still, he offered nothing but silence, as he sat and took in with satisfaction all she could throw at him.

"Did you miss my breath? Did you miss the scent of me? Have you been thinking about me lately as you go to sleep? I've been thinking about you. Come close to the screen, to me. Isn't it warm in here together, Father? Almost as warm as you've imagined, but this screen *is* in the way, isn't it? I didn't come for a confession today. At least not mine. I think it's *your* turn. Or, shall I say, your turning." She let out a low chuckle. "Tell me, Father, what is your secret sin? Confess to me so I can help you. What's the matter, my lonely, longing Peter? Lost your tongue?" She purred through the screen. "Shall I find it for you? Very well, then. You…want…me."

The last word was blown across the screen with a breathy whisper that felt all at once both cool and warm against his face.

"You want me with all your mind, soul, and strength. Confess it. You moved to York because you were afraid you couldn't resist me. You can't, so I've come to relieve you in temptation's hour. Just confess it, Father, and you'll belong to me."

"Why do you torment me? Who are you?" he whispered back in response.

"I am your nightmare and your dream. I am your loving master and your obedient slave. I am what you have always wanted but dared not seek. Your life can now begin in me, for us, if you will just confess it. You want me, and only this wooden screen, your free will, and your need to confess and submit stand in the way of endless felicity.

"Tell me, Father, what do you imagine I taste like when we kiss? Tell me how my hair smells when I hold you close. Tell me what my skin feels like under your touch. You don't have to imagine anymore. I'm right here, ready for you to touch, to hold, to kiss. And when you do, you'll do as I say. You'll hold me, touch me, and kiss me when, where, and how I tell you to, obedient to only me. Because it's what you want so desperately. Confess to me, my love."

"What do you want? What is your purpose?"

"We're both here for a higher purpose, aren't we, Father? What matters is what *he* wants, what is *his* purpose. It's all intertwined, you see. Remember your Apostle Paul in his second letter to the Thessalonians. 'Let no man deceive you by any means: for that day

135

shall not come, except there come a falling away first, and that man of sin be revealed, the son of perdition; who opposeth and exalteth himself above all that is called God, or that is worshiped; so that he as God sitteth in the temple of God, shewing himself that he is God.' He is here, with me, with you. We will be together, Peter. You must confess and give yourself to me. It's his purpose for us, our reconciliations, our redemption."

"You forget the rest of Paul's words. 'And then shall that Wicked be revealed, whom the Lord shall consume with the spirit of his mouth, and shall destroy with the brightness of his coming: Even him whose coming is after the working of Satan with all power and signs and lying wonders, and with all deceivableness of unrighteousness in them that perish; because they received not the love of the truth, that they might be saved. And for this cause God shall send them strong delusion, that they should believe a lie: That they all might be damned who believed not the truth, but had pleasure in unrighteousness.'" The sound of a book closing echoed from his side of the booth. "Where is James Aston?"

The woman sat in stunned silence for a moment. "You're not Peter Hobson!" She leapt from the confessional and opened the door to reveal the man inside. Her shocked eyes opened wide before she turned and ran toward the exit of the church, clutching her bag.

Fred sprang from the confessional and sprinted after her, keeping close on her heels but not closing the distance, like a sheepdog herding her toward the door.

As they both exited the door Fred saw the reinforcements, two uniformed policemen. She turned away from them and headed for the alley beside the church, appearing to run as fast as her feet would carry her. Now the two officers joined him in pursuit, again keeping close but not closing on their prey. As the group turned a slight corner in the alley there appeared a man, arms folded and standing with his legs shoulder-width apart, blocking her way. She was trapped. She was surrounded.

"Mrs. Jones, you're as beautiful as when we first met in America. Death seems to follow you in your native England as well. I'm afraid this time it's you who's been deceived, though." Inspector Jenkins unfolded his arms, removed an unlit cigar from his mouth, and touched the brim of his bowler hat, giving it a slight tip before replacing the cigar and crossing his arms again. "I believe you've previously met my priest *du jour*, Mr. Fred Miller. Amazing resemblance to your Father Hobson, and so kind of him to play the role. A little bait and switch, I'm afraid. You shouldn't put so much stock in church gossip. It's not always accurate, I've found. Now, let's not make a scene. I'd like to ask you a few questions. Can I count on you coming willingly, or shall I instruct these two officers to drag you along?"

She pulled a black box from her bag. Dropping her purse on the ground and raising the box to her face she screamed, "Redeem me!"

CHAPTER 10
HELP

MARY CUNNINGHAM SMILED as she watched her husband in the New York morning sunlight. He was, as she always knew he would be, a good husband, and she reveled in his company. "More tea, my dear?"

Sam looked up from the paper and smiled back. "No, thank you, darling. I must be off to my rounds shortly. I'll just finish this cup. I won't be long, though. Shall we go to the park this afternoon if it warms up sufficiently, unless you have a meeting to attend?"

"The park? Why yes, that would be lovely. No, I've no meetings this afternoon. Perhaps we could celebrate."

"Celebrate? Wait, let me think. Three months...of course! How could I have forgotten the prediction by Doctor Glass?"

"Three months to the day, and you're still here. You do remember what he said, and on our wedding day of all things."

"Of course. 'Sam, you'll never domesticate a wild suffragette like Mary Scott. She'll be off to her meetings with those wild-eyed women agitators. I give you three months before she throws you out of the house.' I do think he was a little tipsy at the time."

Mary laughed and took Sam's hand. "I don't hold it against him. He did get it half right. I don't think you'll ever domesticate me. But you can stay, nonetheless." She felt Sam's warm hand press back in acknowledgment. "We can go to the park and celebrate as soon as you finish your rounds. How are your patients? Any unusual cases of late, or can we finally relax a bit?"

"Nothing seems unusual to me any longer, but no, all garden variety stuff. Mrs. Temple complaining of her back, young Rodney Street broke an arm yesterday, oh, and then there's—" Doctor Cunningham stopped in mid-sentence as his housekeeper entered the room.

"Sorry to interrupt, sir, but a message has arrived for you." She handed him an envelope and waited.

"Thank you, that will be all," he replied, setting the envelope on the table and watching her until she left the room. "Does she always have to be so damned snoopy? I've got to speak with her again about that. Yes, and then there is the Jones girl, bless her heart, sick with a cold again."

"What about little Molly Bell? How is she faring?"

"Quite well, thank goodness. She hasn't had any coughing or breathing difficulties lately, and she seems to have recovered nicely." Sam fished some crumbs off his plate with the tip of his fingers, kissing them off before they could fall back on his plate, all the while casting a casual glance at the envelope on the table. "These scones are quite good. You know that's why I married you, don't you, despite your suffragette tendencies."

"I'm quite sure of it. And I married you despite your table manners. You could use a fork, you know, or even ask for another scone."

Sam grinned. "Yes, but then you'd have the perfect husband. Surely I need to leave myself some room to grow and mature under your gentle guidance. Hardly seems sporting if fifty years hence you have nothing to show for your efforts, no improvement of the man you set out to mold."

Mary let out another laugh while tossing back her head and squeezing Sam's hand.

"I love that music, your laughter. It's composed by God if you ask me."

"I'm glad you think so, my perfect husband."

"Well, what's this then?" He picked up the envelope, which was not sealed, pulled out the single unfolded page, and began to read.

"What is it, Sam? You look white as a sheet."

"A telegram, from London. Here, have a look." He slid the paper across the table.

Mary picked up the note and focused on the short, typed text. "Many Mollys in London. Stop. Need your help. Stop. Come to London at once. Stop. Jenkins."

* * *

"Sam, I'm so glad you proposed lunch before you leave for London. I don't see you as often as I'd like, and it's always a delight. I'd have been quite upset with you if you ran off to England without saying goodbye."

"Thank you, Doctor Glass. And thank you for listening. This whole thing is all so strange. You've been such a help just listening." Doctor Cunningham took another bite as Doctor Glass looked on, appearing calm and content.

"Yes, strange indeed. Tell me, this telegram you received yesterday, has this inspector fellow, Jenkins, has he sent you telegrams in the past?"

"No, now that you mention it. We've communicated, but by other means. Notes left here and there asking my opinion about this or that, it's all such skullduggery. The cable came as quite a surprise. Of course, it was phrased such that I certainly can't refuse."

"Yes, that may well be. Are you sure this is right, though? You leave your patients. You leave your lovely wife. This seems like a dangerous game you've gotten yourself into."

Doctor Cunningham chewed and swallowed a bite and then took a sip of water before answering. "Mary will get along quite all right while I'm gone, amazing woman, stronger than I, no doubt. I've contacted several doctors to look to my patients. My affairs are all in order. I'm hopeful this is a short stay to confirm any diagnoses and then I'll be back before anyone misses me."

"Speaking of your patients, may I do you a favor, please, Sam? I know of your particular concern for Miss Molly Bell. She lives in my neighborhood. Let me look after her while you're gone. I know I'm a poor substitute, but I promise to visit her on a regular basis."

141

"That's quite kind. I would be much pleased and relieved to have her under your care. I'll send word over to Mrs. Bell this evening. In the meantime, I've packing to do."

"Packing? I assumed you would catch the fast ship leaving this afternoon. Why the delay?" Doctor Glass asked with a look of puzzlement.

"Mary insisted I wait until tomorrow. Most uncharacteristically irrational, she was. But there you have it. She was adamant, and I've concluded that the inspector will just have to wait a day."

"Curious, not like her at all. Not sure I understand, either. Is it wise to delay? Won't the inspector expect you on today's departure? You may be upsetting certain plans he has for your arrival."

"Mary's mind is made up. I know when she is immovable, and in this instance she has reached that point for whatever reason. Woman's intuition, I suppose, although I can't get anything more out of her."

"Will you cable him to let him know?"

"No, he's asked me never to contact him. He'll figure it out. He always does, somehow."

"Sam, I don't know, this sounds very risky to me. Perhaps he's made some provision for your safety on today's passage. Why put yourself at risk?"

Sam was slightly taken aback by his companion's changed and serious demeanor. "Doctor Glass, I appreciate your concern, but I'm not sure I share it. Surely the risk, if any, arises upon my landing in England. Inspector Jenkins will deduce that I have been delayed by one day and will take appropriate measures. I may not understand Mary on this issue, but I see little benefit to opposing her advice."

Doctor Glass sat in apparent contemplation for a moment with his eyes fixed elsewhere. Then he turned his gaze back on Doctor Cunningham. "I suppose you're right. Tell me, Sam, does anyone in New York other than Mary know about this trip, about Jenkins, about the strange episode with Molly Bell?"

"Not a soul, and I know I can trust you and Mary to complete confidence."

"Of course, Sam, but of course. I'm sure it's best that way. You're certain that you'll be leaving tomorrow, then?"

"Most certain, I'll pack this afternoon and then dedicate the entire evening to calming my wife."

"Promise me you'll be careful. I have an odd sense of foreboding about all this."

"I promise, and before you and Mary know it I'll be back."

"Well then, let's toast, to a calm wife, your health, a safe passage, and a quick return."

"May I add, and to Miss Molly Bell, whom I leave in the most capable hands. Thank you."

"To Miss Molly Bell."

* * *

"Inspector Jenkins, it is a pleasure to meet you. Thank you for making the time for my visit." Father Tate extended his hand as the inspector got up from behind his desk to greet his guest.

"The pleasure is mine, Father. Thank you for traveling from Leicester to London to see me. I hope you had a pleasant journey. Please"—he pointed to a nearby wooden chair—"please, take a seat. I'm most curious to hear what you have to say. Your urgent telegram was short on details."

"Yes, indeed, but I will, I hope, make myself clear momentarily."

Father Tate sat down in the offered chair. Inspector Jenkins sensed that he was being watched intently as he returned to his seat behind his desk.

"Inspector, I've come to offer my services. I believe you need my help, and I'm here to offer it to you."

Inspector Jenkins sat silently waiting for Father Tate to explain. Noting that the priest was waiting for some reaction, after a few seconds he broke the silence. "Can I offer you something to drink, Father, perhaps some tea or a glass of port? I also have an excellent scotch."

"Very kind of you, Inspector, but no thank you. I stopped at a pub on the way and, well, I feel sufficiently fortified for now. As I was saying, I've come to offer my services."

"And what services might those be, sir?"

"Well, you see, Inspector, Father Hobson of Saint Martin's Church was a dear friend of mine."

Father Tate appeared to wait for a response before proceeding, but the inspector again gave him no satisfaction, staring blankly at him.

"I was his confessor, Inspector, and I tried to support him. His recent passing came as a shock to me. Perhaps you know something about it?"

"He's dead," Jenkins offered matter-of-factly. "That much I know."

"Forgive me for not speaking more plainly; this is an unusual course of action for me. Let me try again. In his confessions to me, Father Hobson was quite open about his revelations to you. Did he not speak of me?"

"He made it clear that matters of the church were matters of confidence for him. We dealt on a business level."

"Yes, that much I understand. I must admit, I tried initially to dissuade him from going to you at all. We spoke frequently of what he was facing. I tried to help him as best I could. Slowly, however, I began to understand the immensity of what he faced. I began to realize that he was right. I was wrong to keep him from you. My only fear is that by insisting that he deal with you with such discretion, on a business level as you call it, I may have..." Father Tate stopped in mid-sentence and dropped his head as if in prayer. "I may have put his life in danger."

"Father Tate, I need you to come to the point. I understand you were close to Father Hobson. I am sorry he's dead. To me, though, he was a source of information."

"That may be, but to me he was a friend." Father Tate's voice trembled with a hint of anger. "Sir, I am here today out of respect for my dead friend. As a young priest he walked a tightrope between the religious world and the secular world. He may have been simply a source of information, but I, sir, I offer you understanding.

"Let me be blunt. I know you are on the hunt, the hunt for someone who has caused you significant difficulties and frustration. Father Hobson told me everything, all about you and everything he told you. But he also revealed much more to me than he told you. Now that he is gone, I feel I must pick up his banner. I must complete his mission, your mission, our mission. This evil must be stopped. I believe with my help, we can stop it. That is what I offer you. That is why I'm here. I've come to help you."

Again the two men sat in silence, watching each other intently.

"I suppose you'll want to be paid, then?"

"Paid?"

"Yes, your friend was on my payroll. Surely he told you. At first he was reluctant to answer my questions fully, but every man has his price. Call it a bribe if you like. Whatever you call it, he died before he could collect, and now it is available for you, if you plan to help finish the job. A substantial sum, I might add."

"I don't want any blood money. You misunderstand me, sir. He was my friend. I have no need for support, either. I've obtained a paid sabbatical from the Church, and my modest salary will suffice." Father Tate stood and looked toward the door. "I'm sorry, Inspector, to have wasted your time. I apparently misjudged your needs."

The inspector rose from his seat, came out from behind his desk, and walked toward the priest. He stopped in front of Father Tate, looked him straight in the eyes, and extended his hand.

"Welcome to the mission, Father. I would be honored to have your assistance."

Father Tate smiled and eagerly shook the inspector's hand. "Excellent. Now, I believe I'll accept that drink you offered, but only if you'll join me."

"Of course, Father. I neglected to mention that I have an exceptional bottle of red wine. You are a red man, are you not?"

"Yes, but how did you guess?"

"It's my business, sir, and I thank you for your offer of assistance."

"Glad to help, my dear inspector, glad to help."

* * *

Doctor Cunningham awoke to the quiet hum of the luxury liner whisking him toward the British Isles. He had some trouble falling asleep, thinking about the concern Doctor Glass had shown for his trip. He had taken all the precautions he could think of. At Mary's suggestion he booked the trip under her maiden name. The ship's manifest showed one Samuel Scott traveling in a private second-class berth. He would keep to himself, seldom leaving his cabin, and make the passage in obscurity on a ship that no one expected him to be on.

It wasn't quite light outside yet. He tried to see his watch, wondering what time zone he must be in after nearly a night's passage. It must be early morning, just before sunrise. If only he could go back to sleep for a while longer.

Another noise soon caught his attention. His room was black, but his eyes were drawn to the direction of the door by the sound. It was a soft scratching coming from the door, as if a mouse with metallic claws was gently testing the door surface. Then he heard a sound that caused his heart to stop and brought him to full consciousness. The lock in the door clicked.

He grasped for the heavy cane he left propped next to the bed just as the door burst open and the form of a man rushed toward him. In the dim light coming from the hallway he saw a knife raised and he moved to counter with the cane. But then, suddenly, the intruder's body jerked back. There was a muffled moan, and now he saw two men in his cabin. The second man, larger than the other, had hold of the first intruder from behind. The two struggled briefly, and then the first intruder slumped to the floor.

"Mr. Scott, you all right, sir?"

The cane was still poised to defend. He didn't recognize the hushed voice and could make out only the outline of a man before him. "Who are you? What are you doing in my cabin?"

The man turned the switch lighting the electric lamp in the cabin and closed the door behind him. "Quite sorry, sir, you're all right, then?" this time louder with a noticeable Irish accent.

Standing before him was a brute of a man with a barrel chest and forearms like anvils. His thick neck was as wide as his head, which was topped with curly auburn hair.

"Was hopin' to get at him before he did you much harm, sir. Sorry if I let him get too close."

"Who are you? What do you want?"

"You can put the cane down, sir. No cause to be alarmed on my account. Oh, who am I, sez you? Well, I'm your guardian angel, so to speak. Here to help, I am." The big man took a bow, offering the crown of his head as an easy target for Doctor Cunningham's cane.

"Who is he, and how do I know you aren't of the same design?"

"Him, well, that fellow, God rest his soul, that fellow meant to kill you. Me, on the other hand, I meant to see that he don't. Now, good sir, we must be off. We'll lock this fellow in your cabin, and you'll just have to share mine until we get you safely to port."

"I'm inclined to do nothing of the sort until I've figured out who you are, who he is, and what has happened here. We should fetch someone from the crew."

"Someone like him, sir?" The brute pointed at the body on the floor, dressed in a crewman's uniform. "Sir, Doctor Cunningham, in all earnest, we must leave. The likes of him works in pairs, and it's just a short time until his second learns that he's now to do the job. You stay here and you're a dead man. Please, Doctor Cunningham, come with me. I mean to keep you alive on this voyage whether you like it or not."

* * *

"Manchester, all off for Manchester!"

Fred Miller smiled at hearing the familiar conductor's refrain. "Well, Inspector, home sweet home."

"Lead the way, Mr. Miller."

Fred obliged, gleefully hopping down from the train but checking himself from skipping through the station.

"You seem rather chipper today."

"I love this city. I've lived here all my life. My parents and siblings are all buried here. With God's grace I'll be buried here too someday, never to leave again. I know we won't be here long, but I'll revel in it while I can. Ah, here we go, the finest restaurant in town, conveniently located in our very own station hotel, the Midland. Inspector, after you."

They were no sooner inside a large dining room with a marble floor and pillars interspersed among tables draped in white cloths than a familiar figure rose from one of the tables to meet them.

"Inspector, Fred, so good to see you both. Please." Mr. White motioned them to seats at his table. "I trust your journey was pleasant."

"Quite so, in particular for Mr. Miller. I felt like I was holding back a nursing puppy from his mother as the station came into sight."

"Yes, he's always shown an inexplicable enthusiasm for our city. Judgment like that can hold a man back from making partner for a long time."

"Ah, so there is hope, then! Apparently I'm being merely held back. I shall remember that and endeavor to march on."

Fred grinned at Mr. White, who smiled warmly back.

"It's good to see you again, Fred. I must admit the firm sorely misses the mirth that always trails in your wake. It's good to have you back."

"That leads us to why we are here, but it may make more sense to have the inspector explain."

"Explain? Very well, but first let's get the two of you something to drink." Mr. White flagged down a waiter wearing a white dinner jacket. "Gentlemen?"

"A glass of beer for me, thank you," Fred directed to the waiter.

"I'll have the same scotch as Mr. White, please," followed the inspector.

"And lunch, all the way around, these gentlemen must be half starved."

The waiter acknowledged Mr. White with a nod and was quickly off.

"Before you explain why you're here, may I inquire about a professional matter, Inspector, just a point of curiosity?"

"By all means."

"Can you learn anything about a man by the scotch he drinks?"

"I believe you can learn a great deal."

"The first time we met, in my office, the scotch I poured in your tea, do you remember what it was?"

"Of course, that's my job."

"So what did you learn about me?"

"That you have good taste." The inspector smiled obliquely as he sat on his answer.

"Yes, well, I can't argue with that. Now, what is it you would like to explain?"

"Fred and I are here for two reasons, to brief you on developments and to ask your leave for me to keep him longer."

"Longer? Now that would be an impediment to partnership."

Mr. White had been joking the first time, but Fred sensed he was in earnest with the last comment.

"I'm aware that may be the case, sir. But please hear out what the inspector has to say."

Mr. White made a slight gesture with his hand indicating the inspector should continue.

"First the development. We have been successful in locating Mrs. Angela Jones. I had tracked her to York and was able to snare her using our good man Fred here as a ruse for which he just happened to fit the part."

"I'm relieved to hear it. And what did Mrs. Jones have to say for herself?"

"She didn't, unfortunately, she chose death over capture."

"Then you still don't know the whereabouts of Mr. Aston?"

"I'm afraid not. She did, however, confirm the depths of what we're up against." The inspector paused as the drinks were brought to the table. "To your health, gentlemen."

"To your health, sir, and to you and Scotland Yard for having tracked down the elusive Mrs. Jones."

"About those depths, this part is rather difficult to explain. I've seen much of evil in my line of work, inexplicable cruelty and senseless barbarity. As much as I couldn't understand it at times, it

150

all seemed worldly enough to me. I'd have to be rather hard-pressed to ascribe supernatural cause to an evil act, so long as I had the possibility of an earthly explanation. I don't believe in ghosts and demons wandering the earth or werewolves or mermaids for that matter.

"The case of Angela Jones is altogether different. It is evil in a way and to a degree that I've never seen before, and it seems to be directed by a hand that belongs to neither this world nor to God's. Whatever that hand or power may be, it has wrought unimaginable cruelty, and I'm convinced it plans much worse. Mrs. Jones was just one player in it all. I'm afraid there are others.

"Mr. White, I need help. Fred here has a real talent. Namely, he's easily trusted. Further, I trust him. I need him for a specific mission, which will require him to take leave of his position. I've come here to explain, as much as I'm able, the situation in the hopes that you will allow him an indefinite leave without prejudice."

"Fred, if I refuse his request for your leave, what are your intentions?"

Fred swallowed hard a mouthful of beer, straightened in his chair, and looked him in the eye. "Mr. White, I am grateful for all the opportunity I've been given at the firm. My goal is now and has always been to become a partner. I very much prefer you give me leave, even at the expense of the timing of my advancement. I've seen enough to believe the inspector is right. I think he faces the devil, or something like it. As a Christian, I cannot deny him assistance."

Mr. White sat in silence staring at him. Fred maintained the eye contact and waited for him to frame his answer.

"And I, as a Christian, cannot deny you leave. You have my permission and my prayers."

A sense of relief washed over Fred followed by a sense of joy as the food arrived on the table.

"Lunch, just in time to save me from death by starvation after having just narrowly saved my position. What a blessed day."

"Amen, Fred, and God bless this food for the nourishment of our bodies and to bring strength to my famished friends from London. May you nourish them in the Spirit and steel them with faith for the work they intend, in the name of your Son, our Savior, Jesus Christ, amen."

"Amen."

"Inspector, if I may make a somewhat obvious observation. You and Fred are but men, mortals. Don't you feel some trepidation about this enterprise? The person you seek, let's assume you have the devil by the tail. What if he turns around and bites you?"

"Mr. White, have you ever felt the passion of Christ? He opens your mind to but a pinhole view of heaven and brings you to your knees in rapture. I have no fear of the devil. Let him do his best."

CHAPTER 11
A DREAM

DOCTOR GLASS KNOCKED on the door a second time and waited patiently on the Bells' front porch until someone finally appeared.

"Doctor Glass, I'm so sorry. I wasn't expecting anyone and so was in the back. Please come in. Can I take your coat?"

"Don't worry yourself, Mrs. Brown. I've come to call on Miss Molly. Doctor Cunningham should have told you to expect me, and since he's been gone now for a few days I thought I'd pay my first visit. Is Mrs. Bell in this morning?"

"Oh, Doctor, so good of you to come. I'm afraid you've missed both Mrs. Bell and Molly. They left two days ago."

"Left?"

"Yes, they've taken a holiday. Oh my, what an adventure. They're to join Mr. Bell in Texas at one of his business ventures and then take a train to California to look into another prospect. It all makes me very nervous, with her asthma and all. I wish they'd taken me, but someone has to look after this house."

"Texas? California? How can I reach them? I'd like to inquire about Miss Molly. I did promise Doctor Cunningham."

"Well, that's the thing, Doctor Glass. It was all so sudden. One minute I'm preparing supper and the next thing I know, it's off to Texas! They left in such a rush, I'm not even sure they were completely packed. I have no idea how to reach them. They said they'd let me know where they might land. Oh dear, I suppose in all the rush we overlooked sending you word that you didn't need to check on Molly."

"Mrs. Brown, it is quite important to me that I contact the Bells. Isn't there any way I can reach them? Did they give you any clue where they might be and when? I simply can't break my promise to

Doctor Cunningham, and if anything were to happen to that little girl...I don't even want to think about it."

"I wish I knew myself, Doctor. I'll worry half to death while they're gone."

"Mrs. Brown, you must promise me one thing. Promise me that you will contact me as soon as you have any information on their whereabouts. I must know where this little girl has gone. Will you help me?"

"Yes, of course, Doctor Glass. You'll be the first to know."

* * *

"Doctor Cunningham, you look exhausted. Please have a seat. Here, have some tea."

Inspector Jenkins passed the doctor a steaming cup. The doctor took it without looking up and slumped into a leather chair.

"I'm glad to see you. I was worried they'd get to you first. I trust my man Mick made your passage as comfortable as possible."

"He's a little rough around the edges, but I came to be most grateful for his company."

"Yes, a good man in a tight spot, very dependable and discreet as well."

"I came as quickly as I could. Thank you for the protection. Who is 'they' by the way? I never could get that out of your man, Mick. Funny, I don't think Mick ever told me his name. As soon as we arrived in England he handed me off to two of your men, and then off he rushed to get on another ship with barely a goodbye."

Inspector Jenkins chuckled out loud. "No, I suspect you wouldn't ever get much out of him. He doesn't know, in any event, who 'they' are. The best men don't ask questions. Answers lead to liabilities, which is why I frequently leave you in the dark. There is one thing at which Mick excels, however, and that is protecting people. If I need someone protected, he never fails me. He has an unnatural knack for it, and he can do it without anyone even noticing."

154

Doctor Cunningham looked at the inspector, waiting for his answer. "So, I suppose I'm still to be left in the dark. I drop everything at a moment's notice, leave my wife, my patients, and travel all the way to London with an assassin or two trying to kill me en route so that you can leave me in the dark! Why did you summon me? How can I help you if I don't even know why I'm here?"

"Doctor Cunningham, I didn't summon you."

Doctor Cunningham dropped his jaw as he sat in stunned silence. Regaining his composure, he sat upright in the chair. "The cable, then who sent the cable?"

"That would be 'they' who sent the telegram. Fortunately, I found out about it with sufficient time to react. What a difference a day makes, as they say, a difference that allowed me to deploy Mick. Not that I couldn't use your help, mind you. I just had hoped to seek it on my time and on my terms. I'm afraid they forced the issue." Inspector Jenkins took a sip of tea. "So, who are 'they'? That's a good question, and one I'm not entirely certain I can answer. But you're right, you can't help me unless you know more. And I do need your help."

"Sorry, sounds as if we've both had a rather trying week."

Inspector Jenkins kindly waved off the apology. "Tell me, what do you remember about the man with the black box?"

Doctor Cunningham looked into his teacup and then back at the inspector. "Still not a lot, I'm afraid. I remember arriving at the building, entering, it was dark inside. I remember a man, and we spoke. I remember being afraid. The next thing I remember is sitting on the floor talking to you. I just don't have any specific recollection of the man or what exactly transpired."

"Do you remember the black box?"

"Only that you showed it to me with one end gone. I don't recall if I had ever seen it before then. I know there is a gap in my memory. I just can't seem to close it. Except, well…"

"Go on."

"I've seen it in my dreams, but nothing I can be sure of."

"Then tell me what you can't be sure of. What do you see?"

"They are very vivid, these dreams." Doctor Cunningham set his cup down and took a deep breath. "I'm holding the box in my hands, not the broken box, but a complete, solid box. It's light, but feels well-constructed. I don't want to look inside, but my arms keep slowly bringing it toward my face. I fight my arms, but the box keeps coming closer, and closer. I try to close my eyes, but something holds them open. After what seems like a long time, the box is pressed to my open eye. Then there is a blinding white flash and, well, that's when I wake up. In the dream, I mean, as if it's a dream within a dream. I find myself sitting on the floor of a dark room, and in my lap is the box, now a broken box." He paused and stared at the inspector. "That's it. There's nothing else, just a dream."

"Interesting. Doctor Cunningham, I have reason to believe that there is some reality in your dream. I believe you *did* look into that black box back in April at Seventeen John Street in New York. I don't know what the box is or how it works. What I do know is that you survived looking into the box, and I've yet to find any evidence that any other man has done so and lived beyond the encounter. I also believe that when you looked into the box it was in one piece, all one whole box. When I arrived shortly after the event, it was not. One end was missing, as if it had been blown out. The box had been rendered impotent, causing me no harm when I looked into it. One other important fact for you to know, there is at least one other black box."

"What! And how do you know that?"

Inspector Jenkins got up from his chair and walked to a solid-looking wood cabinet in one corner of his office. He produced a key and unlocked a door to the cabinet. He next reached into the cabinet and manipulated something with his hand, turning it one way then the other. He then opened a second door within the cabinet and reached inside, pulling out something covered in a linen cloth. He walked the bundle over to his desk and placed it at arm's length in front of him.

"I know" — he removed the linen cover — "because I have it."

Doctor Cunningham sat frozen, transfixed on the black box. It was identical to the box in his dreams, and, other than appearing to be all one piece, identical to the one he'd seen in that dark room back on John Street.

"And this," the inspector said as he reached for something hidden somewhere under his desk, "is your black box." He set the second box next to the first. They were identical in every regard from a front view. The inspector turned them slowly around to show the only difference. The second box was missing one side and was shown to be completely hollow.

"More than one box? How many are there?"

"I don't know, at least two, so I suppose there could be dozens. We'll know more when the children start to fall again and dead men are last seen associating with a man with a black box. Then you and I will go hunting."

"Where did you get it, the first one?"

"From them, one of them, anyway, a woman. Doctor, I know this is frustrating, but knowledge leads to liabilities. I've kept many things from you, that's true. That's a necessary part of my calling and your safety. You must trust me. I can offer you no other comfort. I don't know who 'they' are exactly. But I believe the man with the black box does not operate alone. He has associates, and they have black boxes. I don't yet understand their methods or their motives. I don't even know how this infernal box works, but it kills, that much is certain. At this stage I don't know how to combat this man and his associates other than to track them down as quickly as possible and capture or destroy these infernal boxes.

"And they are infernal." The inspector glared at the boxes. "I lost one officer, good man, who looked into that one." He pointed at the box he had removed from the cabinet. "We've tried to open it. We can't find any type of seam. When we test it, it gives every indication of being solid through and through. We've tried cracking it open with tremendous force, but not even a sledgehammer puts as much as a blemish on it. It's not made of anything that our best lab men have ever seen before. Yet, we must destroy them. Something this dangerous can't be allowed to exist, even if locked solidly in my safe within the walls of Scotland Yard."

Doctor Cunningham struggled to process it all. He wasn't even sure he followed completely, being lost in the contemplation of it. "What about the man who carries these black boxes about? You say you don't know about his associates, but what about him?"

The inspector fell back into his chair. "Remarkable fellow, whoever he is. No one who has ever seen him can describe him. He always seems at least one step ahead of me, which is not where men normally stay for long. I don't know yet, Doctor. Until I do, though, I intend to deprive him of his weapons. I'm resolved to find every black box on this planet and destroy them to the last."

The two men sat in silence, each as still as stone.

"Doctor, I'm afraid that is where you come in."

"How so?"

"This is where I need your help. As I said, I did not summon you, but your arrival is fortuitous. The fact that *they* summoned you as a ruse to kill you substantiates my hypothesis. It also means, unfortunately, that they believed I had stumbled on this hypothesis as well. Up until their attempt at your assassination I only had one source, now dead, to rely upon, which is not sufficient for what I'm about to ask you to do. Now, however, they have confirmed my understanding.

"Doctor, you are going to help me rid the world of these death machines. You are the only man I know who can do it, which also explains why you are now a marked man. With stakes this high, they will stop at nothing to kill you. But before they do, you've got to help me neuter them."

"A hypothesis?"

"A confirmed hypothesis, as I said, but yes, still a hypothesis. Doctor, people look into these boxes and die. They never come back. You came back. I strongly believe, based on an explanation I received from a reliable source, that you are now immune to its powers, whatever they may be. Not only that, but I believe that you can destroy these boxes because of your surviving it once. You, Doctor, can look into one of these boxes and destroy it, just that simple. You now have a unique and unexpected power, a power that makes you a marked man to them, but very valuable to me.

"There truly are many Molly Bells in this world. I couldn't have stated as succinctly that part of the telegram if I had written it myself. Doctor, I said earlier that you're going to have to trust me. This is going to take an enormous amount of trust. I understand that. I wouldn't ask if I had another solution."

Inspector Jenkins got up from his chair and moved to Doctor Cunningham, standing directly in front of him. He then pointed back at the complete box sitting on his desk while keeping his gaze focused on Doctor Cunningham.

"Doctor Cunningham, I need you to look into that box."

"I don't suppose you have any scotch. I think I could use a splash or three in my tea."

* * *

Fred Miller stood patiently at the appointed street corner with his hands buried deep in his heavy overcoat. It was an unusually cold morning in London. He'd left his winter cap in Manchester the week before, and, to make matters worse, in his rush to be on time, he had evidently misplaced his right glove, or at least it wasn't in his right front pocket where he normally stowed it. He did have his muffler and top hat, and he hunched himself down in the upturned collar of his coat to stay as warm as possible.

Passing horses snorted short bursts of steam from their nostrils as they clip-clopped along the busy street in front of him, pulling various carts, wagons, and coaches. The normal street banter was absent as pedestrians hurried briskly by, likewise scrunched down into their recently deployed winter clothing as they darted about trying to get back indoors as quickly as possible, dodging the occasional sputtering motor car.

As he stood waiting, he wondered what the day had in store for him. All the cloak and dagger involved when working with the inspector was becoming almost normal to him. This was just another prearranged meeting with someone, with specific instructions on time and place transmitted by a note pressed into his hand by a passing stranger the day before. At times it was all rather amusing, but this was not his game, and he'd resigned himself to playing by the rules set down by the professionals at the Yard.

In the distance he heard Big Ben strike the hour, and, with the normal similar precision, a black carriage pulled up in front of him. As it came to a stop, the door opened. He dutifully got on board.

It took him a moment to adjust to the dark interior after the door closed. The curtains were all pulled, and that morning's light was not particularly suited to penetrate them. As the carriage jolted forward two figures came into focus, sitting shoulder to shoulder and facing him from the seat on the other side. The first was the familiar figure of Inspector Jenkins. He was surprised to see him this morning, as they had visited just the night before. The second was a smaller and older man whom he did not recognize.

"Good morning, Mr. Miller. Thank you for coming out in such a chill. I trust the day finds you in good health and spirits."

"Indeed, sir, good morning to you as well, and to your guest."

"This is Father Philbin Tate on loan to the Yard from Saint Martin's Church in Leicester. Father Tate, this is Fred Miller on loan to the Yard from the patent firm of Clark and White in Manchester."

Fred Miller extended his cold, bare hand, which was met by the gloved hand of the priest, who gave it a firm, welcoming squeeze.

"Pleasure to meet you, Father."

"The pleasure is mine, Mr. Miller. I've heard good things about you, and, I must say, you bear a remarkable resemblance to a dear, departed friend of mine. You hadn't mentioned that, Inspector."

"I'll get straight to the point, gentlemen. The two of you have a connection. You both have dear friends who have been the target of one Angela Jones. You both have been invaluable to me for both the information that you've provided and the services rendered. Your zeal is a testament to your dedication to your respective friends.

"Mr. Miller, Father Tate recently set forth a proposition that, upon reflection, I find quite sensible. To wit, I'd like the two of you to henceforth work as a team. Your motives are similarly founded, and the information that you each have dovetails nicely. From outward appearances you will be social acquaintances and can communicate with each other at your own discretion. I will continue to keep in contact with each of you either individually or together in the usual manner. We can start the association today, if you have no objection. Your thoughts, sir?"

Fred was taken aback. It wasn't like the inspector to cross-pollinate information between his contacts. He knew there were many others working with the inspector on the bigger case, but he rarely had any information on who they were or what they were doing.

"Inspector, I trust your judgment, as always. I'd be delighted to work with Father Tate."

"Excellent. I've booked a quiet table at a nearby private club where the two of you can enjoy breakfast and get to know one another. The driver will take you there directly. When you arrive, please present this envelope to the doorman and all the arrangements will be taken care of." The inspector handed a small envelope to Father Tate, who tucked it away in his coat.

"Now, before I leave the two of you, any questions?"

"Then, we're to await further instruction for now, after our breakfast this morning, that is?" Fred felt the carriage slowing and coming to a stop as he posed his question.

"Yes, although feel free to make arrangements for future meetings between the two of you on a social level. I'd like you to get to know each other better, and I hope you'll find your time together enjoyable."

"I'm quite sure we will, Inspector. It's very kind of you to arrange for our breakfast this morning, and I look forward to getting to know Mr. Miller better and, I hope, to becoming his friend."

"Please call me Fred, Father, and I too look forward to our becoming friends."

"Excellent. Gentlemen, I'll be off here and leave you two for now." Inspector Jenkins opened the door and stepped out of the carriage. Before shutting the door he turned back to Fred Miller. "Have you checked your left interior pocket?"

"I beg your pardon?"

"Your right glove, sir, last night you placed it in an interior pocket, which is not your custom. Perhaps it's still there."

Fred reached into his coat. "Ah, yes, my glove, thank you, Inspector. You're quite right, as always."

"Good day, gentlemen."

The door closed, and the carriage lurched forward.

"Remarkable man, nothing seems to escape his attention," Father Tate remarked with an earnest tone.

"Indeed, Father, most remarkable, unnervingly so at times."

"The best always are, Fred, quite unnerving at times. You know, the first time we met he guessed that I prefer red wine. It startled me a little. How did he know?"

"Smile again, please."

"I beg your pardon?"

"Smile, and then stick out your tongue. Yes, as I thought, purple stains on both. You not only drink red wine, you enjoy it, sloshing it around in your mouth awhile before you swallow it. Even the

162

stains on the tongue can take a day or more to fade, evidence of recent drinking. But the teeth stains take time to develop."

"Ah, quite straightforward. I don't know why I should have marveled about it."

"Occasionally the inspector lets me in on tricks of his trade. Always testing, he is. He's fascinating to watch in action. Upon meeting someone he doesn't know, he'll ask them a series of unusual questions. Before you know it, he's sized up the character, talents, and habits of the interrogated. Sometimes I think he's testing just to see if I notice that he's testing. Funny you should ask about the wine, though. He brought up the stain on teeth and tongue markers just the last time we met."

"I'm glad to know he's not as supernatural as he first appears. Curious, I don't recall him asking me any questions when we first met in his office."

"Perhaps the collar was sufficient information for him, or maybe his questions weren't so noticeably unusual that day. I'm sure he quickly sized you up and found you to be everything he was looking for."

"I pray so. He does seem to have quite the talent for keen observation, that much I'll say. But then we each have our talents. Tell me, Fred, what is yours, do you think?"

"Earnest gullibility, as best I can tell."

Father Tate let out a hearty laugh. "Well, then we'll make an excellent pair."

* * *

Young Jim Talbot was weary of the fare. It was late, he was hungry, and, worst of all, he had no idea where he was. This gentleman had directed him all over London until he had become hopelessly lost.

His father would never forgive him if he admitted to being lost. He thought back to the countless stories about how his father had driven carts and then hansom cabs since age twelve all over

London and had never been lost in his entire life. And here he was, as if he had never seen the city that he thought he knew by heart.

Jim did know that he had started this fare in Shepherd's Market. His father told him to go there last in order to pick up one of the drunk gentlemen who went there to "break the commandments," as his father would say. Funny, this gentleman hadn't seemed very drunk, but surely he must have been breaking at least one commandment. Why else would he be leaving Shepherd's Market at three in the morning? Three in the morning; he was getting very tired. Was this all a dream?

"Stop! We're here. Wait here. I won't be but a moment."

"Yes, sir," answered Jim dejectedly.

"And do stay with the cab. This is private business."

The man went inside, but appeared to be in such a rush that he left the door to the building ajar.

"Private business, we'll see about that," Jim muttered. Everything was his business when he hadn't been paid yet. This was no King and country fare. Jim dismounted the cab like a cat, not a sound, he thought, and tiptoed to the partially open door. Inside he saw that the man had lit a lantern that he carried as he headed down a flight of stairs to a basement. Jim ducked in and followed silently, staying in the shadows but keeping the man in sight. If this drunk, or whatever he was, intended to sneak away without payment, Jim would at least know where he'd gone to hide.

At the bottom of the stairs was a large, solid-looking door, which the man unlocked with a key produced from his hip pocket. The man flung his entire body against the door, and it slowly opened with a metallic pop and then a creaking groan. Once the opening was just wide enough for him to fit, he slipped through. Jim followed and slowly peeked around.

The man was at the back of a basement, facing away from Jim. He had set the lantern on a table and was removing a tarp draped over the back wall. Behind it was revealed a stone shelf built into the wall, starting about halfway from the floor and running the entire length of the room. In the flickering light Jim made out what appeared to be dozens of small boxes stacked on the stone shelf. He tried to make a quick count of them, but decided there must be fifty or more and stopped the exercise. Jim squinted to see what the man was reaching for. Then it hit him—the boxes were black!

As the man pulled a box from the shelf Jim heard the noise of a door closing from somewhere above the stairs. He looked back up the dark stairwell and thought he heard faint footsteps. Then there was a smell, the familiar and repulsive smell of rotten eggs. Weighing his options, he peeked back into the basement, but he couldn't see where the man with the black box had gone. He slowly leaned further through the doorway to get a better view of the room.

"You there! What are you doing? I told you to stay in the cab. Explain yourself."

A strong hand shot from the darkness and held him by the arm. He saw the figure of a man on the basement side of the doorway. From above, the rotten-egg stench increased as the sound of footsteps grew louder.

Jim searched for words. "So sorry, governor, I thought I heard you calling for help. I just came to see if I could be of assistance. I must have been mistaken, sir. So sorry."

The man stood in silence, holding him fast. Jim tried but couldn't quite make out his face to gauge his reaction. The smell from up the stairs was making him queasy. Cold beads of sweat formed on his forehead. The footsteps had stopped, but he sensed someone was watching him from behind.

"I'll just be going back to my cab now, sir. That is, unless you need my assistance."

"Assistance? Why yes, I do." The man pulled him into the basement. "I did call for your assistance, but I was afraid you hadn't heard me. Thank you, my boy. You're so attentive. You see, inside this black box is something I can't quite make out. The light is so poor in here, and your eyes are much younger than mine. Look into this hole and tell me what you see."

CHAPTER 12
THE TRAP

INSPECTOR JENKINS PACED the floor again, seemingly oblivious to Doctor Cunningham, who stood watching him at work as two other assisting detectives wandered about the same floor that the inspector had paced off.

"Twenty-two, again, twenty-two," the inspector muttered while chomping on an unlit cigar.

"Something significant, Inspector?"

The inspector took off his derby and rubbed his chin as he looked back across the room and out through the door leading to the next. He looked intently at the outline of a chimney coming up from the floor below, running along one wall of the room in which they were standing. He looked back again at the end of the room where his pace count had stopped.

Doctor Cunningham shrugged. He'll tell me when he's ready, he thought. What an odd place to be dragged to without warning or explanation. The interior of the building was coated with dust, evidencing its long-abandoned status. Light from the afternoon sun streaked in through greasy windowpanes to illuminate the remains of some type of warehousing and factory function that had long been forgotten, with little remaining of the equipment and furnishings that must once have filled the space. It wasn't a big building by London commercial standards, which possibly explained its limited usefulness in modern industrial times. Only the bottom floor was presently being used, as storage of some kind for a cloth company, and even then it looked as if no one had checked the inventory in months.

"Inspector, I know you said we're hunting today, but I'm still not clear on why I'm along. You normally keep me tucked away. Surely if you find something you can bring it to me."

"Yes, yes, we'll see."

The inspector's habit of keeping him a little too much in the dark was starting to wear on him. Why bring him along if he shouldn't know what they were doing?

"What is it, Inspector?"

"Pardon? Oh sorry, it's quite simple. This building is rectangular in shape with, as you will note, three floors. We find ourselves on the top floor, which is a full four paces shorter in length than the footprint of the building. Based on the placement of that chimney—" The inspector paused and pointed at the chimney with his cigar. "I would place the missing four paces at this end of the building."

"Are you suggesting a false wall, a hidden room?"

"More than suggesting, sir. There is approximately two hundred and sixteen square feet of space between this wall"—the inspector rapped his fist on the wall at the end of the floor he had paced—"and the outer wall of the building. The question is, how does one access the space? The likely answer is to be found not on the roof above, as that would be open to public observance, but in the floor below us, the middle floor. Shall we? Gentlemen!" He fanned his hat at his fellow detectives to follow him.

Back down the stairwell the group went, with Inspector Jenkins leading the way and Doctor Cunningham following closely behind.

"A bit odd, wouldn't you say, Inspector? This building has seen no use or habitation in quite some time. Yet, London, in the short time I've been here, always seems so crowded to me and lacking in space."

"It is a bit odd. The building is the subject of byzantine layers of legal proceedings that we've not been able to pierce. Businesses thus avoid its use. Interestingly, though, no squatters either. Even the destitute and homeless avoid it. The belief in the neighborhood is that it's haunted. The local poor would rather sleep in the elements than risk a night in this building."

"Not sure I blame them."

"Some of their fear may relate to the rumor that things are delivered to this location that aren't here."

"Ah, like our boxes, perhaps?"

As they entered the second floor the inspector again appeared too preoccupied to treat his last statement as anything beyond a casual observation, certainly not an utterance rising to the level of an actual question.

The middle floor was not quite as dusty as the top floor. A few tables still littered three rooms. Each of the rooms was connected to the next by a single doorway, and the doorways lined up when the doctor looked from one end of the floor to the other. More greasy windows lined the side of the building facing the strangely quiet street below.

Appearing to orient himself from the chimney column, Inspector Jenkins led the group to the room at the end of the building, stopping immediately below the projected hidden space on the floor above.

Jenkins stared at the ceiling, moving his head slowly back and forth, systematically examining it in a pattern of straight lines from one wall to the next. His gaze then went back to one corner of the ceiling, which he slowly approached while staring at it more intently. When he was underneath the spot with his neck craned back, he stopped and squinted at the surface above.

"You there, bring me the table from the next room. I also saw an old broom handle of sorts on the floor in the first room, fetch that as well."

The two detectives bounded out of the room, each returning shortly with their appointed items. Inspector Jenkins helped one place the table in the corner. Taking the broom handle, he mounted the table and started to lightly jab the ceiling at various points in the corner on which he had focused. Suddenly a square piece of the ceiling gave way. Quickly dropping the broom handle, the inspector caught the piece before it fell all the way to the table. From what Doctor Cunningham could see, it was roughly square and about two feet wide. The inspector set the piece on the table and looked up at the square hole left behind.

"Gentlemen, I see a space of a few inches between the missing ceiling portion and what should be the flooring material on the floor above. Ah, there are two iron hinges. They appear new, and little used. Let's just tap them a little…no rust dust."

The inspector turned his attention back to the other men.

"I'll need another table, the small one at the other end of the next room, quickly, please."

The assisting detectives sprinted from the room and returned a few seconds later with a second table.

"Here, place it on top of this one on its side, long end up. Yes, like that. Now, let's move it into place here. Good, yes, that will have to do."

The inspector had placed the smaller table on top of the first but on its side, such that the top surface of the second table formed something of a shield to the area directly beneath the open hole.

"Gentlemen, if I could have you all please move to the next room and stand behind the wall with your backs to this room and hands over your ears."

Doctor Cunningham and the two others retreated to the next room. Once there, though, the doctor felt his physician's concern kicking in, or perhaps it was just his childish curiosity. Either way, seeing that the other two had turned their backs to him with their hands on their ears, he carefully peered around the doorway into the other room.

He saw that the inspector had turned his attention back to the hinges and the solid flat section, the flooring from the hidden room above perhaps, to which they were attached. While crouching behind the upturned second table, the inspector slowly moved the broom handle into contact with the flat section, appearing to gradually increase the upward force he exerted. Suddenly it budged slightly, and what had appeared as a solid flat section proved to be a small door opening upwardly into the room above.

The inspector stopped pushing upward on the broom handle, seeming to take stock of the situation. There was no light coming from the crack he had created by forcing the small door, which now appeared to rest easily on his broom handle ready to be opened fully. He slowly resumed his upward push, gradually increasing the crack that emerged as the door began to swing open. The crack had grown somewhat when from within the dark room above came the sound of a metallic click. The inspector dove from the table toward the doorway and the room beyond as the doctor instinctively pulled his head back behind the doorframe.

A concussive bang knocked Doctor Cunningham off his feet. He felt the sting of being pelted with pieces of ceiling and wall plaster, and was soon sprawled on the floor.

His ears were ringing as he propped himself up and checked his body for damage. He had blood on his hands. His face stung. Feeling it added more blood to his hands, but as he felt elsewhere nothing seemed broken. Through a dusty haze the two other detectives were rolling themselves to a seated posture and checking their own limbs for any evident damage.

"Inspector, are you all right?" Doctor Cunningham shouted at the gray fog billowing from the next room. His voice sounded distant over the ringing in his head. "Inspector! Inspector!"

Doctor Cunningham felt himself being helped off the floor. He wobbled at first, but upon gaining his footing, he staggered into the dust cloud toward the next room.

At first there was no sign of the inspector, just debris piled on the floor and a large, gaping hole in the ceiling with sunlight fighting its way through another hole blown through the roof. They began frantically digging through the debris.

"Look, a hand!" shouted one of the detectives. "I've found him!"

The three men converged on the spot and flung the rubble about as they exhumed the inspector. He was face down and still.

The doctor rolled him onto his back and thrust his fingers flat against his neck, checking for a pulse.

"He's alive."

Seemingly on cue the inspector pursed his lips and took a long draw on the cigar that was still in his mouth but somehow now lit. He opened his eyes and cracked a bemused smile while blowing a stream of smoke skyward. "Of course, Doctor, never fitter."

"I'll be the judge of that."

Doctor Cunningham examined his patient. There were no evident cuts, just bruises and a bloodied nose. The inspector's eyes and white-toothed smile beamed through his dust-covered face.

"Incredible, you seem to be in better shape than we are. Well now, you seem quite pleased with yourself."

"Excellent diagnosis, Doctor, quite pleased indeed. I've just found another, no, make that two more pieces of the puzzle." The inspector sat up, dusted off his chest, and wiped his face.

"Good God, man, it's a miracle you weren't killed! And that's a good thing?"

"Two pieces, yes, excellent day's work. Help me up, Doctor."

All three men bent down and helped the inspector to his feet.

"Care to enlighten us, then?"

"Doctor, but it's so self-evident. Can't you see?"

Doctor Cunningham stared blankly back at the smiling inspector.

"First, they knew we were coming. Second, they wanted to kill us when we got here."

"And that's a good thing?"

"Yes, very good indeed."

* * *

"Thank you for lunch, Mary. It's so nice to share a meal with such lovely company, and the food was wonderful, particularly the pie. How did you know apple was my favorite?"

"Educated guess, Doctor Glass. I'm glad you could join me. It's so lonely with Sam gone."

"I can only imagine."

"Please know that you are always welcome at our table. Sam will be so pleased to hear that you stopped in."

"Please give him my regards, won't you?"

"Of course I will. More pie?"

"Ah, no thank you, I don't believe I could eat another delicious bite."

Doctor Glass took a long drink of his coffee as Mary Cunningham sipped on her tea.

"Almost surreal, don't you think, Mary? Here the two of us sit, calmly enjoying our food and company, like so many millions of others no doubt, while the world simmers imminently poised on self-destruction."

"You must be referring to the Europeans. It sounds like quite a mess, but do you really think it's that grave?"

"I do, indeed. Have I told you about my trip a few years back to the exposition in Paris?"

"I don't believe you have."

"The Exposition Universelle in the year 1900. It was held in Paris, oh yes, I said that already. I was there in May, and Paris was beautiful. Everything was in bloom and society was out in all its splendor. Every country in the world seemed to have an exhibition there. Never has there been such a display of innovation and progress. It was magnificent, and frightening.

"It occurred to me then the power of mankind. We now have machines and mechanisms never before imagined. These most certainly can be used for good, for progress. But they can also be used for destruction, destruction on a scale never before imagined. Wars in the past have been such crude affairs, but that has at least made them somewhat self-limiting. Nations weren't capable of fielding more than small armies relative to their populations. These small armies could only be maintained and supplied in the field for short durations, and their ability to defeat and destroy was capped by whatever crude weapons were at their disposal. That's all changed, and it was evident at the exposition. I fear the next war will be larger, longer, and more dreadful than anything the world has ever seen before."

"I pray you're wrong, Doctor. Surely such a prospect would check the inclination to even begin a war in this day and age. Mankind is so rational in the twentieth century. Someone will find a solution to this Moroccan squabble short of war, don't you think? At least they've all agreed to talk of late from what the newspapers say, some sort of conference in the offing?"

"Perhaps, but that will just delay the day of reckoning. And when it comes... Yes, but where was I? The Exposition? Paris amazed and frightened at the same time. There was the Palace of Electricity, its ceiling ablaze with thousands of lights, as if the sun had been brought indoors. There were pavilions dedicated to medicine, science, transportation, all testifying to how far mankind has come in the last few decades. Toward what destination, one might ask.

"But most impressive of all was the Palace of Armies and Navies, housed in what looked like a medieval fortress. It was quite a testament to man's exponentially increasing abilities to destroy man using means never dreamed of until this dawning century. Can you imagine cannons firing shells the size of a horse twenty miles into the distance? Floating castles dropping exploding bombs like fire from the sky? Railcars disgorging men and material at incomprehensible rates? The British exhibit, called the Maison Maxim, if I recall, was dedicated to their newest machine gun, capable of spraying bullets in a never-ending stream at advancing infantry, mowing them down like a scythe through wheat, a modern-day weapon that would leave the grim reaper in envy."

"My, surely it wasn't all so disturbing as that, Doctor."

"No, not all of it. But what was still gives me nightmares. It needs but little imagination to see, Mary, how great are the probabilities that after all man will prove but one more of nature's failures.

"Ah, but enough, you're right, we mustn't dwell on the inevitable. By the way, I stopped in to check on one of your husband's patients, Miss Molly Bell. Very curious, though, she seems to have disappeared."

"Disappeared?" Mary set her tea cup down and focused with concern on her guest.

"Yes, very strange, both she and her mother just up and vanished. Not even the housekeeper seems to know where they've gone."

"Strange indeed, what do you make of it?"

"Precisely what I was going to ask you, my dear." Doctor Glass set his coffee cup down and leaned forward slightly toward Mary. "Do you know where she's gone?"

"Me, know where the Bells have gone, now why on earth would you think I would know such a thing? You just told me even her housekeeper doesn't know where they are. Sounds like quite the mystery trip to me." Mary relaxed and smiled back across the table.

"Mary, this is a serious matter. I have committed to your husband that I will make sure nothing happens to this girl while he's gone. Now, I, as her doctor, have no idea where she is."

"But surely she's with her mother. Perhaps they've gone to see her father. Mr. Bell does travel frequently, as I understand it. I'm sure Mrs. Bell will use her excellent judgment to see that she receives medical care if she needs it."

175

"Yes, he's a geologist as I understand it. He spends quite a bit of time in…where is it? I think Texas or somewhere looking for oil. What do you know of Mr. Bell?"

"Not much more than that. Texas, the Dakotas, even California. I believe he travels more than he stays put. I've only met him once. He seemed quite friendly."

"You know Mrs. Bell quite well, though, correct?"

"I wouldn't say we're intimate friends, but we've spent a fair amount of time together."

"Tell me about her, please."

"She's a lovely companion at tea time, bright, joyful, and sharp, very sharp, actually. But I don't think she lets on how much she knows and perceives until she fully trusts you. Her faith runs very deep, that's for certain. She also loves her daughter fiercely and admires my husband greatly. She trusts him implicitly, and I think she'd do nearly anything for him. She's a lovely woman, and I'm sure she and Molly are quite well, wherever they may be."

"Mary, I need you to be honest with me. I think you know where Molly Bell has gone."

Mary sat back in her chair, tilting her head slightly to one side and smiling in bemusement, but made no reply.

"I'm deadly earnest. You must tell me where she's gone."

"Doctor Glass, really, I can't tell whether or not you're teasing me. If I didn't know you better, I'd say from your tone that you were threatening me."

"You apparently don't know me better." The two sat staring at each other, Doctor Glass with his jaw sternly set while Mary Cunningham's smile became intentionally forced.

"Doctor Glass, it was good of you to come today. Since you've finished your coffee and our discussion I trust you'll be on your way. Do come again sometime." Her tone had become icy.

"Mary." Doctor Glass lowered his voice. "Please don't make this difficult. If Sam were here he would tell you that you must help me in this regard."

"If Sam were here, he would show you the door. I'm afraid our visit has come to an end. Good day, Doctor Glass. Some other time, perhaps."

Doctor Glass rose to his feet, dropping his napkin casually on the table. He walked toward the front door, turning one last time.

"Thank you for the lovely meal, Mary. I will come again, but I may not be able to give you polite notice of when that will be. I'm sorry you've chosen to be uncooperative in this matter. Perhaps you'll give it some thought and change your mind. You know where to reach me. So, until we meet again, good day, my dear."

Doctor Glass took a short bow, turned, and left the house. Mary Cunningham continued to smile after him, but it turned to one of derision. She dropped her smile entirely as soon as the door closed.

* * *

Doctor Cunningham turned over again in his bed and glanced across the dark room at the sliver of electric light slicing underneath the door into his hotel room. Sleep had not come easy as of late. All of the precautions insisted upon by the inspector since the explosion incident, changing sleeping locations every night from one place in London to another, the dedicated watch of at least one guard outside his door every evening, his disguised appearance when out in public, should have eased his worries, but the attention to his safety just seemed to increase his anxiety. He reminded himself that just beyond the door, bathed in the light of the hallway, sat one of the nightly guards on duty.

On nights like this when he couldn't sleep he listened to the hushed voices and shuffling of feet during the shift changes as one guard would replace the next, always at irregular intervals. The rest of the time they seemed quite content to sit silently watching over his door, ready to burst in at any unusual sound that might emit from his room. Once he accidentally knocked a water glass off a nightstand while reaching for a drink in the early morning hours. It seemed like the guard was in his room and at his side before the shattered glass pieces had finished clinking off the hardwood floor.

He rolled over again with his back to the door. He thought about Mary. It had been too long. He missed her smile, he missed that sparkling look in her eyes that always made him feel loved, but mostly he missed being able to talk to her. He could see her clearly in his mind's eye. She was so beautiful, with her lovely face set on that long, elegant neck. Her inquiring eyes perfectly complemented her small mouth upturned at the edges.

He loved talking with her. It was his favorite pastime. He could do it for hours on end. She surpassed anyone he'd ever met in keeping his attention, and he never tired of just being in her company. He thought about her laugh, how it sounded like a phrase of music to him, and always made him smile.

If she were here he could tell her how frightened he'd been when he first looked into that box in the inspector's office. He'd tell her about the flash of light, and the sense of relief followed by the delight he and the inspector shared when they admired the disabled box that was his handiwork. He'd tell her how scared he was now, tonight, and how glad he was that she was safe back at home. Fool, he thought. That is exactly why she can't be here. He closed his eyes against the lonely darkness and prayed for her continued safety, as he often did on these sleepless nights.

He'd never thought of himself as an easily frightened man before coming to London. Then again, he'd never been relentlessly hunted before. He'd never been anyone's prey.

As he slipped into slumber, the image of an exhausted stag, head bowed and panting, hiding in a dark defile, drifted into his mind. Little time to rest with sounds of the hounds growing closer.

The pattering of rain outside his room faded into the background of a hazy dream. A drain spout ran with a continuous clatter somewhere near a window. That's what the stag needed, a good rain to cover his tracks and hide his scent. Yes, what a relief to have the cold rain coming down into the marshy defile. The sound of the hounds began to fade. The raindrops cooled the tired stag and soothed his aching muscles. Everything would be all right. The stag stood still, snorting bursts of hot breath toward the wet ground with eyes closed. Rest was coming at last.

The floor creaked. He rolled onto his back and tried to rise, but someone had lunged onto his bed and was on top of him holding his body down with his weight. Hands were on this throat. He struggled to get them off, but only his right arm was free. His left arm was pinned under the sheet and the weight of the man on top of him. He battered at the arms above him with his right arm and tried to twist his body sideways to free his other arm.

The hands kept constricting around his neck, tighter and tighter. He couldn't breathe. He couldn't call out. His heart raced and head felt on fire. With all the twisting under the weight of his attacker, he freed his left leg from under the covers and began to swing it wildly about. His knee struck something. He heard a lamp falling to the floor. Then…blackness. He felt his body going limp, and the stag began to falter, sway, and buckle to the ground.

* * *

"Inspector, I hope you don't mind me asking, but you see, it's my job to notice when people are troubled."

"I'm sorry? I'm not sure I follow, Father Tate."

"I understand if this is not the appropriate forum, sitting here in a pub with our hungry friend, but I rarely see you otherwise."

Fred Miller looked up and smiled, raising his glass of beer while continuing to chew his food.

"But if it is, and I don't presume to speak for Fred, but if there is anything you can share with us that we can help you with? After all, as you suggested yourself last week, we need to work as a team given the gravity of the situation we face."

"I'm sorry, I still don't follow you, someone's troubled?" Inspector Jenkins held his fork aloft and loosely in his right hand as he tilted his head slightly.

"Inspector, your peas, you've been sitting there stirring them for the last ten minutes. All I'm suggesting is that Fred and I can't help you if we don't know the difficulties you face."

"Ah, the peas, I suppose you're a bit of a detective yourself, Father."

Fred watched Father Tate smile and wait for an answer. Unwilling to wait with him, Fred washed down another bite with his beer before quickly spearing the next with his fork.

"I suppose I was waiting for the right time to tell the two of you. I won't say 'since you asked,' Father, but rather, along those lines, I'm afraid I do have some rather bad news."

Fred slowed the rhythm of his chewing and looked up at the inspector.

"Gentlemen, I know you've never met Mr. Y, but I trust I've revealed enough about him that you understand his importance to our effort."

"Of course, the gentleman you imported to London who seems to have the ability to destroy the infernal black boxes. He's key to the whole plan. We, and others, help you track down the location of the black boxes, and he puts them out of commission."

"Precisely, Father Tate." Inspector Jenkins stabbed some peas and this time thrust them into his mouth. While chewing he looked first at Father Tate and then at Fred Miller. "He's dead."

"What? Dead! How?" Single words were all Father Tate seemed able to muster.

Fred slowly lowered his fork to his plate and absentmindedly wiped his face with his sleeve. All three men sat in silence, the clinking of silverware on plates and the steady rumble of pub conversation spilling over their private booth.

"The how's not important. He's dead. We failed in our job of protecting him. An assassin succeeded this time where others in the past had failed."

"And what of the assassin? Any clues left behind? Do you know who he was or where he went? I'm sorry, I know this is very bad news. I'm being very impertinent. This is truly bad news."

"No, Father, it's quite all right, thank you. Perhaps the only good news is that we do know the assassin. Unfortunately, the assassin is dead as well."

"Unfortunately?"

"Our man killed him seconds after the assassin had dispatched Mr. Y. If the guard had entered the room just a moment sooner, Mr. Y might still be alive. Yes, 'unfortunately,' since we can't interrogate a dead man."

Fred cleared his throat. "How does this change your strategy?"

"Good question, I've been thinking on this very problem. Gentlemen, so far we have been approaching this only from the periphery. We've been chasing black boxes, since that's all we seem to have success in catching, albeit with a lone operative here and there, although none we've been able to question. We are never going to win this fight with that strategy, especially without Mr. Y."

"Isn't there another who can take Mr. Y's place?"

"I'm afraid not at present, Father. To my knowledge, he was the only man on earth with the ability to disarm the boxes. In any event, as I was saying, we need a different approach. And I think I'll need both of you to help execute it."

"We're here to help."

"Amen, Father. We're here to help. What can we do to assist, Inspector?"

"Gentlemen, I make no pretense about the nature of what this may entail. I've lost Mr. Y, and I have no doubt that your lives may be placed in danger as well. I thought I could guarantee safety, but that no longer seems to be the case."

"Inspector, again, I can't speak for Mr. Miller, but I think we've known that from the beginning."

"Yes, I trust you have, but what I'm about to ask will certainly not reduce the risk." The inspector paused as he stared into the distance.

"When I was a child, I used to visit my grandparents' farm in Wales. My grandmother loved birds. She always kept a feeder full year round for the pleasure of seeing them feast outside her kitchen window. I can still see her sitting and watching as, through shine and gloom, her birds would alight on the feeder suspended from a tree near the house. Ground squirrels of various types came to know that the birds, in their sloppiness, would knock some of the feed to the ground. These rodents, which she did not care for because of their destructive habit, would frequently come to the same tree to wait for the birds to spill some grain for them. As a consequence, yet another animal frequented the place, a fox. The fox learned that when the birds appeared so would the rodents. It was all a perfectly set trap for the fox, a trap that my grandfather, having no love for foxes, was quick to take advantage of.

"Gentlemen, I want *him* this time. No more chasing black boxes. We've been the rodents looking for spilled seeds. The fox knows we're about and is picking us off, one at a time, all the while plotting his kill in every henhouse he can. We need to set a trap and get the man who always seems to slip away. And for that I need bait. You"—the inspector raised his glass in salute—"you, gentlemen, shall be the rodents. And, like my grandfather before me, I intend to kill the fox."

Fred raised his glass in return. "I don't suppose I could trouble you for the rest of your peas? I'd hate to see them go to waste."

* * *

Mary Cunningham set the pen down and listened. The house was quiet, but something had caught her attention. There it was again. She wasn't convinced she heard it the first time, but someone was knocking on the front door. Perhaps she had gotten so used to the housekeeper answering the door that she hardly listened anymore. With the housekeeper away this weekend, having taken a short, unexpected vacation to visit her sick mother, Mary would have to answer the door herself.

She got up from her writing desk and quietly made her way through the house to the front door. Who could it possibly be at this hour? The knocking came again just as she reached the entry room.

"A moment please, who is it?"

"It's me, Mary. Please, I must speak with you."

Hearing the familiar voice, Mary turned the handle and opened the door enough to poke her head outside. "Doctor Glass, I was not expecting you. This is very unseemly at this hour."

"Yes, I'm terribly sorry for the unannounced visit. Mary, just a moment please, this is quite important. I apologize for upsetting you during my last visit. You were kind to invite me into your home, and I'm afraid I behaved poorly."

"Apology accepted, Doctor Glass, now if you don't mind—"

"Mary, please, I come to you earnestly with some terrible news. I…I, this is quite difficult, I'm sorry. Won't you please open the door?"

"For a moment, Doctor, but that's all I can do. It's very late." She opened the door wide but made sure to step directly into the doorway where she could be seen in the gas porchlight.

"Yes, indeed, pardon me. I wouldn't under any other circumstances dream of dropping in unannounced at this late hour. Thank you."

Doctor Glass stepped forward as though expecting Mary to usher him in, but she stood firmly in place, keeping one hand on the doorframe.

"What is it, Doctor?"

"I'm, Mary, my…my, I'll just get right to it. I don't know how else to proceed. Do you know who 'Mr. Y' is?"

183

Mary stared back blankly and shrugged.

"It's, well, it's an alias, you see, a code name, if you will."

Doctor Glass seemed to wait for a reaction but Mary continued to stare blankly at him.

"So I take it the name 'Mr. Y' means nothing to you?"

"Doctor, I'm afraid you've lost me. Please, it really is quite late."

"Wait, hear me out. When Sam left for London, I expressed to him my concern for his safety, and, indeed made certain inquiries of my own both before and after he left. These are all such, how do I put it, frightful games for doctors to play. But I feared for his well-being. A code, shall we say, was developed for confidential communications, and Sam was given the alias of 'Mr. Y.'"

"I see."

"Mary, this evening I received a very short telegram, which is what brings me here at this hour, a telegram from London. It said, I'm so sorry, it said simply, 'Mr. Y dead.'"

"I don't believe you."

"Mary, I'm sorry. I know it's a shock. This is partially my fault. I should have insisted he not go."

"I don't believe you. The whole story is ridiculous. Why are you telling me this?"

"Mary, listen to me. I'm telling you the truth, and it may be even worse. I have reason to believe that Miss Molly Bell is in mortal danger as well. Please, I beg of you, if you know where she is, you must tell me."

"You come to me, unannounced, on a Sunday evening to tell me, with no evidence except some fantastic detective story about code names and mysterious telegrams, that you think my husband is dead. Then you presume to pressure me to give you information that I don't have about the whereabouts of one of his patients!" Mary stepped back and put her hand on the doorknob.

"Mary, please, I know how you must feel. Sam was like a son to me. You and I both know how important his patients were to him. Don't you understand? We can't allow one tragedy to lead to another. I can't tell you the details, but I believe Miss Molly to be in grave, serious danger. I simply can't let what happened to Sam happen to her as well. Please, Mary, I need your help."

"Good evening, Doctor."

"Mary, please."

"Good evening, Doctor!"

"Very well—"

Mary slammed the door toward Doctor Glass, cutting him off in mid-sentence. She went to a nearby window, pushed the curtain aside a sliver, and peered out to watch him leave.

The doctor walked off the porch. Looking up, he seemed to have caught the eye of a policeman casually leaning against a lamppost across the street. Doctor Glass tipped his hat at the policeman, who nodded in return.

"I don't believe him. I know Sam's alive. He can't be dead." Mary closed the curtain and collapsed, sobbing.

CHAPTER 13
THE WITNESS

MARY CUNNINGHAM SAT upright in her bed as she tried to focus on the words in the book in front of her. Sighing, she set the book aside and reached for the open Bible on the nightstand. She looked at the clock behind the Bible. Well past midnight, she noted, without bothering to focus on the exact time. Sleeping had become difficult since Doctor Glass played his surprise visit the night before. The housekeeper had been expected back that morning, but Mary hadn't heard from her since she left.

She turned the pages from the Gospels back to the Psalms, half listening to the wind rustling through the oak tree outside her bedroom window. She was flipping through the Psalms searching for one that would speak to her in the moment when she thought she heard footsteps on the porch downstairs. Then came a loud rap on the front door.

Mary quickly dimmed her lamp, got out of bed, and, hastily tying the robe she grabbed from the foot of the bed, tiptoed to the bedroom window. She moved the curtain just enough to be able to peer down at the front porch. She could make out a large man. He looked to be in a uniform of some kind.

"Mrs. Cunningham, I'm with the police. Please come down," the man stage-whispered toward the bedroom window.

Mary let the curtain drop back in place and thought for a moment before heading downstairs.

"Who is it?" she queried as she entered the front room.

"Mrs. Cunningham, I'm Officer Shannon with the police department. Sorry to bother you, but I must speak with you, urgently," came the response from the other side of the door.

"Can't it wait until morning?"

"I'm sorry, it's urgent, can you please open the door."

"Officer, if you can just tell me what you want. I can hear you just fine through the door. I'm not dressed for visitors."

Mary pressed her ear to where the door met the door frame while keeping her hand over the sliding bolt located above the door handle.

"Madam, I'm afraid you must open the door. I won't be long, but this is not a conversation for your neighbors to hear. It's urgent business."

Mary turned to run toward the closet near the kitchen where Sam kept the loaded shotgun. As she entered the hallway off the dining room she collided with a man standing squarely before her.

The man's arms shot forward, pinning Mary's arms to her side. He shoved her against the corridor wall, allowing a second man to pass and run to the front room.

"Let me go!" Mary struggled as she heard the bolt on the front door sliding and the front door opening. "Let me go!"

Now the policeman and the man who had opened the door were in the hallway with Mary and the man who was pinning her to the wall. She flung her head from side to side as he tried to get a hand over her mouth.

"Let me go! Who are you? Let me go!"

"Bind and gag her. We haven't much time."

* * *

"Where is he? Where's James?"

"Ah, Mr. Miller, sooner than I expected, please have a seat." Inspector Jenkins motioned Fred Miller to an open seat by his desk.

"Where is he? I'd like to see him, please."

"I'm having the body brought up to an examination room. It shouldn't be long. Please have a seat. Tea? Scotch?"

"No, thank you. I came as quickly as I could."

"Yes, I see."

"Where did you find him? I still can't believe it."

"They fished the body out of the Thames yesterday morning."

"What happened?"

"I'm not exactly sure yet. There's no water in his lungs, so he was likely dead when his body entered the river. There's no sign of trauma with the exception of, well, you'll see soon enough, Fred, but the face is missing."

"I'm sorry? What did you say?"

"The face, someone has removed it, rather crudely for sure, but the skin is gone from the hairline to the chin and from one ear to the other."

"Good God." Fred looked down at the floor.

"I am truly very sorry to have to ask you to come."

Fred jerked his head back up and looked straight at the inspector. "You don't know, do you? You asked me here because you aren't certain."

"I have my opinion, but yes, I need you to confirm it. I'm sorry, it was either his best friend or his wife, and given the condition of the body, I made the decision to impose upon you."

"But you aren't certain."

"The clothing matches the description of what he was last seen wearing. The height and weight of the corpse, hair color, age, and eye color, are all perfect matches. His grandfather's pocket watch was in his pocket, as was his usual custom. But enough of that, you'll see for yourself momentarily."

Fred was perplexed, and anxious. He wanted to run to the room where the body was to see for himself. Was his best friend dead or alive? He had to be alive, why else would the inspector need him to look at the body? Wouldn't he know if it were James?

"Tell me, how are you and Father Tate getting along?"

"Father Tate? Well, I suppose. He's an engaging man, very learned about so many things, birds, wine, chemistry, poetry. We do differ slightly on our theology at times. Odd thing for me to bring up with the corpse of my best friend down the hall somewhere."

"Not at all. Differ, how so?"

"For example, it seems to me a rather fundamental point, but he thinks not. As he phrases it, he believes that Christ's gift of salvation was to the community of believers, not to individual persons in isolation."

"Interesting. I've noted you have a keen interest in theology and the Bible."

"Yes, I was quite a disappointment to my mother. She wanted me to join the clergy, not the crass commercial world of inventions and patents. She did plant the passion in me, though, which stayed rooted despite my strong resistance as a boy. In any event, to put it differently, Father Tate believes that Christ died for our collective, general sins, to redeem the community, and—"

"And is not personal to you or me individually."

"Exactly, and that, to me, seems like a rather slippery slope. I mean, if Christ is not personal to my salvation, then the focus is no longer on the personal relationship with the divine, but with a broader relationship with man in general. What does that do to individual responsibility for sin? To individual repentance? He assures me that he's on the leading edge of Christian thought in this regard, but it strikes me as a dangerous road to take, uncharted, as far as I can see. But then, he is much more learned than I."

"Inspector Jenkins, sorry to interrupt. The body of James Aston is ready in Examining Room B, sir."

"Very good." The inspector waved off the visitor at the door. "All right, Fred, it's time. Follow me."

He followed the inspector through several doors leading to several hallways until they entered a brightly lit room with the body of a fully dressed man lying on a table. Fred removed his hat for the first time and cautiously approached the body. The corpse was on its back with its arms at each side, hands palm up. The clothing was indeed familiar, although soiled with mud and blood. A gaping, fleshless face stared at the ceiling.

"May I?" asked Fred of the inspector, motioning toward the body.

"By all means."

Fred moved to the right side of the corpse, reached for the right hand, and turned it over. "It's not him! Thank God, it's not him!"

"Yes, I know. Thank you."

"But why? Why do this to someone? What is the purpose?"

"It's a distraction, evidently."

"What do you mean?"

"Aside from the lack of the identifying marks on the right hand, is it really plausible that James Aston, after being missing all this time, would show up in the same suit of clothing as when he had first gone missing, floating in the Thames having suffered at the hands of a terrible murderer, with a valuable pocket watch on his person?"

"But why? Is he still alive?"

"That I don't know. But as to the why, as I said, it's a distraction. We were intended to discover that this was not James Aston. It's a reminder that he may still be alive. You've stopped looking for him. This is a teaser, to remind you why you originally volunteered to help me."

"I don't understand."

"Fred, when a pickpocket wants to steal a man's watch, what does he need most of all? He needs a distraction, something to turn attention away from the real event. You, sir, are about to have your pocket picked, so to speak. Now, the trick will be for you to appear distracted."

* * *

Mary squinted from the intensity of the light shining in her face when the hood was removed from her head. She was flat on her

191

back with her arms secured slightly away from her sides to the surface beneath her. She seemed to be on some kind of table with padding on it. Her legs were strapped down as well, but spread slightly more than shoulder width apart.

She had struggled as best she could to keep the men from strapping her to the table, but now she could do nothing but strain against the many leather straps that held her body in one place. The towel that had been tightly gagging her was now sopping wet. She had bit and chewed at it, but it still prevented her from crying out. Muffled moans were all she could muster.

"That will be all, gentlemen. Your services won't be needed any further."

Mary recognized the voice of Doctor Glass, but still had to squint as her eyes adjusted to the bright electric light. She heard the shuffling of feet and a door closing.

"Now we're alone, my dear. Let me assure you, there is no one in the building but you and me. There's no need to do research at this hour of the morning, and we have several hours before the first shift arrives."

Mary began to make out the outline of Doctor Glass standing beside her.

"The question is whether by then you'll be just another patient recovering from the emergency surgery that brought you to my care at this odd hour, or, and I hate to say this, Mary, I really do, dead, having not survived the ordeal."

Mary heard Doctor Glass arranging things on a nearby stand, metal clinking on metal.

"I'm sorry it's come to this. I tried as best I could to get what I must have from you, but I'm afraid I've failed up to now. So sad, all this business, but you see, Mary, the ends will justify the means. No time now to explain, but all this is justified. You and I, we will help bring what is coming, what must come. My dear, this is much bigger than you can imagine, and trust me, if you could imagine, you'd be helping me instead of being so stubborn."

She felt spit begin to run out the side of her mouth and slide down her cheek. She bit hard on the cloth between her teeth and pulled again at the bindings that held her fast.

"I know that you know where Miss Bell has gone. You must, there is no other logical conclusion. You, unfortunately, have refused to tell me where she is yet. The fate of many rests on my ability to find her. I am therefore forced to extract that information from you, using as much 'motivation' as you decide it takes. I've about run out of time, you see. The wheels are in motion, and all of us must keep strictly to the schedule of shipments and so forth. Miss Bell's disappearance cannot put me any further behind. So, I'm left with no option but to use drastic measures. I don't want to, Mary, but you are leaving me no choice. Trust me, this is most unpleasant for me as well.

"Now, Mary, let me tell you what will happen and how you can influence that. Please listen closely. This"—Doctor Glass held up a syringe for Mary to see—"this I'll first inject into your bloodstream. No, not poison, but neither is it a pain killer. To the contrary, it's concocted to actually magnify the pain you experience from anything that may follow. Amazing stuff, apparently. It comes highly recommended from a colleague of mine in London, a religious man, curiously enough. I had looked forward to seeing it work, but not under these circumstances.

"In any event, on the stand next to me are the tools that I'll use as needed thereafter. Here's a clamp, for example, excellent for gripping skin and exposed nerves. Here's one of my scalpels, a particularly nice double-sided one we call a lancet."

Mary shuddered at the sight of the small, broad blade with a sharp point.

"This speculum spreads and holds things open, and, of course, the usual variety of hooks, tweezers, rasps, forceps, drills and so on, so many dreadful little devices to choose from.

"I know my trade quite well, Mary. I know how to cause pain that no human can imagine, because I know the exact level that can be maintained without having you lose consciousness. The beauty of this pharmacological agent is that you will sense even that level of pain much more acutely, all while it keeps you from the relief of passing out. It's just a matter of how long you wish to fight me on this. I know you're a strong-willed woman, and that, I'm afraid, will make all this much worse for you. You must believe me that my deepest desire is not to put you through this. You've left me no choice."

Doctor Glass paused and gazed at Mary in full with what looked nearly like a sad expression.

"You are quite a lovely woman. I understand why poor Sam was so smitten. It's such a shame to put me to the test like this. You have so much life before you. This is all so unnecessary, such a shame."

Doctor Glass bent toward Mary's face and looked her in the eyes.

"Mary, there is an easier way. All you have to do to stop the procedure is tell me what I need to know. I'll then administer a harmless sedative, and the next thing you'll know, you'll wake up in your own bed, in your own home."

Mary shivered. The room was cold, and her body began to cool as she tired from the vain struggling against the bindings.

"Listen, I'll need to remove this gag now. I have to hear you when you break. Know that you can shout and scream as loud as you want. No one will hear you but me, and I don't mind. You're entitled to do that, and won't be able to stop in any case. It's going to hurt. And we need to be able to communicate and understand each other.

"Now"—Doctor Glass lifted Mary's head and began to untie the gag—"I'm going to take this off before I inject the solution. You can still tell me what I need and get nothing but the sedative. There, now, what have you to say, Mary? Are you ready to tell me where I can find Miss Bell?"

"Mick! For God's sake, help me now! Mick! Please! Are you there, Mick?"

Doctor Glass frowned at Mary, then looked up suddenly at what sounded like the door bursting open. Mary could see the doctor bending and reaching for something under the stand. The figure of another man flashed by her, tackling Doctor Glass before he could stand back up. She could hear the two men struggling on the floor. The deafening report of a gun going off caused her body to reflexively jolt against the restraints. Then there was silence and the smell of gunpowder.

* * *

Fred sat with the other two men on the bench in London's Hyde Park. He munched casually on an apple while watching the occasional couple strolling by in the dwindling light of the late afternoon. The bench was off the nearest path far enough that he couldn't make out the specifics of the passing conversations, but the occasional laugh or giggle rose above the gentle breeze swishing through the trees. It was truly a beautiful day.

He was flanked on his right by Inspector Jenkins, who sat holding an open newspaper. On his other side sat Father Tate, who marked time by flicking specks of bread at a lone pigeon cooing and pecking in the grass a few feet away. Fred kept his gaze away from his companions, and he assumed they did the same.

"I'm sorry, gentlemen, I've decided I can't ask you to do it. The risk is too great."

Father Tate abruptly suspended his bird feeding. "Inspector, with all due respect, I'm not a young man. My best days are behind me. I have no family, no siblings, no budding career. You may not believe this, but I've faced my share of danger, yes, as a priest. I think that I should be the judge of whether I should take risks with my life."

"I second that sentiment. I may be a young man, but like it or not, close attachments are in rather short supply for me these days. I'd gladly risk my life for the endeavor."

"Yes, and you have a score to settle, Father, and you a friend to find. I understand what you're both saying, and I don't doubt the courage or determination of either of you. I simply don't think the risk is worth the slim chance of return, which means I no longer need your assistance. You've both been a great help to me, and for that I thank you. But I simply won't send you on this errand. I can't expose you further."

"Inspector, you don't understand, this is more than just finding a friend, for me. Although I'd very much like to find James, for his child, for his wife, and for his friends, it's more than that. It's hard to explain, really, what I feel, what I think I know.

"When I was young, my mother asked me what I thought of God asking Abraham to sacrifice Isaac, his only son. I said, 'Well, God stopped him. He didn't make Abraham do it.' 'Why did he stop him?' she asked me. 'Because God loved Abraham. Abraham didn't need to actually sacrifice his only son to convince God of his love and faith, he just had to show that he would have,' I answered. 'Ah,' Mum said, 'and what does that say of us? What did we do when man demanded the sacrifice of God's only son? Did we stop it? Did man say, now I see you are willing to kill your own son to show how much you love us? Did we say, stop his suffering, bring him down from the cross? No, we demanded his death. We stood by and watched him die.'

"She taught me never to forget that, man killed God's only son. God knew we'd fail him then, and sacrificed his son for our sins. But we don't have to fail him again and again. We can try to live up to that sacrifice. We can try when faced with evil by making an effort to stand up to it. And, Inspector, this, what we're up against, is evil. I've sensed it all along, and so have you. You mustn't refuse us this chance to serve God now, please."

Father Tate took a deep breath. "Inspector, listen, the lead you wanted us to follow up this evening, let us take this one last assignment. If there is nothing to it, then Fred and I can report back and either remain at your service or be dismissed, as you wish. But if we find the missing link that gets us to him, then it seems to me that we can still, and should, continue to help you."

"It's just another lead, Father, and a small one at that. We can track it down later without further risking your lives."

"Maybe, Inspector, perhaps, but you'll have wasted all the groundwork. Only Fred and I can gain access to this particular meeting. If you send anyone else we'll be found out and the meeting won't happen. Fred and I have worked hard to gain the confidence of this contact, and he expects us to be where he instructs at the appointed time. You run the serious risk of losing a credible lead if you don't let us at least finish this assignment."

"Gentlemen." Inspector Jenkins folded his newspaper and rose, facing straight ahead, speaking neither to his left nor his right, and announced, "I'm afraid my mind is made up. Your motives or personal feelings on the matter are not relevant to my decision. It has been an honor working with you. I bid you farewell, and trust that all of this, all of this remain in your confidence."

Fred Miller watched as the inspector began to walk toward the nearby path. The cooing pigeon seemed to call out the "Godspeed" that Fred felt too dispirited to voice as the inspector continued out of sight. "I think I need a drink."

"Excellent idea, Mr. Miller, I think I'll join you. In fact, I'm expected at an establishment not far from Albert Gate. We can have supper and a pint while we wait. Shall we?"

"Lead on, Father."

* * *

"Excellent, this ale. Had your fill, Fred, or shall we order some more chips or perhaps some spotted dick to finish off the evening?"

"No, Father, I think I've had quite enough to eat this evening." Fred felt slightly groggy, but then he'd had quite a bit to drink too. "Perhaps one more pint, then I'll be on my way." Fred waved his hand at the bartender and pointed at his empty glass.

"Fred, what you said to the inspector about this all being evil, I can understand how you feel. I too have trouble understanding it all. I would note one thing, though, that I've learned as a priest."

"What's that, Father?" Fred waved toward the bar again and pointed to his glass, just to make sure he'd been understood.

"Judging circumstances too quickly can lead to the wrong conclusions."

"Meaning?"

"Your conclusion, about this all being evil, perhaps you're right. All appearances certainly make it look that way. But we also don't understand it. All I'm suggesting is that sometimes what we don't understand has a wider, broader, more important meaning than that which we prescribe to it."

"Like God moving in mysterious ways, you mean?"

"Perhaps. We shouldn't treat everything in strictly black and white terms. We need to keep an open mind to other explanations for what we don't fully understand."

"Hm, all right, I'll drink to that." Fred picked up a full glass that suddenly appeared on their table. "To open minds, and the ladies who keep them."

Father Tate laughed and raised his glass in toast. "You do fancy the ladies. Why aren't you married?"

"Just never met one who'd have me. It's dreadfully fun searching for one who will. How about you? Haven't you ever been tempted? We're Church of England, after all, not Rome."

"Tempted, that may be the operative word. No, women are far too dangerous to become entangled with. I avoid them at all cost."

Fred laughed. "And that, Father, is why you're in the pulpit and I'm in the pew. Dangerous, though? That's a bit strong."

"They are the stronger sex in my opinion."

"You may have a point there, but I'm not sure that makes them 'dangerous.'"

"All women have a tremendous power over men, just very few know they have it and even less how to use it. That they are the weaker sex is a myth in my opinion. We force women to our will with brute force. They force us to their will by our own desires. Consequently, I avoid the danger by avoiding women altogether."

"Sounds like fun to me."

"I suppose you think yourself immune from their powers?"

"Assuming that I met a woman who could force me to do things based on my desires, it seems that first I would have to want that to happen. I do have free will of my own. But further assuming I were to surrender that free will in any particular, I hope my judgment would be such that I would only do so to a woman who had my interests at heart. Perhaps I'm not immune, but I don't see the danger."

"Let me give you an example, then, to make the point. Take your Angela Jones, the lady you spoke about who was last seen working with your missing friend. You've described her as quite attractive."

"No doubt on that point. I'm not sure I've ever laid eyes on a more handsome woman. If you're suggesting I should test your theory on Mrs. Jones, I'd be delighted!"

"Any idea where she is today?"

"I wish I knew, Father." Fred averted his eyes, wishing the inspector hadn't been so insistent that he never tell a soul about the York affair.

"You think you could resist her wiles if she fully applied herself?"

"I don't know, but I'd love to give it a go." Fred lifted his glass again in toast.

"And you don't think perhaps James Aston gave it a go?"

"I pray not, that's all I can do."

"I'm sorry. This conversation makes you uncomfortable."

"Am I flushing again from too much beer? Perhaps I have had too much."

"Fred, you're more transparent than you think."

"Am I? I do admit to finding the idea of Mrs. Jones seducing Mr. Aston distressing."

"I understand. I would as well if in your shoes. In a sense, though, wouldn't the possibility make it more likely that he is alive, in hiding somewhere?"

"The thought has crossed my mind."

"You'll find him, Fred. And know that I'll do anything I can to see that you do."

"Thank you." Fred paused for another drink. "By the by, earlier you said you were expected here this evening?"

"Yes, I've been debating whether I should elaborate."

"What, keep a secret from me, after all the complaints this evening about the inspector not trusting us? After all this conversation and confession about Angela Jones and the power of women? Father Tate, how could you?" Fred grinned and raised his glass again before taking another gulp.

Father Tate laughed once more and raised his glass in response. "Yes, you have a point there."

"Well, then let's hear it. I'm all ears." He emphasized the statement by setting down his beer and pushing his ears forward with cupped hands.

"You bring me joy, my friend. All right, since you're clearly all ears, I was afraid the inspector wouldn't let us fulfill our mission. I don't blame him. He has too many deaths on his hands. This is becoming a costly pursuit in the body count department. Had he not dismissed us this evening I would have told him, but once he did, I couldn't."

"Told him what? You're delaying my next drink quite unnecessarily."

"Oh, put your hands down. Our mission, Fred, the contact is meeting me here tonight. We may be very close."

"Excuse me, good sir."

Father Tate turned to face a grubby man wearing a worn cap too small for his head. His clothes were greasy, weather-beaten, and torn. The man coughed into his sleeve, which was too short to cover his sooty arm. After wiping his nose with his sleeve he flashed a mouth full of brown, broken, and jagged teeth framed by a flabby, unshaven face.

"Excuse me, good sir." His breath caused Fred to recoil from the putrid smell of rotten eggs.

"What is it? Just because I wear the collar doesn't entitle you to interrupt our—"

"A gentleman, what he was, he tells me, 'Charlie,' he says, 'give this note to that kind priest inside.'" The ruffian thrust a folded piece of paper on the table. "No need to pay me, sir. The gentleman's done it. Although I'd never be one to turn down a coin for services rendered."

"Here, take this, be on your way."

"Thank ye, Father, next time." With that the man limped out of the pub, leaving a not insubstantial stench behind.

Father Tate picked up the paper and read it to himself.

"Perhaps he'll use your tip to take a well-needed bath. Know him?"

"I run into all types in my profession. I can't say I don't. His smell does precede him."

"Yes, but I'm not sure I'd forget that face either, droopy left eye and all, quite distinctive." Fred took another drink. Father Tate was concealing something, but he couldn't quite put his finger on it. "Well, what does it say? Is it from your contact?"

"Yes, indeed."

"Right on cue. Well, what does it say?"

"Instructions, detailed instructions. I'm to go to an address in East London by foot, crossing over the Thames, crossing back, and then crossing again, all by different bridges. It's all very specific. I'm sure the route will be watched."

"You'll be walking all night by the sounds of it. Anything else?"

"Yes." Father Tate grasped Fred's glass as he was raising it for another drink. "It says you must come if you expect to ever see James Aston alive. I'm sorry, Fred. I shouldn't have brought you here. It appears that now he won't let me leave you here either."

"I suppose I best finish this ale, then."

* * *

It had been overcast and dark the entire evening, and the narrow alley was darker still. Fred Miller felt his way along the moist brick wall, stumbling along the rough brick walkway on weary legs behind the figure of Father Tate. Nothing stirred from the dimly illuminated street behind them. Ahead he could just make out a faint glow coming from somewhere on the left. Then Father Tate came to a stop and straightened before craning forward his neck. Fred pulled up beside him and strained to look further into the gloom.

He heard it before he saw it, a low growling at about waist height from somewhere ahead. As the growling grew louder the form of a large black dog began to materialize, creeping slowing toward them from the center of the alley. White teeth glinted in the dim light with every renewed growl.

"Calm now, pup, no need for alarm. We've just come for a visit. Here, now." Father Tate spoke in even tones and extended his hand to the dog. The dog came to a stop at the extended hand, sniffed it briefly, and then turned to face Fred. "Easy now, Fred, he'll be fine if you're steady, like this. Just extend your hand. That's it, just a short visit now, pup. Best not to look him square in the face. Come now, keep your hands at your side and follow me."

Fred walked carefully along behind Father Tate as the two passed the dog, which maintained its station as they continued up the alley. Just short of the glow on the left two more large dogs appeared. They made no noise, but just watched the men approach. Fred looked back to see the form of the first dog trailing them now by a few paces. "I think they've got us surrounded," he whispered in half-jest.

"No need for alarm. They're merely doing their duty. Here we are." Father Tate stepped down to his left toward the glow. After taking three steps below the street level he reached for the handle of a door and opened it. The dim glow brightened somewhat as he pushed the door open wide.

Fred pressed forward down the steps, glancing back at the faces of the three dogs now congregated to their rear watching them from the street. He was relieved they didn't seem interested in following them inside. After passing through the low doorway, Fred closed the door behind them with a sense of further relief that didn't last long as he took in the room. It was poorly lit by a single candle sitting on a single table centered in the otherwise spartan room that smelled of lamp oil and stale animal urine.

"Ah, Fred Miller, so good to see you, and Father Tate, punctual as always."

Fred turned to the direction of the voice and saw the figure of a man leaning in one corner of the small room. The man stood up and walked toward the table.

"Shall I light the lantern?" asked Father Tate politely.

"Yes, please, on the shelf over there."

The man now stood on the opposite side of the table from Fred, who strained to see his face.

Father Tate moved to the shelf, from which he produced a small lantern consisting of a plain, metal base with a bare wick sticking out of the top. He moved back to the table and stuck the wick at the candle resting there. The lantern flickered to life, adding its light to the room. Father Tate set the lantern by the candle and sidled next to the other man. They both faced Fred.

Fred tried to make out the face of the man who had earlier spoken his name. At one moment it was strikingly familiar. The next, it looked like no man he'd ever seen. How strange it was, both familiar and unfamiliar at the same time. Whenever he thought he'd seen some familiar feature he could latch on to, the lamp light would flicker and the entire face would seem to change.

"Wondering who I am? You're not alone. Everyone does, but it doesn't matter. You've come, which serves my purpose."

The man looked down at the table at a black box sitting there. Fred hadn't noticed the box until that moment. He felt his heart racing and sweat beginning to form at his hairline.

"Oh, that, no need to worry, young man."

"Shall I?" asked Father Tate, gesturing toward Fred.

"No, you fool, it's not for him."

"I don't understand." Father Tate stood stiffly, pausing for a reply. "Didn't you want me to bring him to you? Haven't I done what you've asked?"

"Yes, indeed, you've done well, once again. You've brought the witness I wanted."

"Witness?" Father Tate looked puzzled.

"*Father* Tate, do you really think you stealthily outwitted Scotland Yard this evening? You do tend to underestimate others. That Inspector Jenkins, very good, he is, a very thorough, imaginative man. Rather unworldly, don't you think, Mr. Miller? Nothing to say? You don't know him like I do. I'm told you tend to stop talking when you're at a loss. Too bad more men don't follow your example.

"Anyway, back to Scotland Yard. I have no doubt they have both ends of the alley covered and the entire building surrounded by now. Just as I had hoped, and you, my dear Mr. Miller, you are to be my witness."

"But—I don't understand," stammered Father Tate. "There isn't an exit to this room. I've seen it in the daylight, one door in, one door out. We should leave now!"

"Calm yourself, Tate. We are leaving." The man picked up the box from the table. "Here's your exit. I've saved this one for you. It's time. It's your time. It's my time. All is in place now. All the parts are in motion. The fury is coming to a boil. I just need a witness, one reliable, trusted witness who can attest to it all."

Fred couldn't stop staring at the man's face. He couldn't place it. He couldn't retain it. His mind was swimming in incomprehension.

"Tate, take the box."

Father Tate reached out silently and took the box in both hands. Fred was frozen by the spectacle, unable to move or speak. He watched in horror as Father Tate slowly lifted the box to eye level.

The silence of the room was broken by a chorus of growls and the sound of clawed feet stripping across the brick surface of the alleyway. Soon the dogs were in a full-throated bark that ebbed as they ran down the alley.

"Don't tarry, Tate. They'll be here any moment. Look into the box." The instructions were matter-of-fact, devoid of any emotion.

Father Tate drew the box to his face as the distant sounds of growling and barking turned to yelping and then silence. As the box leveled at his eyes he let out a loud shout. "Redeem me!" Then he slumped to the floor, clinging to the box as his head banged heavily off the table.

"Now it's my time. Curious? No box for me, that's for others. I prefer my, shall we say, human approach."

The man reached out to the lantern on the table and removed the burning wick from the top, leaving it flaming on the table.

"You have no idea what an honor I've bestowed on you. You'll remember this all your life, and what a long life it will be."

"But why?"

"He speaks! Is that all you can say, 'but why'? Here, let me help you. Why the black boxes? Why the dead children? Why the dead adults? Why the coming death and destruction? Why the end? There, is that what you mean?"

There was no further sound from outside once the growling and yelping of the dogs had stopped. There remained only silence, and the soft hiss of the lantern wick flickering as Fred stood frozen, unable to respond.

"Yes, you want an answer, I see."

Fred struggled to move, but his mind seemed disconnected from his body.

"Because *He* weeps!" The man smiled, raised the lantern base above his head, and turned it sideways. An oily fluid poured out, and soon the man was drenched from top to bottom.

"Delicious, don't you think? He weeps. Man's communion with man, tasting man's flesh, not some transubstantiated baked wafer. You, all of you, you do it to yourselves and to Him. And *He* weeps. The words from Jeremiah sing forth once again: '*Oh that my head were waters, and mine eyes a fountain of tears, that I might weep day and night for slain of the daughter of my people!*'

"Who am I? I am every man, and yet I am no man. I'll get no credit for what I've done or what I'm about to do. I've supplied the heat, the fire. It simmers strongly now, and soon the fury, the fury of man shall boil. But you, Mr. Miller, you will witness my departure. You will live to witness what follows, with sadness, frustration, and horror all to my honor. Just imagine, Mr. Miller, an entire world aflame! Millions upon millions trudging to their deaths, like dimwitted slaves directed by the hand of an uncaring and stupid master. So senseless, so deliciously destructive, so inevitable. The end of mankind comes, and no one will have the sense or the will to stop it, thanks to me. And *He* will weep.

"As for you, Mr. Miller, people will say, 'Where was he when man demanded this sacrifice? Did he stop it? Did he say, 'Now I see you are willing to die to fulfill destiny'? Did Fred Miller say, 'Stop his suffering, bring him down from this painful cross'? No, you demand my death. You stand by and watch me die.

"Understand now, Mr. Miller? You are the witness. It was preordained by me. We could have had you at any time we wanted. You would have been putty in her hands, just like Mr. Aston, just like Mr. Clark. Father Tate could have drugged your wine several times over. You would have been easy prey for one of our assassins. But I had other plans for you.

"And now, you'll stand by and watch me die and, by merely watching, kill me. Never forget, you killed. Your debt will now be repaid a millionfold. Congratulations, Mr. Miller. You get to witness it all, from start to finish, the chronicler, my Mark. And then we will meet again, after the debt is repaid."

The man's face suddenly came into focus, but it was the face of a thousand men, some familiar, others quite strange. The man smiled, his eyes ablaze.

"Goodbye, Mr. Miller. Goodbye, man."

Fred tried to scream, tried to move, but could do nothing but stand and stare in stunned horror. The man reached for the flaming wick and touched it to his chest. The flames engulfed the man as he began to heave and laugh, laughing loudly as his form twitched and jerked, his arms spread open with his palms facing upward. The laughter rose in pitch as the flames spread across the table and stretched toward the ceiling. Fred's eyes stung. He tried to pull back from the intense heat that scorched his face. The smell of burning oil, hair, and flesh seared his nostrils. Black smoke began to fill the room.

"Fred Miller!" came a yell from the other side of the door. The door burst open. Rough hands yanked him back from the flame. Out the door and up the steps more hands pulled him, dragging him out into the sweet night air and onto the cold brick surface of the alleyway.

"Fred, are you all right? Fred?"

Fred blinked and looked up. The alleyway was alight now from the fire that raged from behind the doorway. "I don't know. Inspector, I don't know."

CHAPTER 14
IT BEGINS

"YOU ASKED TO see me, Mr. President?"

President Roosevelt jumped to his feet and charged at his guest with his right hand extended. "Yes, Tom, please have a seat. How are you? Can I get you a cup of coffee?"

"No, thank you. I had one earlier in the pressroom. You know the others are going to be quite jealous with you pulling me out for personal discussions like this."

President Roosevelt allowed himself a chuckle. "They all know you're my favorite newsman in the whole United States. They'll just have to get over it. Please, take a seat."

"I thought Bill Dunham was your favorite, or was it Max Westing, and then of course there's Ronald Parish at the *Post*."

"Oh, yes, all fine fellows, but none like Tom Mathis, none like you."

"I'm honored to have your confidence. What is it I can do for you, Mr. President?"

"Tell me, how do you think this Morocco thing turned out?"

"Quite an accomplishment. The international conference resolved the issue, and the word on the street is that you managed to breach the impasse with your behind-the-scenes diplomacy. With Lord Lansdowne no longer in the Foreign Office, you stand alone to collect the accolades. Well done, sir."

"Yes, poor Lansdowne, elections do have consequences. I'll miss him. He sends me the finest scotch, you know."

"And this success will no doubt inure to your next electoral victory. Well done, Mr. President."

"That's enough, Tom. Let's not play that flattery game. I wouldn't ask you to tell me what you think unless I wanted to know." President Roosevelt lowered his chin slightly and focused his gaze, making it clear he was in earnest.

"All right, then, the French got everything they wanted. The Kaiser ended up looking like an ass and a bully who had to slink away. The British and French are closer than ever. You came out smelling like a rose as the hero of the hour by staying as neutral as possible. Finally, and unfortunately, the world kicked the problem down the road."

"Yes, kind of what I was thinking, hardly an achievement. The Kaiser seems to have accomplished the exact opposite of what he set out to do. Now with the French and English such close allies, I suspect his military is furious at him for not going to war over the thing."

"Yes sir, I'd say the road to Armageddon is wide open."

"Armageddon? I guess I asked for it. Maybe we were better off playing games."

"Now, Mr. President, you didn't call me in for a private conversation just to say 'I told you so,' did you?"

The President laughed and slapped Tom Mathis on the shoulder. "No, I'd never do such a thing to you. To Ronald Parish, perhaps, but not to you. I'll tell you this, though, I agree. This affair is not over. Europe seems on top of a powder keg to me, and this whole Morocco episode looks like a postponement of the inevitable. This thing is far from over, and it won't be pretty when we get to the end. No, but that's not why I asked you in for a chat." The President paused to take a sip from a nearby coffee cup. "Tom, I need a favor."

"Of course, Mr. President, what can I do for you?"

"I need you to report something for me, and I can't tell you why. It is in the national interest, though, and you know I don't ask for favors at a whim. You've heard I'm going to the Dakotas on a hunting trip this week, yes?"

"Yes, and no reporters allowed, is my understanding."

"Well, Tom, you understand, my aim isn't as good as it once was. I'd hate to shoot one of you by mistake." The President grinned and took another sip of coffee. "That's right, no reporters, and I'll be out of the public eye the whole glorious time."

"With a press conference to display your trophies when you're done, I hope?"

"Why, of course, perhaps another bear added to the collection. I'll have one stuffed just for you." The President grinned again and then set his jaw in earnest. "Now, this is what I need from you, Tom, and you must keep this request in strict confidence, understood?"

"Yes, Mr. President, strict confidence."

"Good." The President sat back and paused for a moment, now donning his signature smile. "Tom, I want you to report that I'll have a special guest with me on this trip, a friend of mine from England. His name is Inspector Edmund Jenkins from Scotland Yard. He's quite a good shot, and I'm pleased that he'll be part of my hunting group. He's never been to the Dakotas, and I think he'll quite like it."

"Edmund Jenkins of Scotland Yard, and will he in fact be on your trip?"

"Tom, you know better than to ask me such a silly question."

"Yes, sir, I do. I hope you and the inspector, Edmund Jenkins, have great success. The American public will want to hear all about it."

"That's it, Tom. I knew I could count on you. That's why you're my favorite!"

* * *

He was off as soon as the train slowed sufficiently at the platform. A wooden sign announcing "Welcome to El Paso, Texas" greeted him as he looked up to take his bearings. He hurried to a shady spot, set his luggage and package next to an empty bench, and sat down facing the train.

He had an excellent view of the platform as he causally watched the other passengers disembark. Although they couldn't know it, he was carefully examining each, making mental notes that would help him identify anyone he might encounter later.

He continued his observations until the last passenger was off. He reflected on how he had gone through this routine at several other stops along the journey. But this time, instead of quickly reboarding the train just as it was pulling away from the station, he stayed put on the platform. This was his destination stop, no more false exits, no more switching trains going in random directions.

He watched as passengers boarded an assortment of coaches and buckboard wagons waiting at one end of the platform. When all the other passengers had departed, he gathered his belongings and wandered away from the station.

The day was crisp but sunny, with the noonday sun warming his face. The wig riding under the straw hat kept his head warm, just as his scraggly beard insulated his face. The chill creeping up the sleeves of his black jacket was refreshing after the long train ride.

"Excuse me, sir," he asked of a smartly dressed man who crossed his path. "Can you tell me where I can find some lunch?"

"*Allá, señor*, there. Look, *mira*, at saloon *con* sign big. *Comprende?*"

"Ah, yes, *comprendo. Gracias, amigo.*"

He walked down the street toward the large, faded sign. He entered the dimly lit saloon and pulled up a stool at the bar. "A whiskey, please, and what's for lunch?"

A heavyset man with a white apron around his waist reached for a bottle and a glass from behind the bar. "Bowl of beans, you can have that with a tortilla or cornbread."

"I'll have the cornbread."

"Beans and cornbread," the bartender hollered over his shoulder as he poured a generous glass of amber liquid.

"Cheers." He raised the glass in salute and took a swallow. "Ah," he sighed as he set the glass down, "I'd give you five dollars for a good scotch, but I guess this will have to do."

The bartender frowned. "Sorry, friend, no scotch in this town. You might could get some across the river. Them Mexicans can find anything if you're willin' to pay 'em enough."

"So I'm told. When does the next train come through?"

"Hm." The bartender pulled a pocket watch from his pants. "Eastbound in about forty minutes. Need to catch that one?"

"No, thank you." He took another swig and set the glass back down. Soon a large clay bowl of beans appeared along with a slice of dry cornbread.

He ate quickly and paid the bill. His timing would be perfect to grab one of the lingering wagons at the station before the next train pulled in. He walked with his baggage back to the station and mounted one of the buckboards.

A young man, not much more than a boy, with sandy hair, a weather-beaten gray hat, and well-tanned skin sat next to him holding the reins of two swayback horses. "Where to, mister?"

"Alamogordo."

"Alamogordo, New Mexico? Mister, if we leave for Alamogordo now I'll have to stop and rest the horses afore midnight 'cause we're gettin' such a late start. Even if we get up first thing, we won't be makin' Alamogordo till mid-mornin' the day after that. Then I'll have to rest, feed, and water the horses. I sure ain't spending two more nights in that desert, so I'll be spendin' the night in Alamogordo. Then I've got two full days back. You're talkin' five days and four nights till I get back to El Paso."

"Precisely. How much?"

"Mister, if you don't mind me sayin', it would make a heck of a lot more sense for you to check into that boarding house up the street and let me take you first thing tomorrow."

"I'd like to leave today, thank you. How much?"

"Five dollars, and I'll be needin' that now."

He reached into his pocket and handed the boy five coins.

"You got a gun, mister?" the boy asked as he pulled out a carbine rifle from under the bench they were sitting on.

"Yes," he answered as he reached into his jacket and produced a revolver.

"Right, when we stop to water I'll take the first watch and you can take the second. You can wake me when you're ready to hitch up in the mornin'. You never know who's out there, and there ain't no help until we get to Alamogordo."

* * *

"Mister, mister, your turn. Wake me when you're ready to go. Then we'll hitch up for Alamogordo."

He blinked at the star-filled night sky. It was clear and cold. The smell of creosote bush seared sweetly through his nose, a burnt menthol smell that was quite pleasing in the night air even though it was rather pungent. A windmill creaked in the light breeze as it slowly powered the pump that filled the nearby stock tank.

He sat up and pulled out a watch. It was four in the morning. The lad had taken more than his share of the night watch. He'd let the boy sleep at least a couple of hours before insisting that they move on to their objective.

The lad had been an amiable travel companion, whistling the few simple tunes he knew and quoting Bible Scripture intermingled with weighty descriptions of his mother's legendary cooking, "God rest her soul." The boy didn't ask any questions, and that was fine with him.

He seemed like an honest and earnest young man, turned loose in the world by circumstances beyond his control by his telling of events. After his mother died, his father left for the interior of Mexico in search of gold, leaving his son the wagon, the team, the rifle, and the family Bible, which the boy proudly displayed when they stopped that evening to water and rest the horses. The boy hadn't seen his father for more than a year, and didn't know if he was dead or alive.

After stretching and shaking off the stiffness that comes from sleeping on cold ground, he clambered up from the dry riverbed that formed their encampment onto the slightly higher ground above. The high desert was ghostly in the moonlight. Clumps of bushes anchoring small mounds of sand, distinguishable from the rest of the surroundings as being slightly darker than the desert floor, dotted the scenery as far as the eye could see. If he focused on any one bush long enough it seemed to move randomly about the landscape.

To the west the jagged Organ Mountains knifed toward the brilliant starlit sky. The mountains to the east were less defined, gloomy and brooding in the distance. The only sounds were the random whisper of a breeze through the scrubby brush, the rhythmic creak of the windmill, and his own heartbeat thumping between his ears until the pulse settled down from the exertion of climbing up the side of the arroyo.

He stood his uneventful watch, listening to the occasional coyote howl in the distance. As the day began to break in the east he woke the boy and together they hitched the team. The boy shared some hard biscuits with him and they boarded the wagon. Steam shot from the horses' nostrils as they exhaled into the dry morning air. The wagon lurched and jerked forward.

They hadn't been on the trail long when they dipped down into a gulley, more of a slight depression than anything else, only about a dozen feet lower than the surrounding terrain. He immediately spotted the three saddled horses to the left of the trail, even before he saw the single man, a cowboy, standing in the middle of the trail holding a double-barreled shotgun at the ready. The boy instinctively reached for his rifle under the seat.

"Not yet, lad. No room to turn around, and we can't see the others. Let's see what he wants."

The boy urged the team forward, coming to a stop a few paces from the cowboy blocking the road.

"Good lad, put those horses close to him and perhaps we can duck and draw if we need to," he whispered. But then he saw the second dismounted rider to the left, squatting down below a bush with a rifle in his hand pointed in their direction.

"Interesting, the third will be behind us then. I think they've got us well covered," he said to the boy.

"What do you fellers want?" the boy called out.

"Well, what you got?"

"We aint got nuthin. I'm just takin' this feller to Alamogordo."

"Well, then what's in that there blanket," the cowboy asked as he pointed at a rectangular shape hidden underneath a coarse cotton blanket on the bench between the two.

He'd carried that bundle concealed in that blanket on the entire journey, London to New York to El Paso, in a roundabout way, and now it sat next to him on the wagon bench in the middle of a desert sea at the end of the earth.

The boy looked at his passenger, waiting for him to answer. "They mean to kill us, mister," he whispered. "I just know it. Somethun's tellin' me."

"Stay calm, lad, I won't let that happen," he whispered back.

"You two quit jabberin' and tell me what's under that blanket."

"You don't want this. It's just something to look into. It's not worth anything."

"Well, hell, mister, I'll be the judge of that. Take the blanket off, fancy talker." The shotgun was raised and pointed for emphasis.

He picked up the package and unfolded the blanket, revealing a black, rectangular box.

"What the hell is that?" asked the shotgun-wielding cowboy.

"It's just a box."

"Well, hell, mister, I can see that. What's it fur?"

"You look into it, that's all."

"Toss it here," the cowboy on the road said as he shifted the shotgun to his right side.

He caught the box with his left arm and gazed down on it. "You look into it, you say? What's in there, some of them naked women pictures? You know I seen some pretty good ones in Las Cruces last month. Look in this hole here?"

"I wouldn't look in there if I were you. Firstly, I normally charge a dollar just for one peek. Secondly, it takes a pretty strong constitution not to pass out once you see what's in there. I can tell you've been on the trail for a while. I don't think you'd be able to handle it."

The man on the road grinned wide, showing crooked, yellow teeth. "Damn, fellas, we got ourselves a damn carnival man, a pretty talker to boot! A dollar, you say? Damn, they must be pretty fine for you to talk that talk."

"A box with pictures so sinful it'll make you faint? Well I'll be dammed," came a voice from behind the wagon. Soon a cowboy revealed himself from behind a bush and came running at the cowboy with the crooked yellow teeth. "Damn, I want me some of that, here, let me look fust. I done that gal in Mesilla last week, I can handle it." The cowboy scurried closer, flopping under a broad, flat-brimmed hat, holstering a revolver as he ran.

"Shut the hell up," replied Yellow Teeth. "I'm lookin' fust, and I ain't payin' no damn dollar, either."

Both of the cowboys now stood in the center of the trail looking at the box. Yellow Teeth shoved the shotgun to Floppy Hat and held the box in both hands. "Look in this here hole? Let's see what them gals look like."

Yellow Teeth pulled the box to his face. He stood still for a second and then crumpled to the sandy trail, dropping the box as he went down.

"Damn!" shouted Floppy Hat. "He fainted! Damn! Let me have some of that box. I'm twice the man you is. I ain't gonna faint."

Floppy Hat picked up the box and pulled it to his face, blinking first, and then staring intently inside. After a couple of seconds his back stiffened with a snap, as if his spine had suddenly become a broom handle. He fell straight backward, landing hard on the sand while still clutching the box.

The two cowboys lay motionless on the ground. Their companion to the left of the trail stood in shock, staring at the pair and the box clutched in the rigid grip of Floppy Hat. He looked back at the wagon and a revolver pointed at his head. His head jerked back as the bullet slammed into his forehead, propelling his body backward as he fell away from the bush.

"Well, I'll be, mister, that's some fine shootin'!"

"Quick, we have some rearranging to do. This is a busy trail, and someone else will be along today or tomorrow." He and the boy got down from the wagon. "Secure your team. I'll be discharging some firearms."

First he trotted over to Floppy Hat, unholstered the cowboy's revolver, and fired it twice into the air. Then he carried Floppy Hat back to the other side of the depression and put him prone on his stomach behind a bush with his arm extended holding the pistol pointed at the man with a hole in his head.

In the meantime the lad had returned from securing his team and started inspecting Yellow Teeth. "Mister, this fella ain't faint. He's dead! He's dead as a doornail!"

"Yes, and so is the other," he shouted as he crossed back to the man he'd shot in the head. Taking the dead man's rifle out of his lifeless hands he carefully aimed it at the prone man and fired into his body.

"Mister, if he's dead, why're you shootin' him? Mister, this ain't right. We need to take these boys with us to Alamogordo and report what happened."

He ignored the lad's plea as he moved back to the trail and picked up Yellow Teeth. He moved Yellow Teeth to the side of the trail, propping him up against a large cactus. He then stepped back a few paces, drew his revolver, and fired into Yellow Teeth's chest, causing the body to push backward into the cactus.

He next retrieved the shotgun and fired it without aiming in the direction of Floppy Hat's dead body. The shotgun was placed next to Yellow Teeth.

"Mister, this ain't right. What are you doing?"

Again he ignored the lad as he went to the three horses, untied two, and smacked the two freed horses on the rear, sending them trotting off into the desert. Back he went to the trail as he retrieved the black box and, on the way back to the wagon, grabbed the boy's arm, moving him along. Once they were both onboard, still strongly holding his arm, he pulled the boy close to him, looking him square in the eyes.

"Listen to me, young man. This is larger than you. This is larger than me. No one must know about this black box or what happened here today. Lots of lives depend on no one ever finding out what just happened. I had to kill all those men because they saw this box.

"Now you've seen it too. One of two things must happen next, and you're going to choose which. The first"—he reached under the seat to retrieve the lad's family Bible with his left hand while still holding fast to the lad with his right—"is that you're going to swear on this Bible in the name of your dead mother that you will never tell a living soul what you saw here today. When we get to Alamogordo you go straight to the constable's office and tell him you heard gunshots from behind you on the trail and that you didn't hang around to see what it was. You've got to swear on this Bible you won't say anything else and that you'll make no mention of the black box, of me, or of these dead men ever, to anyone."

The lad was trembling as he looked into the determined eyes of his passenger. "And what, what's my other choice?"

One of the horses whinnied softly and the morning breeze picked up briefly, feeling cool on his face as he glared at the boy.

"Young man, I don't want to do this, and I surely hope you'll swear on this Bible, just as I'm confident that if your father were here he'd want you to as well. But if you don't, I've got no choice but to shoot you and leave you here to rot with these scoundrels."

"Hand me that Bible, mister."

* * *

Having hired a horse at the local livery stable, he quickly rode north out of Alamogordo with his bundle and luggage strapped to the rear of the saddle. After riding for half an hour, he took a hand-drawn map out of his shirt pocket and studied it. He looked at the mountain peaks to the northeast and east. Turning back around he urged his horse to the east side of the town he had just left. He would skirt Alamogordo and, once south of it, head southeast toward the gloomy mountains he had contemplated the morning before.

An hour after turning onto the southeast leg of his journey he rode over a small hill and saw his first destination, a small pool of water formed by a spring he could hear but not see. He dismounted, removed his straw hat and wig, undressed, and plunged into the pool. The cold water urged him to a businesslike pace as he hurriedly bathed and shaved the beard that he had cultivated during his trip.

Emerging from the pool while he still had feeling in his chilled limbs, he dressed in a fresh set of clothing. He took his old clothes, including the wig and straw hat, and buried them nearby. Donning a derby and sticking an unlit cigar in his mouth, he remounted his horse and continued on his way, occasionally referring to the map to keep him on course.

As the afternoon wore on the sun began to dip in the west. He urged his mount on, knowing his destination was but an hour or so away. Looking to his right, toward the southwest, he saw, for the first time, another rider. The rider was sitting tall in his saddle looking back at him from quite a distance. The rider wore a red scarf, barely visible as a small dot accenting an otherwise gray man on a gray horse. Both men paused, contemplating the other from afar. Then he urged his horse forward, looking ahead as if he had never seen the gray man on the gray horse.

Occasionally he would glance to the right in order to keep tabs on the gray man and gray horse. The gray pair was on a converging course, slowly but steadily getting closer. The red bandana grew from a tiny speck to a recognizable triangle that covered the man's face. Onward the two horses plodded.

After about thirty minutes the gray horse was close enough he could hear its muffled hoof beats on the desert floor. Occasionally they made a crunching noise when a shod hoof came in contact with a rock half buried in the sand.

The gray man and gray horse kept coming on their course, now a nearly parallel but still intercepting path. He could see the gray man in fuller detail now, sitting forward in the saddle in the manner that good horsemen in the west displayed with pride. He held his back erect and let his head bob in unison with his gray steed. On the left side of the horse was mounted a rifle in a leather sheath, probably a Winchester. The rifle's wooden stock protruded from the sheath at an angle pointing generally at the horse's head, putting the stock near the gray rider's left hip. There was a gun belt around the rider's waist, which he surmised supported a revolver on the man's right hip. His gray appearance could now be attributed to the color of his faded flannel shirt being covered by dust accumulated from a long period of work in the desert.

Eventually the gray rider pulled in behind him on the trail. Now the two horses moved almost in unison with the gray one in the rear by a few lengths. Neither rider spoke. They just kept moving forward.

A ranch came into view ahead in the failing light. There was smoke coming from a chimney in the main building and from several squat outbuildings huddled under a scattering of trees. As the riders got closer, a fence surrounding the buildings, now showing their whitewashed exteriors, became discernable as well as a gate providing an entrance to the compound. On the two horses went, one following the other on what was now a clearly defined trail to the entrance to the ranch.

As he and his shadow rider approached the gate, he saw two cowboys walking toward it from inside the enclosed ranch. One stopped at the side of the gate, while the other swung the gate open toward the interior of the enclosure.

The two riders entered the enclosure as the two dismounted cowboys watched the lead rider with noticeable attention. He directed his horse toward the main building where eight other cowboys had now gathered in a loose line formation in front of the building. He heard the gate close behind him and the jingling spurs of the two cowboys following on foot.

Every man standing outside was clearly armed. Some held shotguns, others pistols or rifles. The shotguns and rifles were generally canted at him, and they all watched him with cool but determined stares.

He stopped his horse short of the group of men, tilted his derby slightly, and surveyed the situation. He was now surrounded with a group of armed men to his front, two armed men on foot behind him, and the stalking gray rider one length to his rear. Surely there were others unseen in the compound. He could smell meat cooking in the dry air. Smoke wafted down on the group from the roof of the main building. All the men watching him stood silently at their posts, seemingly content for him to make the first move.

Just then the front doors to the main building swung open and a large figure in boots, chaps, and a weather-beaten gray hat over curly auburn hair came rushing forth.

"Inspector, blessed Mother Mary, so good of you to drop in! Look at me! I'm a cowboy, through and through." The burly man spun around once holding his arms out to his side and bowing when he came back around.

"Why, Mick, I believe you're right. You are a cowboy, and a fine cowboy to boot."

The rest of the men holstered their weapons and began to shuffle off in different directions upon Mick's recognition of the strange rider.

"Mrs. Bell, Molly, Mrs. Cunningham, look who's come to see us! Why, for the love of Saint Patrick, it's Inspector Jenkins, all the way from London to the end of the earth."

* * *

"Please, Inspector, have a cup of coffee. Dinner will be out shortly." Mary Cunningham placed a steaming mug before the inspector as he adjusted himself on the long wooden bench that lined one side of a massive, rough-cut wooden table. "Tell me, how is my Sam?"

"Quite well, thank you. We got to him just in time. A moment later, and I'm afraid his assassin would have succeeded."

"He wouldn't a gotten so close had I been there, sir."

"You have a point, Mick, but then who would have saved Mrs. Cunningham in the nick of time?"

"Weren't no nick of time at all, sir. I was merely waiting for to be summoned, I was." He let out a hearty laugh as Mary Cunningham shook her head and smiled.

"Of course, badly phrased on my part." The inspector flashed a toothy grin back.

"My leaving London with this box should remove any doubt about the doctor's assumed demise. There'd be no reason for my doing so unless he was dead. But in fact, he's safely tucked away in the Highlands of Scotland. Many a man has gone long hidden in those parts. You need not worry, Mrs. Cunningham. And, with a little diversionary help from high places and a few precautions of my own along the way, I think the last place anyone will look for Molly is here. I dare say Doctor Cunningham is as safe as you are here with Mick and that rough crew outside."

"They're not rough! They're my friends! They're good men. Some rode with President Roosevelt and my father in the war with

223

Spain," piped Molly Bell. "They even gave me my pet dragon, Joshua. Can I show the box to Joshua, Inspector? He's not afraid of anything, just like me."

Inspector Jenkins raised an eyebrow. "Joshua?"

"Now, now, Molly, the inspector is just having his fun," interjected Mrs. Bell. "Joshua is her pet horned toad. Strange creatures, certainly the only real dragons I've ever seen. He and Molly have become quite a team. Speaking of that box, I must say the whole idea brings me to insanity. I understand the principle. I'll assume for a moment that it is true, that she can look into the box and it is instantly disabled with no harm coming to her. I understand we can't let anyone else be struck by this evil contraption. But this is my only child. Surely there's another way. I know it's worked this way with the good doctor, but you don't know for sure that it will work with Molly until she actually tries it. I'd much rather let Joshua look into it."

"If only Joshua would do. I give you my word, madam. I have confirmed this theory through several sources, starting with a young priest who gave his life to give me this information. This box is as harmless to your daughter as her favorite dragon, Joshua. When I leave this ranch, I must leave with this box exploded so that I can take it back to London in that condition. Doctor Cunningham's life could well depend on it, as well as the lives of many others, such as Lord Churchill's son, Winston. We've had our work cut out protecting that man, difficult and reckless fellow, but he's evidently been marked for elimination, and that means I've got to protect him as well. There will be more like him too, men I must not let them have.

"I've discerned a pattern in all this. It's not random, but quite methodical. The children victims I can't yet explain, but I'm starting to make out a pattern with the adults that is slowly materializing from the darkness. I'm not certain yet of the ultimate goal, but if I can come to understand the pattern better, perhaps the motive will come to me."

"Like an epiphany!"

224

"Yes, Miss Molly, just like an epiphany. We have a lot of work ahead of us, and it starts here with this box. Mrs. Bell, I can't leave this infernal box functional. I'm sorry, I can see no other way. Doctor Cunningham may be able to assist with others in the future, but Molly has to explode this one."

"Please understand, Inspector, she's my only child. Can I pray about it for a day or two?"

Jenkins let out a long sigh and rubbed his forehead as he suppressed a frown. "There's another reason. It's just a theory, but it does lend urgency to the matter."

"Go on, please. I think if my daughter is at risk I should know all the facts."

"You're right. I am so often in the business of concealing facts, but I think it best to share something with all of you. When Molly looked into a box, she was in a coma until the box was exploded. Once the box exploded, she awoke. This"—he held the box up for all to see—"is a different box."

"Oh no!" gasped Mary Cunningham. "There's another child."

"Mrs. Bell, in London there is a young man, a hansom cab driver, who looked into a box, probably this box, almost thirty days ago. He has a father who cares for him every bit as much as you care for your Molly. I'm guessing the only way to bring him out of his coma is to destroy this box before he dies, assuming he hasn't already. Time, his time, is short."

"Inspector," Mary Cunningham interrupted, "if this young man survives, won't he then be able to disable boxes as well?"

"I think so, we can only pray. If for every box we find and destroy we save another child who can then destroy more boxes, eventually we render the boxes ineffective."

"And eventually my Molly is one of many, and no longer a target."

"Precisely, Mrs. Bell. One step at a time, though. First, we explode this box."

"Explode! I love making things explode. May I have the box, Mother, please? I'm not afraid. You heard the inspector, it's as harmless as Joshua."

* * *

Mr. Davies scampered through the streets of Liverpool on his stubby legs. The old English port never slept, and he moved through the lamp-lit lanes unnoticed in his faded red jacket and faded green vest. They were faded to the point of being barely recognizable as colors in the daylight, and not distinguishable at all on a night's walk in bustling Liverpool, which is the way he liked it. The gold chain leading to a pocket watch in his vest was nothing unusual, either. There were lots of men like him in the port, men of business for whom time was critical. There were loading schedules to be met, bribes to be paid at the right times and places, customs men to be avoided on their usually predictable rounds.

Mr. Davies prided himself as a man of business, and his business was moving cargo for clients who didn't want any questions asked. A business that kept on booming even after the Moroccan affair had blown over. What was in all those crates he didn't care, as long as the clients paid his substantial invoices.

He was determined to see that his most recent client was adequately briefed on their successful engagement before the sun came up on another busy day of business. As he hustled around another corner the street began to clear of people. He stopped under a street lamp and pulled out the paper on which he'd written the address he'd been given, an address where he was to meet his client for the first and probably the last time.

This client was another Mr. Williams. They were all the same to him, Mr. Smith, Mr. Jones, Mr. Brown, Mr. Williams, common aliases with uncommon cargo to ship. He'd confirm his shipments, collect his pay, and move on to the next engagement with the next Mr. Smith, Mr. Jones, Mr. Brown, or Mr. Williams.

Stuffing the paper back in his pocket, he walked across the street and entered a nondescript building. He walked down a dimly lit hallway to the second door on the left, where he stopped and knocked quietly. Hearing a voice respond from within, he turned the weathered handle, entered the room, and closed the door behind him.

"Mr. Davies, I presume, right on time, excellent. Please take a seat."

Davies made for a single wooden chair parked in front of a desk. The room was illuminated by a single lamp that sat directly behind a man sitting behind the desk. As Davies sat in the chair the light from the lamp made a silhouette of the man on the other side of the desk, leaving his face hard to discern in the shadow. He was evidently rather tall and slim, but his facial features eluded him as the lantern continued to burn bright behind the man's head. The room smelled unpleasantly of rotten eggs.

"Mr. Williams, I've come to make my report. All went well." Davies pulled some papers from his vest and set them on the table. "These are the shipping forms for each of the final destinations. This is for Berlin. This one is for Paris. This is for Vienna. Ah, yes, and this one, let me unfold it. This one is for Saint Petersburg in Russia. Tricky business, that one, but I've got it done. And, of course, there is the shipment you had me pull yesterday that was bound for New York. It should be in the warehouse you designated as of yesterday afternoon."

"Yes, I've inspected it."

"Excellent, do you have a date yet on which you'd like to get it to New York? I can always have it moved to my warehouse and ready to ship on a moment's notice."

"No, thank you. We've had a problem come up with our American associate, rather unexpected, I'm afraid. It may take us a while to get matters back in order in that part of the world."

"Sorry to hear it, Mr. Williams. I trust you'll overcome the issue soon. I'll be glad to be at your service again when you do."

"Yes, we'll overcome the issue. It's thrown off our schedule for now, but I'm sure it can be managed."

"Most excellent, all in order, then. All the documents you need for the other shipments are right here. If you've nothing further for me, I'll take the rest of my pay now and be on my way. Here is the outstanding balance on this sheet, and you'll see I've given the appropriate credit for the held American shipment we returned to you."

"Mr. Davies, I do have a question about the American cargo."

Mr. Davies sat upright and shifted nervously in his chair, rubbing his eyes that were becoming watery from the smell. He tried to look Mr. Williams in the eye, but couldn't make out the exact location with that pesky lamp positioned where it was.

"When I inspected the returned New York–bound cargo I noted that the seal on the crate had been broken. There is some minor damage to the crate, and the lid appears to have been taken off and put back on."

"Yes, you see, Mr. Williams, the men at the dock dropped it offloading. I knew you would be sensitive about revealing the cargo, but I also had to make sure I was not returning damaged goods. So I had it quickly moved to a secluded room. I dismissed the crew and opened the crate to inspect it myself. All two dozen of the smaller boxes inside appeared to be unscathed, so I closed the crate before I reengaged the crew to deliver it to your warehouse. Here, if you look at this sheet you'll see that I've documented, yes, here it is, 'crate damaged, bottom left corner, goods inspected, crate resealed.' It's all in order, Mr. Williams."

"So you saw the cargo yourself?"

"Yes, sir, but I didn't go beyond checking the exteriors of the smaller boxes. And"—Davies let out a nervous laugh—"trust me, sir, I have a very bad memory for cargos. I don't even remember what the smaller boxes look like now."

"I see, perhaps I can refresh your memory. Did these smaller boxes look something like this?" The man behind the desk placed a small black box on the desk to his right, plainly illuminated by the lamp.

Davies paused, wondering if he was supposed to identify the box or deny that it looked exactly like the others he'd seen. "Well, sir, are you sure you want me to remember? I don't know. I inspected the items very quickly."

"Mr. Davies, did anyone other than you see these boxes?"

The tone of the statement made Davies quiver. He assumed a sense of bravado. "Oh, why of that I can be absolutely certain. The crate was never compromised. I was alone when I inspected it, and alone when I sealed it. No one but you, me, and your American agent will ever know what was in that crate. On that you can rest assured, Mr. Williams. I give you my word."

"Yes, Mr. Davies, and you have a reputation for keeping it, which is why you were hired."

"Thank you, Mr. Williams. That reputation is required in my line of work."

The silhouetted man across from him sat silently for a moment, motionlessly. Davies felt that he was being measured, but for what purpose he couldn't tell.

"Mr. Davies, do you play chess?"

"Chess, sir? Why, when I was young I played a little, no time for such pleasures now. No, I'm afraid I'd be quite at a loss now."

"You know the basics, though?"

Mr. Davies nodded while shifting uncomfortably in his chair. He rubbed his eyes again and looked intently at Mr. Williams.

"Such a beautiful game, I think it reflects life in many respects, the hierarchy of the pieces, the influence one piece can make if placed at the right place at the right time, the limitless possibilities of outcomes. Do you believe in fate, Mr. Davies?"

"Fate, I, well, I don't know that I've given it much thought? I'm more of a numbers man, you see." The silence from the silhouetted man left Davies with the impression that thought on the topic was in fact required. "I, um, I don't believe I give much stock to it, sir. I mean, you and I can influence what happens to us today, which in turn influences what happens tomorrow, and so forth."

"Excellent, yes, no good chess player believes in fate. Nothing is inevitable until the word 'mate' is preceded by the word 'check.' Only the reasoned movement of the pieces can determine the outcome. We are all pieces on the board of life, don't you think?"

"I suppose that's right, sir. Now, if I could just—"

"Mr. Davies, what do you suppose a game of chess would look like if all the truly influential pieces, the queen, the rooks, the bishops, the knights, the pieces that win or lose the game, if they were all neutralized somehow, either removed from the board, frozen to their positions out of fear, or simply replaced by pieces too simpleminded to know of their own influence? What would such a game become?"

"I suppose, well, mindless slaughter. The pawns could only march forward in a game of mindless attrition."

"Yes, mindless slaughter! Well put. No reason, no logic, no influence brought to bear to end the destruction. Once the major pieces are neutralized, the pawns have no choice but to march to their doom, one after the other, until but one is standing. And one pawn cannot survive alone thereafter, can he?"

Mr. Davies opened his mouth as he listened to the suddenly animated Mr. Williams. Then, just as suddenly, his client sat back in his chair and rubbed his chin with his hand.

"You look puzzled. Perhaps chess isn't quite the right analogy. Let's take an example from the animal world, shall we? We are all just more-evolved animals, after all. Take the life of domestic sheep, it's a life defined by protection from the predators and elements. Without the protection of the shepherd and his allies, his loyal dogs, the sheep face imminent destruction."

Mr. Davies sat with his mouth still open but feeling unable, or unwilling, to utter a sound.

"Have you ever wondered about my business, Mr. Davies?"

"Sir, I make it a point not to inquire about such."

"Yes, I understand that, but my question was whether you ever wondered. Have you? Do you? Surely you've wondered, black boxes going all over the world, to the most influential cities. Surely you have an imagination, Mr. Davies.

"Imagine a world gone mad, mankind marching to destruction like aimless sheep to the slaughter. Can you imagine? 'How would it happen?' you might ask. That's quite easy. It just takes time and some coordinated effort. It takes little black boxes, and then, men willing to act without little black boxes, dedicated little men who follow instructions. Once the rational men of influence are gone, it's the dedicated little men who determine the course of events.

"It's a strategy, Mr. Davies, as in a chess game, that wins in the end. The tactics? That involves identifying targets, the sooner the better, and applying the little black boxes. Many of the targets have been identified, it sometimes takes more than mortal men to do that chore, but it's been done. Many of them, like the children, don't even exhibit their potential now, at least to the untrained eye. You look for the bright, honest, imaginative, fearless ones, future shepherds and sheepdogs, shall we say. Cull the protectors, foster the wolves, simple but brilliant! Sound brutal to you, Mr. Davies? It's required, though; they must not be allowed to assume their places on the board. They must not be able to influence events when the cataclysms come, whether they be five or eighty when you arrest them. The strategy is now set in motion. It's but a matter of time, a few years, a decade or two, perhaps four or five if more than one great spasm of world violence is required. But it's all inevitable, like pawns trudging to their death. We won't be stopped."

Mr. Davies swallowed drily and looked away, scanning the room, looking for a quick exit other than the one behind him.

"Yes, the 'how' is quite easy. The 'why' is the more exquisite question, the more intriguing question." The man across the table paused, seemingly waiting for Mr. Davies to respond. "I said, the more intriguing question. Ah, I see, well, I had hoped for a little

231

more imagination. In our line of work we can use imaginative and dedicated apostles, wolves to feed and nurture. There's a particular wolf out there somewhere, I'm told. Another 'Paul,' shall we say, who rises after the master is gone, the necessary last piece, a man to set the world on fire, an inspiring prophet to lead the world to a new and final solution. I think I'll know him when I see him. Who knows, he could be a peasant in Russia, a gentleman in England, or a starving artist in Austria."

"There's no road to Damascus here today, not even a fledgling wolf pup." A low voice from the corner of the room startled Mr. Davies. The shape of a man walking out of a dark corner toward the desk came into focus. A flabby, unshaven face with a droopy left eye looked down on him. The man smiled, revealing broken and brown teeth. "You're wasting your time on this one. Move on."

"Quite right, it seems," replied the man from behind the desk.

"I'm sorry, gentlemen, but I really must be on to my next appointment."

"Yes, mustn't we all," replied the man behind the desk. "You have goods to ship, and we have pieces to neutralize, and wolf pups to raise. Of course, sometimes I simply have to neutralize a sheep who knows too much. It's just part of my role, part of my, assignment.

"Mr. Davies, before you go, I need you to do one last thing for me." The man from behind the desk grasped the black box with his right hand and slid it toward Davies. "When one is turned it takes constant reassurance, feeding so to speak, from the likeminded. You strike me as quite satisfying for the purpose."

"Sir?" As the box came near him, Davies noticed two red moles on the backside of the man's right hand. They looked strangely like small, angry red eyes.

"Mr. Davies, I need you to look into this box and tell me what you see."

THE END OF THE BEGINNING